SATED IN INK- SPECIAL EDITION

A MONTGOMERY INK: BOULDER NOVEL

CARRIE ANN RYAN

Sated in Ink

A Montgomery Ink: Colorado Boulder Novel

By

Carrie Ann Ryan

Sated in Ink

A Montgomery Ink: Boulder Novel

By: Carrie Ann Ryan

© 2019 Carrie Ann Ryan

PRAISE FOR CARRIE ANN RYAN

"Carrie Ann Ryan knows how to pull your heartstrings and make your pulse pound! Her wonderful Redwood Pack series will draw you in and keep you reading long into the night. I can't wait to see what comes next with the new generation, the Talons. Keep them coming, Carrie Ann!" –Lara Adrian, New York Times bestselling author of CRAVE THE NIGHT

"Carrie Ann Ryan never fails to draw readers in with passion, raw sensuality, and characters that pop off the page. Any book by Carrie Ann is an absolute treat." – New York Times Bestselling Author J. Kenner

"With snarky humor, sizzling love scenes, and brilliant, imaginative worldbuilding, The Dante's Circle series reads as if Carrie Ann Ryan peeked at my personal wish list!" – NYT Bestselling Author, Larissa Ione

"Carrie Ann Ryan writes sexy shifters in a world full of passionate happily-ever-afters." – *New York Times* Bestselling Author Vivian Arend

"Carrie Ann's books are sexy with characters you can't help but love from page one. They are heat and heart blended to perfection." *New York Times* Bestselling Author Jayne Rylon

Carrie Ann Ryan's books are wickedly funny and deliciously hot, with plenty of twists to keep you guessing. They'll keep you up all night!" USA Today Bestselling Author Cari Quinn

"Once again, Carrie Ann Ryan knocks the Dante's Circle series out of the park. The queen of hot, sexy, enthralling paranormal romance, Carrie Ann is an author not to miss!" *New York Times* bestselling Author Marie Harte

DEDICATION

To those who need that push to take a chance.

SATED IN INK

The Montgomery Ink saga continues in a seductive romance where a runaway bride and two best friends might just take the chance of a lifetime.

Ethan Montgomery thought he had his life figured out until the moment he and his best friend met a woman in a wedding dress drinking wine out of a paper bag. He might work too many hours and always seems to put his family and friends first. Still, when he finally opens up to Holland and Lincoln, he may just get everything he's ever wanted.

Holland Yeaton made a horrible mistake, and running out on her wedding seemed like the only thing to do at the time. Taking the next step of her life on her own won't be easy, but now she has two sexy and bearded strangers to help her figure out exactly what she desires.

Lincoln McClard has loved his best friend for as long as he can remember. Only he's never dared to do anything about it. Instead, he puts all of his sexual frustration into his art. As soon as he meets Holland, he realizes exactly why he waited for Ethan and what has been missing all along.

However, it's not only the three of them in this tangled and steamy relationship. And if they aren't careful, it won't only be their feelings that get hurt...and broken.

PROLOGUE

The breeze slid through my hair, and I tried to let it calm me, tried to let it through the shell I'd wrapped around myself the moment I walked into the storage room of the church. My fingers crinkled around the paper bag in my hand, and I looked down at what I carried as if I'd forgotten about it.

But I couldn't. No, I couldn't.

Not when it was a reminder of what I'd lost. What I'd walked out on.

I had cheap wine in a paper bag in my left hand. The diamond ring on my fourth finger mocking me with its sparkle. The puffy, white dress that held me like a straitjacket rustled in the breeze.

My heart ached as if something wrapped around it with spindly fingers and squeezed until it robbed me of breath, of sanity, of life.

My fiancé wasn't my fiancé anymore.

The man I loved, or thought I loved, didn't love me the way I thought he did.

Instead, he loved himself. And maybe even loved my sister. How else could I have walked in on him getting a blowjob from my sister as if it hadn't been the first time? And likely wouldn't be the last. I let out a rough chuckle, then looked down at the wine, wondering if I should drink it.

Would that make the ache go away? Would that make *anything* go away? In the end, however, it didn't matter.

The man I loved wasn't the man I thought he was.

Apparently, I wasn't the woman I thought I was either. Because if I were...maybe I would have seen it long before this. I wouldn't have run out on my wedding day.

I wouldn't have become a runaway bride.

I slid into the bench in front of me and discreetly sipped at my wine.

I just wanted to breathe. To be alone.

I never wanted to talk to anyone ever again.

As I looked down at my dress, I knew I didn't want to be this Holland.

And I truly, *truly* never wanted to speak to or like or love a man again.

Ever.

CHAPTER ONE

"I'm not that bad at Mario Kart." Ethan Montgomery panted as they turned the corner on their jog.

Lincoln shook his head. "You're pretty bad. I mean, it's a family joke for a reason."

Ethan just sighed at his friend's words, kind of hurt. And...mostly not. After all, he was *really* bad at Mario Kart. He had no idea why. It should be easy.

"And there you are, telling yourself in your head that it should be easy because you have degrees and you work with computers for a living. That you program things. You could literally save the world with your research. Yet you can't figure out how to hit a single little Miss Peach with a green shell."

Lincoln didn't sound out of breath at all, and Ethan

wanted to shake his best friend. Just a little. How was it that even though he and Lincoln jogged together three times a week on this path, Lincoln was always in better shape?

Okay, it was probably because while Lincoln's job could be sedentary, he did his best to work out and stand while he did it, as well. Ethan, not so much. After all, being a computational chemist meant you had to be at a computer. And he didn't really like using a standing desk. It hurt his feet. He sat. A lot. He wasn't out of shape, not really, but it sure as hell sounded like it when he was standing next to his best friend.

His very hot best friend.

Yes, he had noticed. He had noticed a lot. Ever since that first time he had seen him without a shirt, when they had been fourteen or so, Ethan Montgomery had had a crush on his best friend Lincoln. But there was no way he was ever going to tell him that. There were rules about that sort of thing. You never fell for the best friend, especially when Lincoln was practically a Montgomery. He was family. And messing that up with crushes and hormones and hard dicks really wasn't worth the pain. He would rather have Lincoln as his best friend than know what Lincoln's dick felt like in his hands.

He held back a groan as his own cock started to

harden behind the fabric of his jogging shorts, and he kind of wished he had worn tighter underwear. Now, the rest of his jog would hurt even more than it already did.

"Are you even listening to me?" Lincoln asked seriously, still not out of breath. How did he do that?

"I'm listening to you. And I'll have you know, I hit Peach last time with a green shell."

"You were playing *as* Princess Peach, Ethan. It doesn't count if you hit a wall and then hit yourself with your own goddamn shell." He looked over at Lincoln, trying to act affronted. Instead, he burst out laughing right along with his best friend.

Of course, then he tripped over his own two feet and had to pause on the side of the walkway to rest his palms on his knees, trying to catch his breath.

"You are not this out of shape," Lincoln said, shaking his head at Ethan. "What's wrong?"

"I think I am. Must have been all those nachos I ate the night before last." He rubbed his belly, and Lincoln's eyes drifted there, narrowing.

"I've seen you without a shirt. You are just as ripped as the rest of the Montgomerys. I don't understand how all of you guys can be so pretty. Even the cousins. It's a little disconcerting."

Ethan fluttered his eyelashes at him, and Lincoln

pushed at his shoulder. "Aw, you think we're pretty? You're so sweet."

"And you're an asshole."

"I am not. You're the asshole."

Ethan shoved at him, and then they both laughed again before heading off to finish their jog.

"How many more miles do we have?" Ethan asked. He wasn't panting as badly as he had been before, but it still wasn't great.

"We have a little bit to go. Don't be a baby. You get like this at mile two every single time. Then, as soon as we get to mile three, you're just fine."

"You know me so well," Ethan said, glancing over at Lincoln.

Lincoln just shrugged and continued on his jog. And he *did* know Ethan well. After all, they had been best friends since elementary school. They met in class and had been forced to sit together thanks to their last names. McClard and Montgomery in all its alphabetical glory meant the two of them had been paired early and often.

It was dumb luck that they had actually gotten along, considering all the forced proximity. But then they had shared their pudding cups and they'd been best friends ever since.

The fact that Ethan had had a crush on Lincoln

since middle school was something that went unsaid. Lincoln didn't have a clue about Ethan's feelings. And for that, Ethan was grateful. It was just a little crush, probably because Ethan knew Lincoln so well. *And* the fact that the man was hot. Ethan couldn't help it. He had always been attracted to any gender. Of course, it hadn't been until he saw Lincoln shirtless that he really wondered why he'd stared at boys just as much as he had at girls.

Maybe Lincoln had been the catalyst for that, but he hadn't really been the first man Ethan had noticed or found attractive.

Come on, Brad Pitt in *Legends of the Fall* with that glorious mane of hair did wonders for many coming-outs.

And it wasn't like Ethan had time to date anyway. He was working on two projects right now, both of which were stalled, meaning he was working so many hours, he had a feeling if he set up a cot in his office, no one would mind. It would simply mean more output.

And while he would have loved to be able to do all his work from home since he worked from the computer, one of the projects was for the Department of Defense, and that meant he had to be connected to a certain server. The other he could set up his run times at home, but having to log in from a proxy server wasn't easy from his home all the time. It was just easier to go in, get his work done, and be able to talk out some of his frustrations and mathematical equations with his coworkers.

That meant that, sometimes, he didn't see his family and Lincoln as much as he wanted to. But that was fine, they understood. They had to. Right?

"How much longer?" Ethan panted.

"We're almost done. And then you can get your crawler like you want to and pretend that you're not eating sugar and greasy carbs."

"You always eat the other half, and then we go and get a sugary coffee. I don't know why you're judging me."

"I would have better self-control if you weren't involved," Lincoln snapped and then blushed.

Ethan's brows rose. Lincoln rarely blushed. He rarely showed *any* emotion. The man was an artist, but he went against the grain with what a stereotypical painter was thought to be like. Lincoln wasn't flamboyant or broody or even moody. He got shit done. That blush was weird, and Ethan had no idea why it had even happened.

Lincoln was a talented painter, one who was

already making waves in his circles, and people had started to recognize him at art shows.

People knew his name, his talents, and Ethan was just glad to be there. Because his best friend was one talented motherfucker, and he loved it.

He had Lincoln's first-ever painting in his living room, after all. Lincoln constantly tried to steal it back—not because he wanted to sell it, but because he said it wasn't good enough. That there were errors and flaws.

But Ethan didn't see any of those. He just saw a gift from a friend, one that spoke of so much raw talent and potential that it sometimes brought Ethan to his knees.

He didn't really get art, or what made things pretty or beautiful. He just knew what he liked, and he liked Lincoln's work.

He just liked Lincoln.

And that was enough of that.

He needed to get his mind off Lincoln and away from that train of thought. Maybe he should get laid, actually go on a date with someone, and/or maybe even find a new vocation where he didn't work so many hours—even if he loved his job.

Spending all of his free time with Lincoln probably wouldn't help this whole getting-over-his-crush thing.

They ran for another mile, Ethan almost out of breath, and Lincoln finally panting by the end of it.

"We can cool down and head over to the donut place," Lincoln finally said, and Ethan cursed out loud.

"Did you not want to stop?" Lincoln asked, his hands on his hips as he cooled down.

"Oh, I was just cursing out of gratitude."

"I didn't sleep well enough last night, I don't think," Ethan said, running his hand over his face and looking down at it. "Seriously. It's Boulder, it's not supposed to be humid. Why am I sweating this much?"

"Well, we did take a week off from running, and you hate cardio. You're much better at swimming and lifting." Lincoln handed over the water bottle that he had strapped to his wrist and Ethan took it greedily. He hadn't been lying when he said that he hadn't slept well the night before. He had forgotten his water bottle today, and the little strap that went to his wrist that Lincoln had bought him the Christmas before so they would have water on their runs.

"Why don't we swim?"

"Because the two public swimming pools that we could use in the mornings are now overrun with children. It's that time of year. There's a private one up in Westminster that I've been looking at. But the dues are astronomical."

Ethan grinned, touched and not surprised at the fact that Lincoln had been looking into it for them. Ethan had put it on his list but had forgotten because he'd gotten so busy. And he hated that forgetting both small and important things because he was focused on his work had become the norm. But Lincoln always tried to make sure that he came first. So that meant Ethan was going to keep trying to do the same for him.

"You're a famous artist and making bank right now on your art. You don't have to worry about things like that. And I do okay myself. I mean, those two PhDs of mine had better be useful for something."

A strange look crossed Lincoln's face, and Ethan frowned.

"What? What did I say?"

"Nothing. Just weird to think that I make money off something that I usually like to do."

"Usually?"

Lincoln shook his head, grabbing the water bottle back and taking a big swig. "No worries. Just temperamental artist stuff and all that. I'm figuring it out."

"Okay. If you're sure. But if you ever want to talk it out. I'm here."

Lincoln gave him a small smile, and Ethan swallowed hard. He loved it when Lincoln smiled. He really needed to go on a date. Because this was getting ridiculous.

"You hate art."

Ethan's eyes widened, a little hurt—and worried—that Lincoln thought that. "I do not. I love your art. I might not understand everyone else's, but I get yours. At least, as much as I can."

"I will always be grateful that you try. Speaking of, there's that show that Damien wants me to go to. You're going to be my date, right?"

Ethan winced. "I hate Damien." He hadn't meant to say that aloud, but it wasn't like he kept that particular feeling to himself.

"I know. You tell me often. But he's my agent, and he's really damn good at what he does."

"No, *you're* really damn good. Damien just uses you to get what he wants."

"We're not having this fight again."

Ethan held up his hands and shook his head. "You're right. Sorry. I'll be your date. Unless work runs late."

Lincoln narrowed his eyes.

"Okay, okay, work won't run late." Probably. He would get out of it, and he'd write the show on every single calendar he had, both electronic and paper, so he remembered.

"I'll see if Bristol or Madison wants to go as backup in case you forget," Lincoln said, but Ethan could hear the curtness to his words.

"No, I'll be there. It's already on the main calendar, and I'll put it everywhere else. I've got you. Trust me."

"I do, I promise."

"Okay, then. Now, what about that crawler?"

"You can have the crawler."

"Let me guess, you're going to have yogurt, something healthy."

"No, I was thinking of a Boston cream-filled. With the chocolate on top. Sounds amazing."

Ethan closed his eyes and did his best not to groan. And no, it wasn't because he was currently being a pervert and thinking of his best friend licking cream off his lips as he bit down. No, that was not what was going through his mind. However, he did want sugar now. And calories. And, when he had time, a date. Because he really needed to stop thinking about Lincoln that way. It hadn't been this bad before, but as soon as his brother Liam had started dating Arden and then got engaged? Things had gotten a little weird. Everybody was talking about marriage and babies and settling down. And Ethan wanted that. He really did. Didn't matter that he felt as if he didn't have time for it these days. He wanted that.

But he didn't know who he wanted it with. Because it couldn't be with Lincoln. That wasn't what Lincoln wanted. Meaning, Ethan needed to figure out what he wanted for himself.

And he just wasn't good at that.

But he wanted happiness, desired that happily ever after. And maybe, just maybe, he wanted to get married.

They turned the corner, and once again, Ethan tripped over his feet.

"Are you seeing what I'm seeing?" Lincoln asked.

"You mean the fact that I see a woman in a very gorgeous wedding dress currently sitting on a bench in the middle of a park, drinking from what looks to possibly be a bottle of wine out of a paper bag?"

Lincoln nodded.

"Oh. Good. Because I'm seeing that, too."

And the fact that Ethan had seen it right after thinking about marriage and babies? No, he wasn't going to overthink that. But, hell. This would be interesting.

"And either nobody has noticed that she's here, or they're all doing their best to not pay too much attention and give her space." Ethan looked over at Lincoln as he spoke, nodding.

"We should make sure she's okay," Lincoln said, even as Ethan kept nodding.

"I mean...it looks like we have a runaway bride on our hands."

"I can't believe how much you love that movie."

"Julia Roberts and Richard Gere coming together again? It was perfection."

"No, it really wasn't. But at least she wasn't a hooker this time."

"I don't understand what your beef is with Julia Roberts' movies," Ethan said as they walked towards the bride on the bench.

"I love most of her movies. But I'm just not a fan of her as a hooker or a bride on the run."

"Maybe not say that so loudly as we're about to go talk with a bride," Ethan mumbled out of the side of his mouth.

"You're right. This is a completely different situation. And there's no Richard Gere here to save her."

"No, just us. Right?" Ethan asked, winking.

"You really need to get away from your desk more." Lincoln mumbled the words, but Ethan smiled even as they walked up to the woman.

And, dear God, she was breathtaking. Sharp cheekbones and lush lips. Shoulder-length, auburn hair that had been pulled back on one side in curls, and she wore a crown—tiara?—rather than a veil. She had on a strapless dress that tucked in at the waist and had a billowing skirt that looked way out of place in the park. However, they were on the least used side of the park because there weren't as many good running trails, and the children's playground equipment was on the other side, so, not many people walked past her.

Thankfully.

"Hey, you doing okay?" Ethan asked, trying to sound casual, as if they weren't just walking up to a bride drinking wine out of a paper bag.

The woman looked up at them, and Ethan sucked in a breath. Ethan noticed that Lincoln stiffened right beside him.

Her eyes.

Jesus Christ, her eyes. They were this deep blue that looked as if they could be contacts, but Ethan knew they weren't. He could tell they went with her perfectly proportioned face and bitable lips.

She looked stunning, even with the mascara trails down her cheeks.

"Oh, hi."

His dick went hard at her voice, and he cursed under his breath.

Down, boy. This is so not the time.

Hadn't been the time with Lincoln, and sure as hell wasn't the time with her.

"Do you need help?" Lincoln asked. Then he bent down to one knee, and Ethan did the same. They looked as if they were proposing to her now, but hovering probably wasn't the best thing either.

She looked between them and shook her head. "I'm fine. Just enjoying the day."

"You look like you had other plans for the day," Ethan put in.

Her lips quirked up into a smile, and then her eyes watered. Ethan wanted to hit himself.

"Can we get you anything? Coffee?" Lincoln asked.

She looked down at the bag she held, and then tossed it and the bottle into the trashcan right next to her bench. "I really have nowhere else to be. So, coffee sounds great. You're not murderers or serial killers, are you? Because I've watched enough *Criminal Minds* that I know, sometimes, serial killers work in pairs. But, usually, it's just by themselves. And I also know that if they do work together, there's normally a dominant and a submissive within the pair." She shut her mouth, and Ethan just shook his head.

"You would really get along with my brother, Aaron. He loves *Criminal Minds*."

"I don't know if I love it. It tends to keep me up at night. Anyway, I really should go home."

"Come on, let's get you some coffee. Make sure you're okay. But first, my name's Lincoln. And this is Ethan. You look like you've had a tough day."

The woman gave them a watery smile before standing up, and they followed suit. "I'm Holland. Today was supposed to be my wedding day."

"We got that much," Ethan muttered, and Lincoln elbowed him in the gut.

"I mean the dress isn't really that great for just a Thursday afternoon out." She sighed. "I could use that coffee. And I *really* hope you guys aren't serial killers."

"Well, I'm not," Ethan said and then gestured over at Lincoln. "Can't promise the same for him."

Holland's eyes widened, and Lincoln muttered something that Ethan probably didn't want to hear.

"I'm not a serial killer either. Though, of course, that's the first thing a serial killer would say. Anyway, we can go have coffee now right outside of that café. We don't even have to go in. I promise. You're safe with us."

Even as Lincoln said the words, they warmed Ethan, and he knew that even if he wasn't there, she would be safe with his best friend. Because Lincoln was the person you went to when things got bad. And from the way Holland was standing there, looking lost in her big wedding dress, he knew things had gotten bad.

"Okay," she whispered.

Ethan knew, right then, that no thoughts of him wanting his best friend, or things with work, or even the fact that he was getting out of shape mattered.

This bride needed them, and he was a Montgomery. Lincoln was pretty much a Montgomery, as well. And that's what Montgomerys did. They helped.

Even if their libidos happened to get in the way.

CHAPTER TWO

Holland Yeaton had lived through bad days before in her life. Plenty of them. So many bad days interspersed with the good ones, it was actually a little scary. But normal.

The fact that this day was probably the worst of her life felt like a dramatic understatement.

But as she sat across from two of the most incredibly attractive men she had ever met in her life while sitting at an outdoor café as people stared at her, she figured that maybe she wasn't overreacting.

After all, she was wearing her insanely and annoyingly expensive wedding dress, the one that she loved but hadn't thought she should get. In her mind, a wedding was only supposed to be one day, and she had wanted to have a *life* with her spouse—now, her ex.

She had wanted more than just that single day. She wanted years, *decades.*

At least, in theory. Just because she and Dustin had had problems before the wedding day didn't mean they always would have had problems. It just meant they'd have had things to work on right out of the gate. And that should have been fine.

Because all couples had things to worry about.

But despite not thinking it was important, she had been coerced by her sister and mother into purchasing this far too expensive dress. The one they'd said looked spectacular on her in a high-couture sort of way but made her feel like a lacy cupcake.

She had wanted a simple ceremony, a simple dress, and a lifetime of happiness and love with Dustin.

None of that had happened.

Instead, she sat across from two strangers. Men who had come up to her to make sure she was okay when everyone else had walked by. Onlookers had gawked and likely wondered if she, in her stupid wedding dress, was for a photoshoot or perhaps some form of farce or TV show.

It was none of those.

It was her life. And maybe this is what she deserved.

After all, she had tried for happiness and had been left wanting.

Why not add humiliation and a little drunkenness to that?

"Would you like another cup of coffee?" Lincoln asked. Holland looked up, her eyes widening as she stared at the sexy man in front of her.

The fact that she kept calling them *sexy* and *attractive* in her head just meant that maybe she'd had a little too much wine—which, yes, she'd been drinking out of a paper bag.

She hadn't really thought through what else to do outside of drinking her worries away in a public place because she had nowhere else to go.

She'd only had her small purse with her, not even all of her credit cards, so she hadn't been able to find a hotel. Plus, that would've just been weird. She hadn't been able to go home either, because that's where Dustin lived. And she couldn't even go to her parents', because her mom and dad were furious with her.

After all, walking out on your wedding while still wearing the damn dress probably wasn't the best thing to do when your parents were already mad at you for a thousand other things. Stuff that seemed like nothing but was inconceivable in their minds.

But as she looked at Lincoln, Holland tried to push that out of her head and just be...okay. She likely already seemed a little insane to them. She didn't want to add to that. She just wanted to be normal. But *normal* wasn't sitting alone in a wedding dress in a park, drinking wine out of a paper bag.

At least, not anybody *else's* normal. Maybe it was hers now.

Snapping herself out of her thoughts, she focused on the man in front of her again. Lincoln had longish, dark hair that curled right above his collar, a strong jawline, piercing eyes, and very sensual lips.

Not that she was looking. That was the wine. All the booze.

And on that thought...

"I'd love another cup of coffee," she mumbled.

Lincoln smiled softly. It reached his eyes, the expression full of compassion rather than judgment, and she counted that as a win. He raised his hand.

The waitress quickly scurried over, and Holland didn't blame her for the extra hustle. After all, the woman wasn't the only person gawking at the two men —Holland was right there with her.

"Could we have another round of coffees? Thank you," Lincoln said, smiling at the waitress.

"And extra cream." Ethan gestured towards the empty creamer container between them. "I use an exorbitant amount of creamer in my coffee. And it seems I'm not alone," Ethan added, smiling over at Holland.

Holland could feel the heat on her cheeks as her blush spread, but that was fine. So she liked a little coffee with her cream and sugar. Sue her.

But Ethan seemed to like his coffee the same way, even if Lincoln only added a dash of cream to his.

And the fact that she currently cared way too much about how they took their coffee just told her that the wine was still in her system. She was focusing on everything that didn't matter so she didn't have to focus on the huge, glaring, obvious elephant in the room. Also known as the wedding-dress thing—and what had led up to it.

"Thank you," she said after the waitress had walked away, and Holland could speak to the guys alone. Not that she was sure she really *wanted* to talk with them. She was actually a little worried about what they might say. Were they just nice guys offering her a cup of coffee? Or were things about to get weird? She knew she probably shouldn't have just gone off with two strangers, but she had a good feeling about them. And if this was her end via serial killer, well, it served her right. After all, she'd had a really bad day.

"So, do you want to tell us what's up?" Ethan asked.

Holland just grinned and looked down at her empty coffee cup.

Lincoln closed his eyes and groaned. "Ethan," he grumbled. "Seriously?"

"What? I'm just saying."

Holland blew out a breath, wanting the awkwardness to be over. She wanted everything to be over so she could get to the next step and figure things out.

"My name is Holland, as you know."

"Hi," Lincoln said, his smile still in place.

"I own a boutique...and I was supposed to get married today. But, as you can see, it didn't happen."

"Well, I actually didn't know if it happened or not," Ethan said. "For all I knew, you got married and *then* ran off. Not that you did. Maybe I should just shut up. You're right, Lincoln, I do tend to spout off nonsense."

The waitress came back and handed out their drinks, still staring at the two guys while ignoring Holland altogether. It was only her quick reflexes to move her hand out of the way right at the last moment that stopped her from getting burned with hot coffee. The waitress walked off without even a "sorry," and Holland just shook her head. Well, the guys *were* pretty attractive, but that was a little ridiculous.

Ethan quickly handed over napkins while Lincoln grabbed her hand and looked it over.

"You okay?" Lincoln asked. "Did she get you?"

Holland looked down and shook herself mentally.

Just because these guys were being sweeter to her than anyone had been in a long time, didn't mean she had to continue down this line of conversation. Or even stay here. This wasn't smart. She really needed to go home —or *find* a home—and figure out what to do next.

"I'm fine." Holland pulled her hand away, and gratefully took a napkin from Ethan to finish cleaning up the mess.

Ethan helped her clean. "No harm, no foul. Messes happens all the time. But are you really okay?"

"I'm fine," she repeated.

"Okay," Lincoln said, looking into her eyes. "If you say so."

She wasn't fine. But...whatever. She was all right when it came to the coffee and the spill, and that's all that mattered at the moment.

"How about you guys tell me what you do?" she said, trying for small talk so she didn't have to actually answer their question. Namely, telling them why she was in her wedding dress and had been drinking in the middle of a park.

The guys looked at each other before seeming to have some sort of silent conversation she wasn't a part of. Were they...together? Maybe. They seemed to be at least best friends. But the thought of the two of them together? Hottest thing ever.

Not that she was actually going to think about that. Her brain was already too full as it was.

"Well, I'm a computational chemist," Ethan said, saying it quickly as if he were afraid that Holland would judge.

"What type of computation? Like in industry, or do you do research with a university?"

Ethan's brow rose, and Holland just grinned, not surprised in the least at the reaction.

"One of my good friends was a chemistry major in college while I got my business degree. We met in one of our math classes. I don't remember the type anymore because it was one of those statistics and theoretical mixed hybrid things where they were trying to give less credits for double the amount of material or something like that."

Ethan nodded, smiling full-out, an expression that did wonderful things for his eyes. "Well, I work for industry, not so much in the university sphere. So, while I do write papers, I don't have to teach."

"Thank God," Lincoln muttered, and Ethan mock-glared.

"Excuse me?"

"You have no patience for teaching."

"I do."

"Remember that time you tried to teach your sister how to work her new Fire Stick?"

"She didn't understand it, and I didn't know why. She knows how to use her computer, knows how to use the internet. I just didn't understand why I had to be the one to show her how to use a little thing that you plug into the back of a TV."

Lincoln looked at Holland, and she held back a smile.

"And that is why he would not be a good teacher."

"Fuck you," Ethan said and then looked over at Holland, blushing. "Sorry."

"You're welcome to curse all you want. I promise. I'm not going to get offended. I usually have a mouth like a sailor, but I'm having a really weird day."

The guys looked at her, expecting her to say something else, but she didn't. She would wait until the last moment if she could. Or not at all. It wasn't as if she really knew how to explain what had happened.

"Well, I paint," Lincoln said, filling the void of silence.

Holland grinned. "Really? What kind?"

"Right now, I've been working with mostly oils. But I've done some acrylics and mixed media, as well. I usually do some sketching and charcoal too, when I'm working on drafts. But right now, it's mostly oil."

"He's pretty good at it, too," Ethan said. Lincoln gave him a look that she couldn't read. Was Ethan being sarcastic? Or maybe Holland was supposed to know who Lincoln was. After all, she liked art, knew art, but she couldn't remember every artist's name. Maybe if she hadn't had so much wine earlier, she'd be a little bit better than this.

"You don't have to talk if you don't want to. But do you want to talk about what happened? Why you're sitting here in your wedding dress," Ethan asked, and Lincoln sighed, pinching the bridge of his nose.

And because that made her smile, because Ethan looked so earnest in his desire to help, Holland figured... why not? It wasn't like the rest of the people in her world wouldn't find out soon. After all, they had been at the wedding that morning.

"As I said, I was supposed to get married today. But, instead, I walked in on my maid of honor, also known as my little sister, going down on my future husband."

Both guys just stared at her, their eyes wide, mouths agape.

"I've never seen blush and bashful in that position before, and I never want to see it again."

Both guys grinned at her really lame movie joke, but she couldn't help it, she just wanted someone to laugh. It was either that or break down crying.

"You know, Lincoln and I were talking about Julia Roberts' films before we saw you," Ethan said.

"*Steel Magnolias* is a heart ripper. But I didn't choose my colors because of that. My mom did, actually." Holland shook her head. "I really didn't have a lot to do with this wedding. It was all what everyone else wanted. I was just happy to be married, looking forward to spending the rest of my life with Dustin. But that's not happening. It can't. He's a cheater. As is my sister. Honestly, I don't know what I'm going to do next. So, excuse me while I try not to cry, and maybe find more wine or something. Because if I drink it all away, perhaps I'll wake up from this horrible nightmare, and I'll be married, and everything will be fine." Holland gratefully took a napkin from Ethan and wiped her tears. "I know I look ridiculous. I don't know why I ran out of the place in my wedding dress. I grabbed my small bag. Not even my big one. So, I don't even have my phone. Or anything, really."

"What can we do?" Lincoln asked. Holland looked up.

"What?"

"What can we do? What do you need from us?"

"I don't need anything from you guys. I don't even know you. You let me speak and have some coffee. And

I'm grateful for that. I have a little cash. Like a five or something that was in my small bag."

"I'm pretty sure we can pay for your coffee," Ethan said dryly. "Now, you may not know me, but my family and I—and that includes Lincoln over here since he's my best friend—we don't just *not* help people.

"Oh." What else could she say? But she did get some information out of what he'd said, even with the crazy double negative. They were best friends. That was good to know. At least for her own mental catalog. She really needed a nap or something. She was losing her mind.

"Now, do you have a plan?" Lincoln asked.

Holland shook her head. "I just ran. I saw the smirk on my sister's face, and I knew that wasn't the first time it'd happened. And it probably wouldn't be the last. I couldn't marry him. My mother screamed at me, called me horrible names and told me I had to get back there, even though she saw exactly what I did. After that, I ran and left everything behind."

"Okay, then. If you don't have a plan, we'll find a new one," Lincoln said. He gave her a tight nod, then looked over at Ethan. "Let's call your brother and see if he still has that condo available."

"Condo?" She was so lost, and these guys talked as if they had a plan. She didn't even know the meaning of the word at the moment, and that was *so* unlike her.

"You mentioned that you didn't have anywhere to go," Ethan said, pulling out his phone. "My brother has a few properties around. I'm sure you can stay the night at one of them. That way, you don't have to stay at one of our places and feel weird or even more like we're serial killers trying to lure you into our webs."

Holland snorted, feeling as if she were twenty steps behind again. "Well, I didn't really think that you guys were serial killers, but it would be par for the course after my day."

"We're not serial killers. However, you know that probably doesn't mean anything coming out of a serial killer's mouth." Lincoln's lips quirked as he said it, but she didn't relax. "So, you'll at least have a place to stay tonight as long as Ethan can arrange it. And if not one of those places, we'll find you somewhere safe to sleep. Now, why don't you tell me where you were getting married, and we'll go get your stuff."

Holland just sat there, stunned. "Why are you doing this?"

"Because you need help," Ethan said, looking down at his phone and not at her. "And I've always wanted to save a princess in a white dress."

"You have not," Lincoln said. "Your jokes are getting worse."

"They really are. Sorry."

Holland just looked between the two of them, confused. "I don't get it."

"You don't have to get it. And you don't have to be alone. We'll help you figure this out."

"But how can I ever repay you for any of this?"

"You don't have to," Ethan said. "Or I don't know, pay it forward or something. Or let us know what happens later." Ethan just shrugged. "You might not know the Montgomerys, but once you're in, it's really hard to get out," Ethan said with a wink. Holland frowned.

"If you haven't guessed, the Montgomerys are his very large family," Lincoln said dryly. "This guy over here sometimes forgets that not everybody knows about them."

"Oh." She was still confused.

"Okay, we have a plan. You'll have a place to stay, at least for the night. We'll get your things, and you can take some time to figure out what to do. And if you need to talk it out, we're here. I promise we won't punch your ex in the face. Or in the dick," Lincoln said, and Holland burst out laughing. She had thought Ethan was the one with the sense of humor, and Lincoln a little more stoic. But, apparently, they each had layers.

"I don't really know what I'm going to do, though. About anything."

"You don't need to make any decisions right now. But if you want to get out of that wedding dress and into something comfortable, we can figure it out. You don't have to go it alone. That, I can promise you."

She looked between them, still confused. But she knew that maybe, just maybe, they were right. Perhaps she *didn't* have to do this alone.

Later, sitting in the back of Lincoln's SUV as he drove the three of them towards the church, she had to wonder if she was making a mistake.

What was she going to do without Dustin?

He was supposed to be her future, her everything. But she couldn't think about that.

Because it wasn't just the cheating. It was the look. Not just her sister's smirk, but the look on Dustin's face, too. As if he didn't care about her, didn't care about anything.

As if she weren't worth it. Wasn't worth anything.

She hated that feeling. She didn't want to feel that way, didn't want to wonder if he would cheat again or if he was thinking about her sister when he slid inside her. How long had it been happening? And how long had she been the dupe, the one he planned to marry because everyone thought it was expected?

And how was she supposed to face her sister?

The woman who always wanted everything

Holland had, who was always jealous, even though Holland never understood why. She didn't understand her little sister, never had. And now, she knew she never would.

As they pulled into the church parking lot, Holland let out a relieved breath, thankful that she didn't recognize any of the cars.

She didn't know what would happen next.

But, as she'd thought earlier, and as she looked between Ethan and Lincoln, maybe she didn't have to do it alone.

Then she looked down at her wedding dress and remembered. She had to do this alone. She was going to be alone now.

She had lost her chance at her happily ever after. As that thought settled in, tears slid from her eyes and ran down her cheeks. And she broke.

She was just so tired.

So hurt.

And angry.

All of it burst like a dam, and her cries came out in hiccupping sobs.

The SUV door opened, and Ethan slid in beside her, holding her in his arms as Lincoln shifted in his seat to reach back and put his hand on her knee, giving it a squeeze through her dress.

Though she knew they were there, that this would matter to her later, right then it couldn't. It couldn't matter that they were trying to help the crazy lady in her wedding dress. Because if she let it matter, then she'd have to feel beyond the icy layer she'd tried to wrap herself in.

She had lost everything that day. It was hard to find hope in the darkness.

And she hated herself. Hated that she'd even had hope to begin with before she walked in on her sister and her fiancé.

She should've known from her experiences long ago that having hope meant it would be a harder fall when everything got ripped away.

She should've learned. But she hadn't.

Once broken, shame on them.

Twice shattered, shame on her.

Again.

CHAPTER THREE

A FEW MONTHS LATER

Lincoln McClard loved art. He loved the fact that no matter what an artist did, sometimes, it didn't portray exactly what was on their mind. Interpretation was up to the viewer, not the artists themselves.

Artists could put everything into a piece: their heart, their soul...their literal blood, sweat, and tears.

But, in the end, it was those who were also a part of the art, the viewer, and the observer, that stated what art was—at least, to them.

But no matter what, the artist was the one that pressed that initial stamp ingenious, that initial stroke of paint or other media. It was their job to do their best to convey what they needed the world to know. But *they* also needed to know that, sometimes, that wasn't what happened in the end.

And Lincoln told himself that often. Because, dear God, some days, he just really hated his fucking job.

Since when had art become so hard for him?

He was creative. It had practically been stamped on his forehead by his parents, teachers, friends, mentors, and classmates.

Ever since he was little with his macaroni necklaces and art projects. Even before they did it in art class itself, he had known he wanted to create.

Oh, he had done pretty poorly at first. Had spent years learning his craft and separating the good from the bad. Yet now, he felt like he was right back in that spot where it was macaroni and no prospects.

But, no matter what, he always did his best. Or at least he thought he did.

He had learned how to paint and draw, had used different media over time, had practiced with clay and kilns and other earth materials. He'd tried as much as he could, attempting to find what worked for him.

He'd even had a go at glassblowing and sculpting, using metal and casts and bronze.

He'd worked with almost everything he could get

his hands on and knew he would keep experimenting with different things as time went on.

But, at the moment, he had a commission that he actually had to get done, and nothing was coming to him. Not a single damn thing.

The only thing the man who'd ordered this piece had said, was that he wanted gray in it. He'd said it didn't have to be entirely gray—it could be rainbow-colored for all he cared. As long as there was gray to match his wife's eyes.

And Lincoln loved that idea. He loved that it would be different. At least, in his mind. Something perfect just for that man and his wife, even if it was going to a huge conglomerate. Some of his art friends weren't fans of working for 'the man' or any form of corporations.

He made art for money, and he was just fine with that. He didn't believe in the starving-artists' deal. The idea that you could only create if you were doing it for the art itself and not to actually put food in your mouth and a roof over your head.

That was like saying someone who worked in business or owned their own company couldn't make their own money. But, no, no one ever thought that. In that, as long as they did the work, they were allowed to make money. But an artist had to starve? No, thank you.

Lincoln growled, threw his paintbrush onto his table, and put his head in his hands.

Thankfully, there hadn't actually been paint on his brush, so he hadn't made a mess.

Because putting paint on the brush meant he had to actually know what the fuck he was doing.

But, like always lately it seemed, he had no idea.

And now, he was having a diatribe in his head when it came to what art was and where his place in the art world should be.

Honestly, he didn't know what art was anymore.

He had been art-blocked. Cock-blocked, art-blocked, all of it. And he knew exactly whose fault it was. And it wasn't him.

Even though it was irrational, and he knew that it was probably all his own damn fault, he knew exactly who he blamed.

Ethan fucking Montgomery. His best friend and the bane of his existence.

Just because he had loved the man for as long as he could remember didn't mean that anything was ever going to happen between them. No, nothing was going to happen with Ethan Montgomery. Why? Because Lincoln had long ago been put in the friend-zone.

Lincoln had watched Ethan go through men and women over time. He knew that Ethan was bad at dating—he spent way too much time at work and was really terrible at the small details needed for establishing new relationships.

And that was fine for some people. Lincoln would have liked it. But that would only matter if Ethan actually paid attention to Lincoln beyond just being best friends.

Lincoln was spending his time thinking about Ethan and how he missed him. The fact that he had seen him just the day prior and already missed his face meant that he'd gone off the deep end. And now Lincoln was wondering what he was doing while being a lovesick fool over a man who was never going to think of him in that way.

And if he let himself imagine that anything could ever happen...he might just throw up. Because he couldn't. Ethan was such a big part of his life, the idea of doing anything to mess up what they had, made him want to break out in a cold sweat.

Lincoln didn't have a second option. He didn't have a backup plan when it came to friends and futures.

Ethan was it.

Lincoln had a cousin he liked, parents he loved even though they lived across the country, and that was it.

Those three people. And his best friend.

And the Montgomerys since, through his best friend, they had practically adopted him.

So, having lustful thoughts about Ethan probably wasn't the best idea.

Even though Ethan's mom probably would have been happy in a sense because that would mean marriage, maybe even babies, and she'd be able to be a grandmother.

But that wasn't for Lincoln.

And the sooner he got those thoughts out of his head, the better.

It didn't help that every time he thought of Ethan, he got hard and couldn't think of anything else. So, he would just push all of that out of his mind and try to get to work.

He glared at his canvas.

No, staring and praying wasn't going to work. Nothing worked.

Lincoln stood from his seat, rolled his shoulders back, and was just deciding whether he should go for another jog—or maybe go visit Ethan since he knew his friend had the day off—when the door opened, the sound of keys hitting his ears a moment later.

He frowned, thinking of who had keys to his studio.

Ethan, of course, since they had keys to each other's

places for emergencies and if one of them was out of town.

And...Damien.

"Ah, you're done for the day. That's good. We need to talk." Damien walked through the bottom half of the studio and looked up, grinning as if he were in his element and didn't have a care in the world. As if he were only there to be helpful. But that was never the case. Damien was good at his job because he always got what he wanted. And Lincoln didn't always mind that because the other man wasn't cruel about it. But he sure as hell wasn't in the mood for whatever Damien had to say at the moment.

Lincoln sighed and wiped his hands on his towel before walking toward Damien. "I thought the key was only for emergencies," he said, a little annoyed. What if he'd actually been working? Someone opening the door like that would have thrown him right off track.

And while Ethan had a key, he never used it. He always let Lincoln know when he was coming by, sending a text so it wouldn't bother Lincoln until he saw it.

They had rules, and when you worked out of a studio in your home, boundaries were important.

That wasn't something that Damien understood, though.

And while he might be Lincoln's agent, might've helped him get to where he was today, it was still really annoying.

The fact that Lincoln had slept with Damien a few years ago didn't help. Things had gotten weird. Lincoln had thought that things were fine. That they had calmed down. But they still seemed a little odd.

Or maybe that was just him.

"The key?" Lincoln prompted again.

Damien waved that off. "Oh, it's just me. I'm practically family." He winked. "Okay, not *too* much like family. Don't want to get too Southern, if you know what I mean."

Lincoln didn't say anything. There really wasn't anything *to* say. Damien did what he wanted to, said whatever he liked, even if it was cruel and derogatory. But he knew the art business inside and out—and he knew Lincoln's work. So, it felt like, sometimes, Lincoln had to make a deal with the devil. And Damien really wasn't *that* bad.

Even though he shared a name with the little Antichrist from that movie.

Something that Ethan mentioned often.

Lincoln *really* needed to get Ethan out of his head.

"So, what are you working on?" Damien asked.

Lincoln was grateful that he had closed off a section

of his studio so nobody could simply walk through. He had rules about his art, something that Damien usually followed: no one saw it until he was ready. But Damien always asked anyway.

Always.

"Work. As you know."

Damien just frowned. "Okay, if you say so. Now, I know you went to that art show a few months ago with your little friend, but you have something coming up soon. You're going to need to have someone on your arm that people want to talk about."

Lincoln pinched the bridge of his nose. He hated this. Hated that Damien called Ethan his *little friend.*

Lincoln growled about it. He so didn't want to get in the middle of this. So, he wasn't going to.

Fuck it all.

"You know what, yes, I went to the art show. It was nice, but I don't really need to go to another one. Not until I'm ready for my next show. And that's not for a bit yet."

Or until he felt like it. He had some pieces ready, but he wanted to get this commission done first. He just needed to get Ethan off his mind so he could concentrate. But that wasn't easy when people kept bringing him up.

Damien just rolled his eyes and went to the fridge to

get out a sparkling water for himself. He didn't even bother to ask or offer Lincoln one. Not that he wanted one, but still...Damien just made himself at home wherever he went.

Which was *never* a good thing.

"Well, I signed you up for one. You have to go, or it'll make you look bad."

Considering that he hadn't been the one to book it, he wasn't sure how that was even an issue. Jesus Christ, he was already tired, and it wasn't even noon yet.

The more he thought about it, though, he usually had a good time at those things, even if he didn't like being forced to go. And he could celebrate and aid other artists, and that usually made up for any annoyances that came with Damien's pushing. *I love art*, he reminded himself.

"Fine, but I'm bringing Ethan."

Damien scowled, making his all-too-pretty face look harsh. "The man knows nothing about art. I don't know why you force him into it. He doesn't have any fun, and it makes you look bad."

Again with the looking bad. "Who cares what other people think? And he has fun, and I have fun when he's there. He's been my best friend forever. Don't start."

Damien set down his sparkling water and held up his hands. "I'm not starting anything. I'm just saying what everybody else thinks. You need to dump that little guy."

Jesus fucking Christ. Little guy?

"We're friends, Damien. And, besides, you really don't have a say. You're my agent, nothing more."

"I was more once."

"That's it. I'm done. I have things to do. Is there something else you wanted?"

"Just to tell you about the upcoming show and to check in as always. No need to get angry. Now, you know your deadline's coming up. So, no pressure but... *pressure.*" He laughed as he said it, and Lincoln's pulse began to throb in his temples.

Dear God, he was never going to be able to finish this project, and even if he did, he might end up strangling Damien or some random passerby in the process. He was tired, annoyed, and had no idea what he was going to do about this art piece—or Ethan, come to think of it.

"I need to get back to it. I'll help you find the door."

Damien narrowed his eyes at the slight insult, but Lincoln really didn't give a flying fuck right then. He was tired and really just wanted Damien out of his apartment.

Maybe he should change the locks.

With that errant thought, he smiled. Damien saw

the grin, and heat filled the other man's eyes. He leaned forward, but Lincoln stepped back, giving the other man a tight nod.

"Talk to you later."

"I'm sure you will," Damien purred before sauntering out. Sauntering. How the man did it so well, Lincoln would never know, but...seriously. Lincoln grabbed his stuff and quickly sent off a text to Ethan, letting him know he was on his way over.

Ethan: *Good. I just finished up some paperwork at home and was about to put on the game.*

Lincoln: *Yeah?*

Ethan: *Yep, some form of sports ball is on.*

Lincoln: *You like all sports, stop acting like an idiot.*

Ethan: *Well, you like me that way.*

He did. And that was the problem.

He sighed and then got into his car to head over to Ethan's. Maybe if he just relaxed a bit, he'd be able to focus on work. Because forcing himself to work wasn't working at all.

He pulled into Ethan's driveway and got out, laughing at the absurdity of what Ethan wore when his best friend walked out to the porch to meet him.

He snorted, covering his eyes as he made his way toward Ethan. "How are you an adult?" Lincoln asked, shaking his head as he walked past Ethan.

He had on SpongeBob pajama pants with a white tank and a Denver Broncos jersey over it, but the jersey was so big, he could see the straps of the tank. He looked like a mashup of orange and blue and yellow, and it seriously burned Lincoln's corneas.

"It's laundry day."

"You can't have so much laundry that you're wearing that. And where the hell did you get SpongeBob pajamas that fit you?"

"Bristol. She's the sister that keeps on giving. And, don't worry, I was going to change. You just got here faster than I figured."

"Well, at least you look comfy," Lincoln grumbled.

"And you look like you've got a stick up your ass. You doing okay?"

"I'm fine. Just art stuff."

"You want to talk about it?"

The fact that Ethan could ask that, even if he didn't know anything about what Lincoln was talking about and was willing to just listen and try to help meant everything. Lincoln hated the fact that he wanted more from his best friend. Why couldn't this be good enough?

It needed to be enough.

"I'm going to go change real quick. There's beer in

the fridge, although I don't know if it's too early for that or not."

"Well, it's college football day. I think you're allowed to start drinking at noon. And, hey, look, it's noon now."

"College football." He snapped his fingers, grinning. "I knew I was wearing the wrong jersey."

"As I said before, you're an idiot. Go change. You're hurting my eyes. Maybe put on the right jersey since I know you own that, too."

"I may be an idiot, but you love me," Ethan said. Both of them just looked at each other, Ethan going a little pale, even as Lincoln's heart raced.

Well, this wasn't awkward at all. Though he didn't know why it seemed strange for Ethan. It shouldn't be. It was just him. Right?

"Sure. Even with all of...whatever the hell you're wearing." He gestured to Ethan's ensemble.

"I'll go change."

"Thank God."

And then Lincoln turned and went to get two beers and two of the reusable water bottles that Ethan kept in the fridge.

They'd watch football, talk about nothing, and Lincoln would figure out his life.

Because he had to.

"So, what do you think Holland's up to?" Ethan asked, zipping up his jeans. He'd kept the white tank on, but now he was wearing jeans that molded to his ass perfectly with it.

Dear God, how the hell did the man do it? He'd looked like a deranged toddler before, and now, he looked sexy as hell.

Lincoln was going to lose his damn mind because of his best friend.

"Eyes up here, bro," Ethan said, laughing. Lincoln blushed.

"Sorry, I was just...you know, confused without the color."

"Sure."

"If I wanted to look at your junk, I would," Lincoln said, trying to cover.

Ethan's brows rose. "Good to know."

"Anyway, Holland. What do you think is up with her?"

"You texted her yesterday, didn't you? What did she say?"

It had been a few months since Lincoln had met Holland Yeaton. A few months where she tried to figure out her new life. And Lincoln was glad for it. He liked her. Really liked her.

And if he were honest with himself, if she hadn't

been in a fucking wedding dress on her wedding day, drinking wine out of a paper bag in the park, he probably would've asked her out. And in the months since, he knew she'd needed time. And frankly, so did he.

"Nothing," Ethan said quickly, and Lincoln's brows rose.

"You've been talking about her often. You got a crush?" Lincoln asked, only partially joking.

"Maybe. She's nice. And you know she's single now." Ethan groaned. "Okay, rephrase that in a way that doesn't make me sound like a giant douche."

"Well, considering I was thinking that if she hadn't been in a wedding dress that day, *I* might have asked her out, I think we're both douches right about now."

"Oh. That's weird. Have we ever liked the same girl before?"

"Maybe. But we have different tastes."

"A little. Though I don't think our types are anything concrete. Mostly we both just want a non-horrible person. That's a good place to start. And Holland seems to fit that. But I don't know if she's really ready to date."

"That's what I was thinking, too. Though she has moved on, at least in terms of getting her own place and all."

"Right, and even though we both offered to help her move in, she refused."

"Well, there is that whole idea of two random male strangers figuring out exactly where you live."

"We aren't strangers anymore. And weren't even really then at that point." Ethan paused.

"Think we should invite her over for game night or something? You know, as friends."

"Just friends," Lincoln replied, not knowing what else to say.

"Well, we don't know if she's ready for more, and the number one rule between us has always been: never let anyone get between us. Right? So, if we both have a thing for her, then we should both stand aside."

"That is a good rule, but I don't know if we've ever used it."

They each took a breath, staring at one another, and he wasn't sure what to think, what to say.

There was so much silence then that it hurt. Lincoln cleared his throat and began again. "Let's invite her over. She can kick your ass in Mario Kart."

"You're an asshole."

"True. But she should be used to it by now. I mean, she's met you more than once so..."

He rolled his eyes. "Okay, I'll invite her over. I think

she could use some friends. We don't need to be lecturers."

"We're not lecturers. Of course, that's probably what a lecturer says."

"True enough. Plus, even if we get beyond the fact that we both think she's hot, it's nice to have other friends. You know?"

"She probably needs to smile. Or needs to laugh her ass off as she watches you try to play."

"I'm going to get you for that. But we'll invite her over. And then we'll be friends. You can never have too many friends. Friends are good."

"Friends *are* good."

As Ethan walked away to pick up his phone, Lincoln hated that he hadn't been talking about only Holland just then.

Because he was in love with his best friend, and the girl Lincoln had been thinking about was also on his best friend's mind.

No wonder he couldn't create anything. His mind was too fucked up. Maybe beyond redemption.

CHAPTER FOUR

Tonight was probably a bad idea, but lately, Ethan felt as if he were full of them. And not just when it came to personal decisions like asking Holland over for game night. He'd likely not only suck donkey balls in front of her game-wise, but he'd also cock-blocked Lincoln a bit.

He'd thought he knew his best friend so well. But he'd clearly missed the fact that Lincoln had a thing for Holland just like he did. But maybe that's *why* he had missed it. Ethan had his own feelings for Lincoln...and Holland. And wasn't that just great?

Hell, tonight was a recipe for disaster, but it wasn't like he could back out now.

He wasn't sure he wanted to.

But none of that would matter if he didn't get home.

Lincoln was going to kill him.

Flat-out *kill him* if he didn't make it on time.

He'd been called into work for a server issue, and even though it was a Sunday, he hadn't had a choice. So, he'd left Lincoln to set up the house for the evening. He was such an asshole. He didn't even have flowers or scotch or anything to say he was sorry for not being there when the whole thing had been his idea.

Work had gotten in the way. As soon as he sat down to try and fix something, he'd become engrossed. He'd lost track of time. When he finally looked up, he realized that the sun was setting—and he was so totally screwed.

Ethan tapped his fingers on the steering wheel as he waited at a red light, wishing it would turn green. He had called Lincoln on his way, but he hadn't answered, and Ethan hoped it was because his friend was just busy with something. Not because he wanted to strangle Ethan.

Okay, maybe not *too* busy. That meant Lincoln was doing all the work while Ethan was doing nothing.

God, he was such an asshole.

He knew he was a bad friend sometimes, but he figured today might take the cake.

Ethan needed to do better. Seriously.

He pulled into his driveway, thankful that he only saw Lincoln's car and not another one that could have been Holland's.

But for all he knew, she could have taken an Uber so she could have a drink. And now he seriously wanted to slap himself.

He did not deserve his best friend. That much was clear. He would just have to make it up to him. Somehow.

Ethan got out of his car and practically ran to his front door, but Lincoln opened it before he even had a chance to get out his keys.

"Hey, nice of you to show up," Lincoln said, and Ethan groaned.

"I'm sorry. I'm so sorry. I didn't mean for it to happen."

Lincoln just looked at Ethan and then gave him a sad smile before nodding.

"I know you didn't. Did you finish what you needed to get done at work?"

"I did. And then a couple of other things because I got distracted."

"You're the best at what you do, Ethan. They're lucky to have you."

Ethan followed Lincoln inside and took his stuff out of his pockets to put in the little bowl by the front door.

"It's Sunday, though. I shouldn't have had to work at all. And since my boss was there, also working, I told him I wouldn't be coming in tomorrow since I put my hours in today."

"Your boss is pretty cool. As long as you get the work done and put in a certain number of hours, you don't have to actually be there nine to five during the week. Pretty nifty for a job in science."

"Nifty. So, if you want to hang out tomorrow, I can make it up to you. Seems I have the day off."

"Maybe. We'll see how my brain is working in terms of art."

"Still having trouble with that painting?" Ethan asked as he went to the fridge and pulled out a beer. And then he looked at the counters and cursed under his breath.

"Jesus Christ. How am I such a horrible person?"

The counters were covered in food, all plated perfectly with a charcuterie board and little appetizers. Lincoln had even set up a warming station. He had everything covered, ready for when Holland and Ethan showed up.

Since none of the stuff out on the counter needed to be refrigerated, Ethan had a feeling that other things were still in the fridge. He was going to hell. A special level where he was forced to pay penance for all the stupid shit he had done to his best friend.

"The painting is taking its time. They sometimes do that. And don't worry about it. I was taking my frustrations out by cooking, so I made way too much food. But I had fun. Check out the pinwheels in the fridge. I put extra bacon in, just like you like."

"Frustrations over your work, or me?" Ethan asked as he went to the fridge and took out two wheels. They were tortillas filled with cream cheese, shredded lettuce, and bacon, then rolled up and cut into little rolls.

It was seriously heaven in his mouth.

He groaned as he took a bite and handed the other one to Lincoln. Lincoln just smiled at Ethan and ate his.

"Both. Frustrations in both. But don't worry. You're here. And Holland will be here soon. I guess we should form a plan."

"A plan?" Ethan asked, taking a sip of his beer to wash down his pinwheel. Such good food.

"A plan, for when Holland gets here."

Ethan looked at Lincoln, frowning.

"We need a plan?"

"Okay, maybe eat a little bit more so you can think. We are bringing a woman over, one we both find attractive and like. And we want her to be our friend. Or maybe we just want to hang out with her. Whatever. Regardless, we have never been fully attracted to the same woman before. So, are we going to acknowledge that or not?"

Ethan took another sip of his beer, this one a bit bigger, and then set the bottle down on the counter as he leaned back. "I don't know. All I know is that Holland said she needed friends. And we could be that for her. If she wants something more? With either of us? I'd be fine with that."

Lincoln stared into his eyes, and Ethan swallowed hard. "You'd be fine with that? If Holland was attracted to me as well, and I asked her out, and she said yes. You'd be fine with that."

No, he wouldn't. Because Ethan loved Lincoln. Loved. But he could never be with him. Ethan just needed Lincoln to be happy. And if that meant being with Holland, someone that Ethan also liked, then that was fine.

It had to be.

"If you guys were happy, sure. I'd be fine with that." That was the truth. *Fine* would be great. He wouldn't be *happy* really, but he'd be *fine*.

"If you're happy, then I am. But you know, this is all

probably moot because she's not going to want to date. Let alone us."

"What's wrong with us?" Ethan asked, affronted.

"Well, we're a couple of bachelors who spend far more time with each other than we do with anybody else. And we invited her over to play Mario Kart. Like we're twelve."

"There's nothing wrong with Mario Kart."

"Other than your ability to play it," Lincoln said with a grin, and Ethan punched him in the shoulder. "Jerk."

"Well, I would say that hurt, but you don't have any force behind your hits. Maybe you should work out more."

"You're going to pay for that later," Ethan mumbled, and Lincoln just grinned, that wicked gleam coming to his eyes that Ethan loved so much. Seriously, he needed to get laid. And to figure out what the fuck was wrong with him. Because he clearly had a problem when it came to his best friend.

Thankfully, he didn't have to worry about that long, though, because the doorbell rang. It had to be Holland.

"Ready?" Lincoln asked, looking ridiculously hot.

"As ever. I'll go get the door."

"I'll take out the rest of the food. Because, apparently, I'm feeding an army."

"Hey, all that racing takes a lot of energy."

"Yes, sitting on your ass and trying to play with a controller takes up *so* much energy. Hence why we're going on a jog tomorrow morning."

"Great," Ethan mumbled but was still smiling when he opened the door.

Holland stood there, those deep eyes of hers staring right at him. That look went straight to his gut—and his dick.

"Hey, you found the place," Ethan said, taking a step back. Holland walked in and handed over a bottle of wine. "I wasn't sure if you drank, and then I figured I might as well bring the same type that I was drinking out of that paper bag. Sort of bringing it all full circle, you know?"

Ethan just grinned and then leaned down and kissed her cheek, surprising them both. He stood back quickly and noticed the widening of her eyes, and the blush on her cheeks, but she didn't pull away. Maybe she was just surprised. Or perhaps she didn't mind. After all, friends kissed cheeks all the time.

"You look great," Ethan said, and he was serious. She wore a cute, long shirt thing that had a v-neck that showed off just a little cleavage but covered her butt, and she wore it over leggings that hugged her sexy legs. She also had on knee boots. The whole thing just really worked. She had her hair down, the soft, auburn waves touching her shoulders, and he really wanted to reach out and play with it.

But he wouldn't. He wasn't that much of a cad.

Okay, maybe he was a little. But...whatever.

"Seriously, though, thanks for the invite," Holland said, grinning. She paused. "You look great, too. Sorry, I'm not really good at this whole thing."

"What thing?" Lincoln asked, walking into the room. He leaned down and kissed her other cheek, and Ethan just grinned.

Okay, this was starting to feel more and more like a date with the three of them. And that was fine. Because Ethan knew the truth. It wasn't. But, in the dark pits of his mind, he could imagine it was. After all, his cousin was in a permanent threesome and was even married to both of them. One legally, but both in her soul.

It wasn't completely unheard of.

So, in his fantasies, he could imagine that this was a real date. And, of course, playing Mario Kart would just clinch the deal. He was so bad at it that she would go running, screaming into Lincoln's arms. And that'd be fine. Seriously. Because as long as Lincoln and Holland were happy, that was all that mattered.

"I like your place," Holland said, and Ethan looked around.

"Thanks. I'm not here often, so most of my decorating came from my mom. Sorry."

"I helped," Lincoln said, and Ethan nodded.

"You did. You picked out my furniture. Mostly because I have no taste."

"It's true," Lincoln said.

Holland just laughed, looking between Lincoln and him. "You guys have been friends for a while?"

"Forever, it seems," Lincoln said and then looked up at Ethan. Ethan swallowed hard again and then pulled his gaze away so he wouldn't get a hard-on while standing between them. Tonight would be difficult enough without his dick getting in the way.

"Okay, Lincoln cooked up some pretty amazing appetizers, and probably made enough for a whole army, so let's pour you a glass of your wine—unless you want a beer or something else I have in the fridge."

"I brought over some wine, too," Lincoln said. "So, you could have some of that, some of yours...anything you want. And, yes, I made too much food, but I was stressed."

Ethan grinned.

"Why were you stressed? And Ethan doesn't cook?" Holland inquired.

Ethan blushed then. "I was at work, and I got lost in

it. I'm a jerk, and Lincoln did all the prep for this get-together, even though it's my house. I'm sorry."

"It's okay," Lincoln muttered. "And I'm just stressed about work. But, no worries. Tonight's about fun."

"And, apparently, Mario Kart?" Holland asked.

"Yes, it's a family and friend tradition. We were actually just joking about it at first, but now I kind of want to play," Lincoln said, grinning. He handed her a glass of red wine, the one that Lincoln had brought, and the three of them clinked their drinks. The guys had beers, Holland had her wine, and they each took a sip.

"To new friendships," Ethan muttered after the toast, and Lincoln rolled his eyes.

"That's not how you make a toast, you have to say the words beforehand."

"Well, you caught me off guard with clinking before I could say anything. I suck at this."

"I'm sure it's fine." Holland tapped her glass to his bottle again. "See? And now it's a real toast." She took a sip, her gaze fixed on his, and Ethan quickly chugged down a gulp. Lincoln did the same next to him.

Okay, then. This night would be interesting.

"We seriously do not have to play Mario Kart."

"No, I want to see how bad you are at it."

"Great. Well, there goes all my prowess."

"You have prowess?" Lincoln asked, and Ethan flipped him off.

"Okay, I think tonight is going to be pretty fun. At least from the way you two act. And, my God, this food looks amazing."

"Lincoln's a fantastic cook. I always thought if he didn't decide to paint, he would have gone to culinary school."

Lincoln frowned. "Really?"

Ethan shrugged. "I told you that."

"You've never once said that."

Ethan just started piling food on his plate after he'd handed Holland one. "I thought I did. Well, I thought it anyway. I never starve when you're around. Thank God."

"I do like to take care of you."

There was an awkward silence after that until Ethan cleared his throat. "Well, I'm glad you do. Because, sometimes, I get too lost in my work, and I forget to cook. Or eat."

"I would think it would be the other way around, with Lincoln being the artist and all." Holland looked between them, interest in her eyes.

Lincoln shrugged, taking a bite of some bruschetta. "Not really. Ethan's the one who forgets little things. I tend to want to make sure I get every little thing completed around me before I can actually sit down and work. It's not a very creative way to go about things, at least according to most stereotypes, but it works for me. Or it *usually* does."

"Well, since I run my own business, sometimes I have to eat while on the job, or I forget altogether. But, I'm glad the two of you have each other."

"Well, now you have us, too." Ethan looked at her, and Holland just grinned.

"I like that. Now, do we eat? Or do we play? How does this work?"

"Come on, let me show you how bad I am at Mario Kart. Ethan's not the only terrible one."

"This should be amazing," Holland sing-songed, and Lincoln laughed, leading her to the living room. Ethan watched them go and took another bite of his food, willing his dick under control. Watching them together, just laughing and talking, made him so hard it hurt. His dick was already pressed against the zipper of his pants, and this wasn't even a date. He had to keep reminding himself that, no, this was not a fucking date.

Everything was fine.

He was not losing his damn mind.

It was tough not to want more when she was here, though. Or when she made Lincoln smile. Ethan would do anything to keep Lincoln smiling.

Even if it meant walking away.

Ethan followed the pair into the living room.

"Okay, I didn't ask if you've played before," Lincoln said as he sat down on the couch. Holland took the spot next to him, and that left just enough room for Ethan on the other side of her. He set his plate down on the side table and took his seat, doing his best to ignore the heat of her near his thigh.

He was going to lose his mind.

"Oh, I'm a pro." Holland quirked a grin.

"Dear God," Ethan groaned. "This is not going to end well."

"Wait until you see how many times he hits himself with a green shell," Lincoln grinned.

"Lincoln, I used to do that a lot," Holland said gently.

"When you were like five, right? Because it's always when you're five. Because you learn things by the time you're in your twenties like us."

Ethan put his head in his hands and groaned, while Holland and Lincoln laughed. "I don't think this is funny anymore. Let's just watch a movie."

"No, no, you lured me over here with Mario Kart and drinking. Let's get this done."

"So you can have more than one glass of wine?" Lincoln asked.

"I took an Uber over here. So, yes, I can have a couple more glasses."

"Then let's have some fun," Lincoln said, and Holland grinned.

Ethan just hoped to hell they weren't making a mistake.

They were four bottles of wine in and a couple of hours of games down when Ethan rubbed his head, groaning.

"I'm really not good at this."

"You're really not." Holland giggled.

Her cheeks were rosy, her eyes bright, and he knew that she was just as drunk as he was. In fact, it was kind of hard for him to string words together, but that was fine. He figured Lincoln could sleep on the couch, and Holland could take the guest room if they got too drunk. He really didn't want her to end up in an Uber all alone when they were drinking this much. Though once they'd started, it was kind of hard to stop. And this was fun.

"Okay, let's make this interesting," Ethan said, the devil on his shoulder suddenly coming out to play.

Lincoln walked into the living room, three shot glasses in one hand, and the tequila bottle in his other.

Even though Ethan had been the one to mention shots, he'd almost forgotten that Lincoln had gone to get them.

"You asked me to get some tequila shots ready, and now you want to make it even more interesting?"

"What, I figured we could make a point system. Loser has to take a shot."

"A point system, in Mario Kart. You're going to get drunk as fuck," Holland said, reaching for a shot glass.

"I'm already pretty much there," Ethan said, snorting.

"Then let's play a game that Ethan can actually play."

"Like Chutes and Ladders?" Holland asked, and Ethan flipped her off.

"I knew I liked you," Lincoln said, giving her a high-five before pouring tequila into each of the shot glasses. Ethan had the good tequila, so they only needed a little salt and didn't even need the lime.

They clinked shot glasses and then tossed them back, the smoothness so good, he could barely taste the liquor.

This was going to end badly.

"No, we'll figure out a way. And we'll put it at the highest-level difficulty and figure out not the points on the actual score, but whoever hits each other the most. They get to keep their sanity."

"So, the people who get hit the most take a shot?"

"Yup," he said, answering Holland's question.

"Game on."

He was in that warm, fuzziness of buzzed, almost to drunk, and all he wanted to do was lean down and take her lips. Or Lincoln's.

He should really stop drinking.

They played one round, with Ethan and Holland having to take a drink while Lincoln looked on like a cat in cream.

"Okay, one more, and I'm going to kick your asses," Holland said, wiggling on her butt where she sat on the floor. They had all settled on the carpet where there was more room. Each of them had taken off their shoes and socks, and Ethan noticed that Lincoln had been playing with Holland's toes, mostly because she wore toe rings. Apparently, his best friend had a foot fetish. Who knew?

They each did another shot, primarily to get the game rolling, and Ethan figured that was probably one shot too many. So, when he and Holland lost again, they looked down at the tequila, and Holland shook her head.

"Okay. Maybe that's enough for me."

"Yes, but we still lost. So, what should we do?"

"Strip Mario Kart?" Lincoln said and snorted. "I was kidding."

"Totally not playing strip Mario Kart," Holland said, leaning against the chair.

"Well, so...what's your penance for losing?"

"I don't know." Holland looked between Lincoln and him and swallowed hard. "I won't strip. But how about you kiss me?" she asked, then her eyes widened, and she put her hand over her mouth. "Forget I said that. It's the tequila. Mixed with the wine. I'm really not going to like tomorrow."

But Ethan wasn't thinking anything. Instead, he swallowed hard and, before he could think too hard about it, he looked at Lincoln. His best friend nodded, and then Ethan lowered his head, pulling Holland to him. He smacked a hard kiss on her mouth. Her eyes went wide.

"Oh. Wow. Okay." She looked over at Lincoln. "But you were the winner. I mean... I guess you're going to lose out."

Lincoln shrugged and then leaned forward, cupping her face and brushing his lips along hers.

"No, I don't think I'm missing out at all." And then he deepened the kiss, sending a moan through her, and right into Ethan.

His dick strained at his jeans, and he was suddenly just a little bit sober.

"Holy fuck."

Holland pulled away while Lincoln sat there, his eyes dark. Ethan just swallowed again.

"Okay, you both kissed me. And that...that's a good way to win at Mario Kart. But now it's your guys' turn." She looked between them, and Ethan froze.

Her eyes widened again, and she shook her head quickly. "Shit. I'm sorry. You don't have to do that. It's the tequila talking. And I really didn't mean that. Let's go back to drinking. Or just playing for cheese or something."

But Ethan looked over at his best friend and figured he was almost drunk enough to have an excuse. Nearly drunk enough to pretend that this was only a kiss. That it was nothing.

So, he leaned forward, and Lincoln leaned in even more. And then his lips were on his best friend's. He knew this couldn't be a mistake. He wouldn't let it be a mistake. But tequila had never done him wrong before. And as he opened his mouth, his tongue brushing along Lincoln's, he had a feeling that, right or wrong, this was going to change everything.

CHAPTER FIVE

It was as if every ounce of alcohol in her bloodstream had evaporated in that moment. Holland sucked in a breath and watched as the two men kissed, first hesitantly, and then harder. Her nipples tightened, everything in her body reacting as if they were the only three in the world, and this was all that mattered.

She had never done anything like this before in her life. She didn't really even know these guys. Oh, she spoke to them often, had gotten together with them a few times, and knew they weren't serial killers or horrible people. She liked them. And she had thought she was well on her way to becoming good friends with them. While it had been a few months since her life changed, she hadn't been ready to date. And she hadn't wanted to choose between Lincoln and Ethan, the only two people who'd even appeared on her radar this entire time. So, she'd decided that she wasn't going to choose. She was just going to be their friend. But as she watched them kiss, watched their breaths come in pants right along with hers, she knew she could never choose. This was a mistake. This was such a huge mistake.

The guys broke apart and looked at each other as if they were the only two people in the world. But then they turned and looked at her. The same hunger-filled gaze that she knew was on her face was on theirs, and it was directed right at her.

"Oh," she breathed out. The guys leaned closer to each other but were still touching her knees, as if they needed her to be a part of this. But what *was* this?

She looked between them and then scrambled to her feet and ran into the kitchen.

She could hear them cursing behind her as her breaths came in shallow gulps. She tried to force air into her lungs, wondering what the hell was going on.

She was not this person. She didn't have three-somes with men. Well, she hadn't before, at least. She hadn't done a lot of things before.

She'd been in a relationship with Dustin for so long. That had been her normal.

But she knew lasting poly relationships existed. She knew of a triad who shopped in her store often who had three children. And there was even a popular TV show that had the main characters in a full triad. They were happy, and while some part of society may look down on them, their family didn't. Their friends didn't. It was normal, just like a partnership would be.

But then again, did she really want to get in the middle of this? Literally?

From the way that Ethan and Lincoln had kissed, she had a feeling there were some long-dormant and deeply buried emotions between the two. Had that been their first kiss? Maybe. It felt like it.

Would she get in the way?

She found a glass and got some water. As she was sipping it, trying to breathe while not choking, the guys walked in, their lips swollen from kisses, their cheeks ruddy—but not from drink.

No, it was from each other.

And maybe her. She was the one who had done this. She had been the one to say they should kiss and all of that.

This was her fault.

She had no one to blame but herself.

"Holland, are you okay?" Lincoln asked, sounding just as sober as she felt.

"Fine. Everything's fine. See? Everything's *fine*."

"Then why are you saying the word *fine* a lot with a very high-pitched voice?" Ethan asked, coming near her. They were so big, they crowded her without even trying. She swallowed hard, her back against the counter as both men stood, not touching but close enough that she could feel the heat of them. Or maybe that was just her desire.

She didn't know, but she was worried. *So* worried.

What if this is a mistake? What if she lost both of them when she'd just found them?

But maybe this would lead the men into a new part of their relationship that they both wanted. Perhaps this was good for them.

Horrible for her. But that was fine. She didn't need anything more than she had. She was just fine.

"I just didn't expect that."

"We didn't mean to pressure you into anything," Lincoln said.

"He's right. We're sorry. It started out as a game, but it turned into something completely different."

"I guess so. I'm sorry, you guys. I'm the one who started it. I ruined it all."

Lincoln took a step forward, and she stiffened. But he just stood there, so close but not touching. Ethan looked between the two of them, worry on his face, and she tried to smile. To lighten the mood. It wasn't easy.

But nothing ever was these days.

"I should go."

"You've had too much to drink, and I know it's not my place to say anything, but I don't feel right about you getting into an Uber like this. It's not safe," Ethan said. "And neither of us is sober enough to drive. You can stay the night."

Her brows shot up on her forehead.

"Excuse me?"

Ethan put both hands up.

"I was thinking you could sleep in the guest room. And Lincoln can take the couch while I sleep in my bed."

The word *bed* dropped like a stone between the three of them, and she swallowed hard, trying not to imagine them in his bed. Or even just the two of them. Any two. Any pair would work.

Holland knew she was letting herself overthink this. And making the wrong decisions.

"Okay, I'll stay. Mostly because you're right, I don't really feel safe getting into someone else's car right now."

"But I want to make sure you feel safe here," Lincoln said, stuffing his hands into his pockets.

The movement actually made her look down, and she noticed a very hard erection pressing against his jeans. And when she turned her head, she glanced over at Ethan's crotch, too—because, of course, she did—and he had just as thick of an erection.

Dear God, everything was moving too fast.

Both guys noticed her looking, and Lincoln cleared his throat. Her gaze shot up to his, and he smiled at her. A soft smile that wasn't a sneer, wasn't mocking.

She felt safe. Not just with him but also with Ethan.

She didn't know how everything had happened. She didn't know how she had gotten here. But maybe she didn't have to walk away. Perhaps this could be fun. Just a distraction.

Or maybe she was losing her mind by even considering it.

"We can go play the game and put the rest of the booze away," Lincoln said.

"That might be best."

She swallowed again, her mouth dry, and Ethan seemed to notice. He handed over the glass she had put on the counter. She didn't even remember doing that.

"Drink some water. We all probably should."

"We should."

But the guys didn't move. And she didn't sip.

Instead, she set down the glass and looked at her hands.

"I didn't mean for this to happen. I don't want you guys to ruin your friendship or never see me again because of this. So, let's pretend it didn't happen."

"I don't know if I can do that," Lincoln said quickly, and both she and Ethan looked over at him.

"What?"

"I don't think I can forget. I'm sorry. I can't."

"Oh."

"I guess we need to talk?" Ethan asked.

Lincoln nodded, but then he leaned forward and pressed his lips to hers.

She was so shocked that, for a moment, she didn't do anything. But then she kissed him back.

Before she could even take a breath, Lincoln took a step back and turned her to face Ethan. The other man stared at her wide-eyed before he seemed to get the message Lincoln was sending and leaned down to kiss her again.

She felt as if she were swimming, her body two steps behind her actions, her mind even further away, but she just kept kissing him, wanting more.

And then Ethan was gone, and Lincoln's lips were on hers once more. She moaned, sliding her hands through his hair even as her other hand was still on Ethan's chest.

She pulled back a bit. "What are we doing?"

"Just kissing. We can do that, right?" Lincoln asked.

"But I don't know what any of this means."

"I don't think it matters. Just for tonight. We'll figure it out." And then Ethan's mouth was on hers again, and she was moaning once more.

A heartbeat later, she was watching the two of them kiss, their way a little bit rougher, with a little more growl.

Her lips were swollen, she could feel it, her chin most likely a little red from their beards, but she didn't care.

When Lincoln pulled her close, his hand on her ass as he molded her to his body, his lips on hers, she leaned into it. Wanting more.

And then Ethan was behind her, slowly running his hands up and down her sides. She leaned back into him. Both men kissed her neck, and then she twisted her head back to kiss Ethan.

When she moved her head to the side, the guys kissed each other around her, but both of their hands were still on her. She couldn't focus, couldn't do anything. There didn't seem to be a need for talking.

The booze caught back up with her, and then she didn't need to talk. Didn't *want* to.

Instead, she just let her body do what it wanted, what they all needed. She gave in to the moment. To the passion. There would be time for talking and repercussions later. But right then, she could blame it on the booze.

"What are we doing?" Ethan breathed into her ear. She turned, kissing his chin.

"I don't know," she answered honestly. "I don't know."

"We don't have to do anything but kiss. We can stop right now," Lincoln said. He looked at them both, and she nodded.

"I know I can walk away. Right now, if I want. I don't feel pressure." That was a lie. She felt pressured, but it was by herself, not them. These two had nothing to do with it. Oh, they had everything to do with *it*, but not in the pressure department.

"I just like the way you taste. Both of you. And I feel like I can taste Ethan on your lips, and it makes me even harder." Lincoln growled out the words.

She looked down between them and then rocked her core against Lincoln's jean-clad cock. Both of them groaned, and when she wiggled her ass back on Ethan's hardness, he let out a sound from the back of his throat.

"I need to get my hands on you," Ethan growled, much like Lincoln had earlier. "Both of you. Is that okay?"

"Just hands. Just for tonight. I don't think I'm ready for more."

Lincoln nodded. "Hands are perfect. But I think we need to move back into the living room. Because I've never really wanted to have sex in a kitchen. I'm just saying, it's probably not the best place for it."

Ethan laughed, and Holland joined in. Who'd have thought she'd be able to laugh during a threesome, and that it'd actually be fun? Who thought she'd be having a threesome at all?

But she didn't want to stop. She couldn't. So why was she even thinking about it? The guys weren't talking about it. They didn't want to stop. Right then, she decided she would go with the flow, seize the moment. She only hoped to hell that there were pieces left of her when they finished.

Without words, Lincoln led them into the living room, and while she might've thought it would dampen the mood just slightly, it almost seemed to intensify it. As if they wanted to touch each other but couldn't. As if they needed to. *She* needed to.

Before she could think, Lincoln's mouth was on hers

again, and Ethan's hands were between her and the other man. He slid his knuckles down Lincoln's erection, and Lincoln growled into her mouth, rocking into Ethan's palm —and therefore, her, too. Ethan's other hand slid under her shirt, over her soft belly, and then cupped a breast.

She groaned and leaned back as he tweaked her nipple, letting Lincoln's tongue slide down her neck as Ethan played with her breasts.

"I need more," Lincoln growled.

She had never felt like this before. Had never been in this type of situation. It was all so new and exciting. And, yes, she needed more, too. Wanted more.

When Lincoln tugged at her shirt, she raised her arms, letting him take it off. Ethan undid her bra so quickly, she almost missed it.

But then she found herself pressed against Ethan's chest even firmer, Lincoln's mouth on her breasts as Ethan's hands slid between them and behind the waist-band of her leggings.

She gasped as he cupped her over her panties, his middle finger playing between her folds.

She couldn't focus, there were so many sensations that it didn't matter. All she could do was just live in the moment.

Ethan rubbed at her clit over her panties as Lincoln

sucked at her nipples, one and then the other, squeezing and molding.

She writhed between them, wanting more, but she couldn't even breathe. Couldn't do anything. So, she slid her hand over Ethan's length, and then Lincoln's, rubbing them over their clothes.

They both groaned and then pulled away from her, leaving her wanting and breathless.

Suddenly, her pants were around her ankles, and she shucked them off. And then her panties followed. She stood between the men, naked, and licked her lips as she gazed at them.

"It doesn't seem fair that I'm naked and you two aren't."

They looked at each other, then at her, and then nodded in unison.

It was so fucking hot.

They each tugged off their shirts and then undid their pants. She couldn't just stand there doing nothing, so she played with her breasts, cupping them, rolling her nipples between her fingers.

Ethan groaned, quickly shucking his pants. Then he was naked before her. Lincoln joined him a moment later. Both completely built, utterly bare. And hers for the night.

Hers...and each other's, as well. It was the three of them. There was no going back.

They were both long and thick, and she knew it would likely be too much for her, but she didn't care. Ethan reached down and gripped the base of his cock, slowly sliding his fingers up and down his length as he stared at her.

Lincoln did the same, but then she moved forward, wanting more. She slid her hands over Ethan's and then Lincoln's and gave them each a squeeze. Both guys let go, and then there she was, holding two dicks in her hands, running her fingers up and down their lengths. She had never felt so wanton, and she loved it.

She pumped them once, twice, and then they both groaned and moved.

Lincoln was behind her this time, rubbing his cock along the seam of her ass as he slid his hand down her body, spearing her with two fingers.

She called out, but no sound escaped as Ethan had his mouth on hers. She gripped his dick, pumping hard as she cupped his balls with her other hand.

Ethan's mouth was now on her breast, and it was so good. So many limbs and tongues and mouths. It was hard not to get lost in it all. But then she let herself. Because, why not?

They'd just said hands. Hands and touch. And

maybe a little taste. But they were all standing there, their hands on each other, all of them clearly wanting and needing more.

The sounds of flesh against flesh and growls in the air was almost too much, and she nearly came right then.

But Lincoln suddenly had his thumb on her clit, and Ethan's mouth was on her breast, and then...she came. Hard and fast, clenching around Lincoln's fingers even as she arched into Ethan's mouth.

She twisted her neck just slightly, and Lincoln took her lips in a bruising kiss that sent both of them to the edge. Her again, him for the first time.

But then she twisted out of his hold. Lincoln slid his fingers out of her and rubbed her wetness on Ethan's mouth. She almost came again as Ethan's eyes darkened even more, and he opened his mouth, sucking Lincoln's two fingers, licking her wetness from the digits.

It was so fucking hot, all she wanted to do was ride them both into oblivion. But not right then. No, this was now. Only touch.

And so when she reached down and grabbed Lincoln's dick, he groaned and pumped into her hand, already getting hard again.

Lincoln reached around and grabbed Ethan's dick,

while Ethan slid his hands along her ass and around so he could spear her with two fingers.

Somehow, the three of them worked in unison, mouths and tongues and hands.

She pumped harder, using her thumb to slide the leaking fluid from the tip of Lincoln's cock down him. She knew he was doing the same to Ethan, both of them working in tandem, even as Ethan pumped in and out of her with his fingers. She wanted him to use his cock, but not just then.

No, somehow, this was even hotter.

As if it were one step above indecency before oblivion.

When both men groaned, their bodies going tight, and Lincoln's dick hardened even more under her hand, they came, both of their bodies jerking. Hers did too as Ethan found that bundle of nerves within her.

She called out some incoherent nonsense, wanting more, and then there wasn't anything else. She was standing in Ethan's living room, covered by them both, Ethan's hand still inside her, and all she could do was sink into Lincoln's hold and know that this could be the last time she saw them.

Something this perfect, this...everything, wasn't meant for her. But she could soak it in, and she could hold them. At least, for the moment.

Because this had been the most erotic, dangerous, and wonderful thing she'd ever done in her life.

And she never wanted it to end.

CHAPTER SIX

Waking up with a hangover was never a good way to start the day. Waking up while naked and sprawled face-down on the couch was really not a good thing. Add in the fact that it wasn't his couch, but Ethan's?

Lincoln was pretty sure he'd made a horrible mistake. But as flashes of the night before came back to him—the skin, the taste, the feel—he wasn't sure he could regret it.

Because he'd finally gotten a taste of Ethan Montgomery, had finally touched him. And then adding Holland to that...

It was as if a lock had clicked into place, something that had been missing this whole time. A person to push them over the edge into obsession rather than longing.

After the three of them had finally settled down the night before, all of them still drunk and covered in each other, they had scrambled into Ethan's huge shower and scrubbed one another clean without saying a word. It was as if they knew that as soon as they started speaking, reality would set in, and they'd break the spell.

So, instead, they hadn't said a word, just made sure they were showered, removing all evidence of what had happened. Lincoln had slid his fingers through Ethan's hair, helping him wash it, then had done the same with Holland with Ethan's help, touching fingers as they made sure she was completely clean. It had felt right. As if it were what should be happening.

But it wasn't. Not really, or at least not yet. Not when he knew that as soon as they talked about it, they'd likely do their best to forget it. Or they wouldn't, and then it would be a mistake. Ethan had been drunk, that had to be it. Because in the entire time that they had been friends, Lincoln had never once thought this would happen between them.

And he hated himself for what he might have done. For what he could have broken by giving in to his desires. Because while he wanted more, he had risked everything, and now he didn't have the alcohol in his system to use as an excuse anymore.

Last night, Lincoln had pulled away after Ethan had kissed him softly and then Holland before saying it was time for bed.

They had listened, and somehow, the three of them had ended up in separate places. Maybe there had been some unspoken agreement that they'd all been aware of where if they started doing anything more than they had, there would be no going back. They couldn't call it just a drunken mistake.

At least, that's what was on Lincoln's mind.

And so, Holland was currently sleeping in the guest room, Ethan had passed out on his bed, and Lincoln was naked on the couch.

He groaned, trying to keep quiet as he ran his hand over his face, pressing his feet onto the floor. Even the sensation of the carpet fibers against his skin hurt, and he knew he had drunk far too much the night before.

When his body pained him to the point where even his skin hurt? That's when he knew he'd put his body and soul through the ringer and had lost his equi-librium.

And on the heels of that thought, he quickly shoved his clothes back on, picking them out of the jumble on the floor. He did his best not to linger too long over

Ethan's or Holland's clothing, tried not to remember exactly what had happened—even though the memories would be the only thing left once this was over.

Instead of dwelling, he slid his feet into his shoes, looked around for his keys and phone, and put them into his pocket.

He would leave. Without talking to them. At least, for now.

Because he didn't want them to say that everything was great, that it was fun for a night, but that was the end of it.

And he didn't know what *he* wanted to say. Because he had already bared himself, and it had taken far too much alcohol for even that to happen. He honestly couldn't bear anything else right now. So, he slid out of the house, got into his car, and crept out like it had been a mistake. And maybe it was. But it had been the most beautiful, precious, and seductive mistake of his life.

Even though he was afraid that he had ruined everything.

He didn't know how he would face Ethan again. But he would have to. Holland, too. Because she was special. So damn special. Just like Ethan.

And he knew that he was likely going to lose them. Because that's what he did. Every time. He didn't have serious relationships. He didn't hold onto those he cared about. Because they did things like move across the damn country where they forgot about you. Like his parents had.

Ethan and Holland must have still been sleeping because he didn't even get a text by the time he got home. Or an angry phone call for sneaking out as quietly as he had.

He groaned and then headed up to his apartment, the one that he had scrimped and saved for because he'd always wanted to live in a downtown city, even if he could see the mountains in the distance. That way, he could get a little bit of both—urban and nature. And he was close enough to all his friends who lived in the suburbs and even some that lived in the mountains that he could always visit other places.

He locked the door behind him and then went in search of coffee. And aspirin. Anything that could help the throbbing in his head go away. Not that he thought anything could really help right then.

No, it would take time, energy, and probably a lot of caffeine.

He looked over at his studio area, at the canvas that he had covered, and figured maybe he would work today.

Perhaps he'd be able to get something more on that canvas now that he knew what Ethan tasted like. What

Holland tasted like. He didn't have to wonder anymore.

And he'd try not to think about the fact that he had a hundred other worries on his mind now.

But that was probably asking too much.

He chugged a cup of coffee, nearly scalding his throat in the process, and then poured himself another mug before going to his studio area and sitting down on his stool.

He couldn't sit for too long on it since it really wasn't great for his back, but he had painted his first painting while sitting on it, so he had pulled it out of storage and brought it into his studio, thinking maybe it'd help him recreate something. Perhaps if he used all the power and superstition at hand, he'd be able to figure out how to get through this painter's block.

And it wasn't even just that this was for a commission. He couldn't even think of art right now. And he hated that. It had always come so easily to him, even when it was hard. Even when he was having trouble, he always knew that he could rely on something within him to get the job done.

But it had been weeks now, and he couldn't even hold a paintbrush without going blank.

Something was wrong with him, and he hated himself for it.

But now, work was work, and just because he was an artist didn't mean he could flake out. He wasn't a stereotype. So, he picked up the paintbrush, looked down at it, and wondered what came next.

He knew he had that art show to prepare for, knew he needed to add more to his portfolio.

But he couldn't think of anything.

And that scared him.

There was something wrong with him, and now he knew it couldn't be Ethan.

No, this was all him. And he had to figure it out.

But first, more coffee.

He was just getting up off the stool after setting down his paintbrush so he could distract himself again, when he heard the key in the front door turn, and someone walk through.

He growled low, pissed off.

Damien sauntered in like he hadn't a care in the world, as if he owned the place.

"Oh, good, you're home. You weren't home yesterday when I came by to check on you, and I was worried. I mean, why didn't you leave a note or something?" Damien came forward, took the coffee cup from Lincoln's hand, and drained the last dregs of the brew.

"Ugh, you need more sugar in this. Though it's not

great for your teeth or your body, but maybe it'll get that scowl off your face."

"What the hell are you doing here, Damien?" Lincoln asked, trying to keep his temper in check. He didn't want to take out his frustrations on Damien, but right then, he really didn't have a good reason *not* to.

"I'm your agent. I'm here to help. Clearly, you need it. Is this what you've been working on?" Damien asked, trying to maneuver around Lincoln so he could see. "There's barely anything on this canvas. Is this another project? What's wrong, buttercup?" Damien asked.

And that was it.

Everything that had been simmering just beneath the surface slid into Lincoln, and he snapped. He was done. So done with this. "Okay, you know the rule. You don't look at my work until I'm ready."

"I'm your agent, buddy. Plus, we're friends. We *know* each other." And given the way that he emphasized the word *know*, Lincoln knew exactly what Damien was referring to. Lincoln knew he never should have slept with him. But there had been attraction at one point. They had been close, and it had seemed like the right thing to do at the time. And he had been younger then. Stupid.

Well, he wasn't going to make any more stupid

decisions. After all, he'd made possibly the worst one ever the night before.

"No, no. We're not doing this. I told you, you aren't allowed to look at my work until I'm ready. And you're not supposed to use the key just to come in. Were you seriously in my apartment last night when I wasn't here?" he asked, the rest of Damien's words finally penetrating his haze or irritation.

"I was checking on you. You're my best client. And my friend. You know I just want what's best for you." Damien moved as if to touch him, and Lincoln swept his arm out, gripping Lincoln's wrist.

"Don't touch me."

Damien looked pointedly at where Lincoln's hand clamped around his wrist.

"I do believe *you're* the one touching *me.*"

Lincoln let him go as if he'd been burned and growled. "Get out."

"My, aren't you in a bad mood?"

"Shut the fuck up, Damien. What is wrong with you? Why are you acting like this?"

"I could ask you the same question. As I said, I'm just here to check up on you. And yet you're acting as if I'm Satan."

"Give me my key back," Lincoln said quickly,

holding out his hand. "You can knock like everybody else. I don't know why I gave you a key to begin with."

"Because I'm your agent."

"You keep saying that, but do you have keys for all of your clients?"

"Of course, not. You're special. We're special."

"No. We aren't. And I'm tired of this. Just give me my key, or I'm going to change the locks. Because this is ridiculous. You don't appreciate or respect boundaries, and you never give me my privacy."

"I'm worried about you. You're not producing. What's wrong? Is it Ethan? Talk to me. You know I'm always here for you."

But Lincoln didn't hear anything anymore. He was done. He should have done this a long time ago. Should have put up his own walls, laid down some laws. But he had been complacent in protecting himself from those who slithered between the cracks of his foundation and never let go. This was his own damn fault.

"Give me my key, now. You don't get to come into my home without knocking. You don't get to barge into my life as if you own it. You help me sell my art. That's it. And if you don't listen to me, then you're not the agent I need you to be, and I will find someone else."

Damien's eyes narrowed into slits, and his jaw

tensed. Now he looked like the man Lincoln had known before. The shark who could get anything done.

But instead of focusing on the job, all his anger was directed at Lincoln. *Great job.*

"I made you. I'm just trying to help, Lincoln. But all you do is push me away. If you keep doing that, no one will be around to help you when you need it. So, you better think about that."

Damien slid his hand into his pocket and pulled out his keys, slowly taking Lincoln's off the ring.

"Now, I'm going to forget you talked about meeting any other agents, and we're going to talk this out later. Clearly, you need more coffee. Or maybe you just need to get laid. Regardless, I don't really give a shit right now, you'll apologize later. But first, know this… You have that commission coming up. And I will fight for you to get more time if that's what you need. Because that's what I do. I do so much for you that you don't even understand. Yes, you're the artist. But I'm the one who sells you. Never forget that. Never forget where you came from." Damien pushed past him, shoving his shoulder into Lincoln's before he walked out, but Lincoln didn't budge. He was so fucking tired.

When Damien slammed the door behind him as he stormed out, Lincoln sighed and then went to turn the lock. Soon as he did, though, someone rang the doorbell. He jumped, the shit scared out of him.

He looked through the peephole, ready to scream if it was Damien, but then he sighed.

He opened the door.

"Hey there, little cousin," he said, holding out his arms.

Madison slid into his hold and sighed against his chest.

"I saw Damien stomping past me, but he didn't even notice me. He never does. You guys get in a fight?" she asked, leaning back to stare at his face. "And, dear God, are you okay? Looks like you didn't get any sleep."

"You always help me boost my ego, you know?"

"Oh, shush. I'm worried about you."

"Apparently, a lot of people are."

"Damien doesn't worry about you. He worries about his bottom line and *his* ego."

"Please, tell me how you really feel about him."

"I will later, but we have lunch with my parents today. You should probably go shower and get ready. Did you forget?"

"Shit. I really don't want to go to lunch with your parents," Lincoln said truthfully.

Madison snorted and went to her tiptoes to pat his cheek. "You know I don't want to have lunch with them either. But they're just going to get worse if we don't placate them with this. And the fact that you're coming with me so I'm not all alone with them tells me you're my favorite cousin."

"I am your *only* cousin."

"Well, that is true. I can't help it that our fathers are brothers and decided to only have one child each. We're all alone in the vastness of our present state of being marriage-less and child-less. Our clan is going to die out with us." She put her hand to her heart, and Lincoln rolled his eyes.

He loved Madison. They had grown up like siblings, and he would call her his sister, but it just pissed off her parents more when he did. And even if he didn't really give a shit about what her parents thought of him, he did care about how they treated her.

Madison had never been good enough in their eyes, never pretty enough, never skinny enough. Had never dated the right guys. Or gotten the right job. Was never the perfect daughter they wanted.

And they made sure she knew that.

Lincoln wanted to beat the shit out of them, but apparently, that was frowned upon and probably a felony besides. Maybe a misdemeanor if he did it lightly.

Lincoln had really good parents. They'd loved him

and took care of him until he turned eighteen. And then Dad had gotten a job out in Seattle, and they had moved. Lincoln wanted to stay in Boulder and go to school, so they had left him behind.

He had visited for every holiday but had stayed in Boulder with the Montgomerys during the summer so he could take summer courses and try to get through college a little easier and quicker.

His parents never visited.

It was like as soon as they found Seattle, they found their new home.

And while he understood, it still hurt.

Lincoln had a feeling it had to do more with his father's brother, Madison's family, rather than Lincoln himself, though.

Because if you visited Boulder, you had to visit Madison's parents. And that was something no one really wanted to do.

So, Lincoln went out and visited Washington often. Ethan even came with a few times.

His parents were amazing. They had paid for his schooling, and they talked at least twice a week. And with the invention of FaceTime and Skype, they saw each other through a screen regularly. They even took a vacation to Canada a couple of years ago as a family.

He loved his parents.

He just wished they were closer.

But his life was here, and theirs was in Washington, and in this new age of technology and travel, sometimes, you didn't get to live near your family. Oftentimes, you didn't have to. However, he did have family here. Madison. And her parents.

"I'll be quick," Lincoln rumbled. He leaned down and kissed the top of her head, and she grinned up at him. She was beautiful. All curves and wide eyes and a warmth that just radiated out of her.

He wanted her to be happy, but he knew she would never get that unless she got out from under her parents' thumb.

It just wasn't easy when her parents were the people they were. They sucked others in and never let go.

And they seriously didn't like Lincoln or the way he lived his life.

But...whatever.

"Maybe we can just play hooky?" Madison asked quickly.

Lincoln shook his head.

"No, we can't. Because then they'll take it out on you later. So, we'll have lunch, I will listen to your father explain to me that being an artist is me ruining my life. And about how I should've become a banker like him."

"Yes, because with the economy the way it is, his job is so secure." Madison rolled her eyes.

"Hey, don't say that to him. He will go on his whole rant about the market and people stealing his money and all that crap."

"Well, yes. And the fact that you're a painter who pays for his own medical insurance, and I'm a small business owner who doesn't have *the man* as my boss to help pay for *my* insurance or anything just means that we're totally breaking the rules."

She twisted her hair around her finger, and Lincoln narrowed his eyes.

"Did you add pink stripes to your hair?" he asked, aghast, though only partly since it looked great, and he loved his cousin.

She blushed, then grinned.

"Maybe."

"Your mother is going to kill you." Lincoln grinned. "I love it."

"Well, I did it for me, mostly. I've always wanted to, and hey, the look is in. I fit in rather than standing out."

"Yes, just like me with my tattoos."

"Well, I have as much ink as you. I just hide it better."

"If your parents ever find out about that, they're going to try and beat you or something."

"Well, maybe. But, again, whatever. Let's just try to make peace."

"Fine. But if they call my being bisexual a *lifestyle* again, I may actually punch them."

"You wouldn't hit them. But you would stomp off and get all growly, and then I'd have to follow you as my mother used that *tone* on me."

Lincoln hated the tone. The one where his aunt's Southern roots really came out. It wasn't that she said anything bad. In fact, it was all compliments, at least on the outside. But Madison's "little shop," and the dress that fit her "despite her curves," and all that crap that she always said just needled at him over and over again. But the tone was sweet, even though it killed.

And butter would never melt in her mouth.

He hated that phrase, and yet it was the perfect description for Madison's mother.

"I just want you to be happy," he said.

Madison looked at him, frowning. "I could say the same about you. Because you're not happy, Lincoln. And we both know why."

She only knew part of it. His cousin was the one person in the world that knew Lincoln loved his best friend. But he couldn't talk about that. Couldn't do anything about it. Because he needed to face Ethan soon. The same with Holland. And he had absolutely no idea what he was going to say. All he knew was that he needed to face the part of his family that was still in Boulder and help his cousin. That was his mission for the day. He just really wished he didn't have to be hungover when he did so.

But maybe once he got through this, once he remembered what true family was and the fact that his extended family was not it—other than Madison—maybe he'd remember what really mattered.

And perhaps then he'd be able to create again.

If not, then he knew he had to at least figure out what to do about Ethan. And Holland.

Because they were only part of his painter's block. He'd have to face the rest eventually.

And *eventually* was coming far too soon for his liking.

CHAPTER SEVEN

After Ethan had woken up that morning with his head and heart hurting, he knew from the first moment he opened his eyes that he was alone in the house.

He had shoved on his pajamas, stumbled out to the living room, and saw the couch completely empty. The single blanket Lincoln must have used was folded and placed right on the cushions.

There wasn't a note, didn't need to be one. He knew he would see Lincoln later. And either they would talk this thing out, or pretend it never happened.

Knowing his best friend, it would probably be the latter.

Then, he had gone into the kitchen, needing coffee

before he faced the idea that Holland would likely be gone too, and saw the note pinned to the fridge.

Had to head home. The shop needs me. Thank you for last night. –Holland.

She had thanked him. For the games? For the food and booze? Or for all the orgasms?

He didn't have the answers and was truly afraid that if he tried to find them, he would just end up hurt.

He hadn't known what he wanted when he woke up. Had he wanted them there? Maybe it would have been better so they could have hashed it out.

But the problem was that he didn't have the answers. He didn't know what he wanted. So maybe having them gone was a good thing. Perhaps it was exactly what they needed. To have some space before they figured it all out.

Ethan didn't have the answers. But he sure as hell needed to figure things out.

However, because he didn't want to look at his house the way it was anymore, he quickly cleaned up all evidence of the night before. He was thankful that Lincoln and Holland had helped him at least put the food away last night before they went to bed. So, there wasn't much to clean up.

He looked at the white scarf on his mantel and knew that it was Holland's. It wasn't cold enough for her to truly need it, but it had fit her look, made her look even sexier somehow.

But he didn't know what to do about it, so he didn't do anything. Instead, he left it where it was, as a reminder, and went to get ready for work.

An hour later, he sat at his computer, wondering what the hell he was going to do for the rest of the day. Oh, he had calculations to run, data to analyze and pore over. Considering that it was a Monday and should have been a normal day at work, everyone else was already in the office. Some people worked nights, and others worked weekends so they could have a few weekdays off. Sometimes, he did that, too. Having a Monday or Tuesday off was freeing. It allowed him to go to the grocery store or get other shit done. Because most everyone else was at work.

But even though he didn't need to be here today since he'd put in the hours yesterday, he was working.

Because he had nothing else to do. And he was scared to return home to face the fact that he might have just lost his best friend because he had given in to temptation.

He now knew what it felt like to have Lincoln against him, his mouth on his, his dick in his hand.

He knew what it felt like to have Holland with him, as well.

It was like she completed them. Became a bridge between the two of them that wasn't just a bridge. Because he had a feeling that if he were only with Holland, it would feel like Lincoln was missing. There were no substitutions, no second thoughts.

It had worked last night between the three of them.

And maybe it was because he already knew of a lasting ménage in his life thanks to his cousin. He had seen it work, even with all the communication hurdles and society issues.

Maybe that's why Ethan wanted this one to work now.

Did he? Is that really what he wanted? For them to, somehow, take the next steps and pretend that it wasn't just a night of dreaming and obsession?

He didn't know, but he needed to figure it out. And soon.

There was only so much holding back he could do. Especially when it came to his best friend.

"You're sure looking contemplative over there," Julia said from his side. He looked over at his coworker.

"What do you mean?" Ethan asked, even though he knew the answer.

"You look sad. And a little hungover. Which you never do. Rough night?"

Ethan rubbed his hand over his face and growled.

"I'm fine. I worked yesterday, I probably didn't need to come in today."

"But you love work as much as I do. You work longer hours than anyone else I know, except for maybe me."

He looked over at Julia and grinned. "Well, we are workaholics."

"That is true. Anyway, I wanted to come over to let you know that somebody ran too many calculations and filled up the server. It's going to take a little while for the rest of our stuff to run."

Ethan frowned.

"Who?" he asked.

"Who do you think?"

He sighed. "The boss man?"

Julia nodded. "Yep. It's like he sometimes forgets that even though his calculations are important, there is only so much space for everybody to get theirs done."

"How much you want to bet I'll be the one who has to redo everything when he fucks it up?"

"Well, I'm not going to bet on that because if you don't do it, I'll have to, and I'm not in the mood."

"Sounds about right. So, I guess that means none of us gets to have our results anytime soon."

"Nope. But, sadly, you should be used to it by now. That's how things operate here."

Ethan groaned. "I really shouldn't have come in to work."

"Well, considering you're not actually getting paid for it, probably not."

He sighed. "We should go home."

"I am. I worked a double on Saturday. I just came in really quick to check on what I did so I don't waste so much time tomorrow."

"Same here, pretty much."

Julia grinned. "I swear to God, sometimes it's like wrangling toddlers in here instead of grown men and women who have numerous PhDs, MDs, and master's degrees to their names."

He snorted. "Well, at least it's not academia. I'm heading home to pretend that everything's okay."

Julia reached out and put her hand on his arm. She didn't touch him often—if ever—so it surprised him. He looked down, and she blushed, pulling her hand away.

"Sorry," she said quickly.

"No, it's fine. What's up?"

"Just know that even though we're not the best of friends, I'm here if you need me. Okay?"

"Thanks." He smiled and let out a deep breath, meeting her gaze. "Seriously. Thanks."

"Anytime. Now, go get more coffee or caffeine in your system. Or maybe a greasy taco. That will help."

He shuddered.

"I don't know how people can do that much grease when it comes to hangover food."

"Don't knock it. It's a time-honored tradition."

"Not for me."

He packed up his things and headed out to his car in the parking lot, figuring he might as well head home and get some stuff done around his house. Maybe even talk with his family.

He hadn't had dinner with them in a couple of weeks. Considering that he usually did as often as possible, that was saying something. But everybody was busy, and he knew there was a Montgomery family dinner coming up.

He sent off a quick text to the family group, just saying good morning and hoping everyone was okay. They all replied back that they were working, and hoped he had a good day, too.

It was Bristol who texted separately.

Bristol: *You okay?*

He knew he probably should have sent a private message. It was best to sound a little less depressed in his texts.

Ethan: *I'm fine. Just figured it had been a while since we all got together.*

Bristol: *We can make it happen. It has been a while. I miss your face.*

Ethan: *I miss your face too, brat.*

Bristol: *Okay, maybe I don't miss you as much as I miss Aaron.*

Ethan: *You can't see me, but I'm totally flipping you off right now.*

Bristol: *There are emojis for that, you idiot.*

Ethan: *You're so sweet.*

Bristol: *I know. Now I've got to get back to work. Practice never waits for anyone. Love you.*

Ethan: *I love you, too.*

Aaron texted next.

Aaron: *Everything okay?*

Ethan snorted. Apparently, checking in on his family on a Monday afternoon meant that he was losing his mind. But at least his family cared. It was better than most of Lincoln's family. Oh, Lincoln's parents were amazing, they just didn't live near them anymore and had their own lives now. Ethan wasn't even going to get started on Lincoln's extended family.

Ethan made his way home, and as he pulled in, he noticed that Lincoln's car was already there.

Oh. Well.

Today was going to suck.

More so than it already did.

Before he got out, though, Liam texted.

Liam: *Just checking in.*

Ethan was never going to text his family on a Monday again. Just because he might *need* help, didn't mean he actually wanted it.

And wasn't that going to be the tagline of his book if he ever wrote one?

Ethan: *I'm fine. Just thought I'd say hi since it's been a while.*

Liam: *If you need anything, I'm here. Arden is, too. We're here.*

We. Hell, Liam was a *we* now. Including the dog that he and Arden now had together.

Ethan was happy for Liam. He truly was, he just really wished he could figure out his damn life.

Ethan: *Love you guys. Talk to you soon.*

And then he slid his phone into his pocket, knowing his mom and dad would probably text next.

He loved his family more than anything, but sometimes...they saw too much.

He looked at Lincoln's car parked next to his and sighed.

Better get this over with.

He walked into the house, closing the door behind

him, and inhaled the smell of garlic. He held back a groan.

"I thought you'd be home," Lincoln said from the kitchen, sautéing something in a pan.

Ethan set his stuff in the bowl next to the door and walked over to the kitchen where his best friend stood cooking chicken and garlic pasta as if nothing had happened. As if everything were fine and normal.

What the hell?

"I went in today since I had nothing else to do."

"I see that. I did the same. Tried to work anyway. Things didn't work out."

"Oh."

"Then I went to lunch with Madison and her parents and ended up not eating because all they wanted to do was talk about how much of a low-life I am. Same as Madison. So, we had a mimosa, and then Madison and I left. But we tried. That should count for something. At least for a while."

Ethan cursed under his breath. "I forgot that you had that lunch."

Lincoln looked over his shoulder. Ethan noticed he looked tired, his eyes full of something he couldn't read. And he hated that he couldn't read his best friend. He'd always been able to before. Had that changed?

"I forgot, too. Until Madison showed up. After Damien left, that is."

Irrational jealousy spiraled through Ethan. He tried his best to push it back. But it was hard to do when Damien was such a sore subject for him. And not just because of the jealousy. Because Damien treated Lincoln like trash, like a cash pony only. And Ethan hated it.

"Oh?" he asked.

"Oh." Lincoln rolled his eyes. "You're right, he's an asshole. He's crossed some lines. I'm working on it, okay?"

Surprised, Ethan took a few steps forward. "What do you mean?"

"Meaning, I took my key back. So, you are officially the only person with a key to my place."

Ethan ignored the way that knowledge felt in his chest. No need to think too much about it. They were best friends. Only friends. Right? Clearly, that's how Lincoln wanted to play it.

"Anyway, Damien is still my agent, but hopefully those boundaries will start to work." He shrugged. "If not...I don't know. I'll figure something out."

Ethan moved forward and reached out to put his hand on Lincoln's shoulder but stopped. He didn't know if he was allowed to touch Lincoln anymore. And that killed him. "Okay. If there's anything I can do for you, let me know."

"I know." Lincoln turned off the burner and then looked directly into Ethan's eyes. "I know."

Ethan swallowed hard and tried to think of something to say. He could only come up with one thing. "So, we're not going to talk about it?"

Lincoln's face went blank. "Talk about what?"

"I don't know, maybe how I had your dick in my hand? Or that you were touching my dick, too?"

Lincoln closed his eyes, muttered a curse under his breath, and took a step away. He started to pace the kitchen while Ethan just stared at him, wondering if he had just lost everything. He felt as if someone had ripped out his heart, slowly massaging it before threatening to twist it and break it into a thousand pieces before shoving it back into the empty cavity that was his chest.

He couldn't think, couldn't focus, he had no idea what the fuck he was doing.

"Do you want the truth?"

No. But he couldn't say that. Instead, he just clenched his jaw and nodded. "I need to know."

"Fine. I want you. I've always wanted you. I've wanted you for so fucking long, but I'm an idiot about it. Is that what you wanted to hear?"

It was as if everything had changed, as if he had heard the words spoken but they weren't really there. Instead, Ethan took a few steps forward, just close enough that he could reach out and touch Lincoln's face. Lincoln didn't move away. The stubble of his unshaven beard scraped across Ethan's palm, and he wanted more. "Okay."

Lincoln frowned. "Okay? That's all you have to say."

"I don't know what else to say. Only the fact that I want you, too. And I don't know what to do about it."

"Well, we did something last night, didn't we?"

"But we weren't alone. What about Holland?" Ethan asked, worried about the answer.

He continued. "I've wanted you, too. But you're my best friend, Lincoln. I can't fix this if we fuck it up."

"What if we do? Though I think we're already past that. And it took booze to make it happen."

"And...Holland? What about her?" Ethan asked again, his heart in his throat.

Lincoln rubbed a hand over his face and stepped away. It felt like a chasm had opened up between them. Neither knew what to say. It just hurt.

"I don't know what to do. I want her, too."

"So do I." Ethan laughed, but it was hollow. "I guess we figure this out. My cousin did. I mean, she has two husbands. Maybe we can figure out how to make it work."

"Maybe."

"I don't want it to just be words, though. Because last night? Best night of my fucking life. But I don't want to risk you. And I don't want to risk what we have with Holland either because we don't talk it out."

"Then I guess we'd better do better about that," Lincoln said wryly.

"I haven't been good about that."

"I know. But I'm no better. Maybe Holland will be good for both of us."

Lincoln nodded, but before he said anything else, Ethan leaned in and brushed his lips softly against his friend's.

Lincoln gasped and then deepened the kiss. There was no booze, no worries—at least not right now. It was just them. Only them. Ethan groaned, wanting more.

"We really going to do this?" Lincoln asked, surprise in his tone.

Considering how taken aback Ethan was right then, he didn't blame the other man. "I think we are. But you have to tell me what you want. You have to talk to me. If it's too much, or if it's not enough, I need to know.

Because I can't lose you. And I don't want to hurt Holland. I want her to be a part of this."

"And she will be. She was last night. And she's always with us. But for right now? You're the one in my arms." Lincoln said the words, but Ethan agreed. They leaned forward and kissed again.

"Tomorrow we talk with Holland," Ethan whispered.

"But right now, right now, I think we should let the dinner get cold."

Ethan groaned, wrapping his arms around Lincoln's waist as Lincoln slid his hands through Ethan's hair.

He groaned and then gasped as Lincoln tugged.

"I thought you said you didn't like doing this in the kitchen," Ethan said, a smile on his face.

Lincoln laughed, his whole body shaking as he tugged Ethan across the house. "You're right about that."

"Holland tomorrow, though?" Ethan asked. "Because while I want this with you, and I want to figure this out, I don't want it to feel like we're cheating on her."

"It doesn't feel that way at all. It feels like we're one connection, one link. And we'll figure out the rest. I promise."

Ethan nodded, then his lips were on Lincoln's, and

there didn't need to be any more talking. At least, not right that second.

Lincoln led Ethan the rest of the way to Ethan's bedroom, their lips on each other, their hands roaming the entire time. This was everything he had ever wanted. It was as if it were finally happening. After so many years, so many wants and dreams, it was so much more than he had ever imagined.

And he didn't want to mess it up.

"You're frowning against my lips," Lincoln whispered.

"I forget you know me so well," Ethan rasped.

"If I knew you that well, we would've already been doing this long before now."

Ethan shook his head. "I don't know. I think we both needed to be ready. Or, at least, figuring out what we wanted. And maybe it's weird to say, but I believe we needed Holland."

Lincoln stared at him then and smiled. "I think we did. I think that's exactly what we needed." And then they weren't talking anymore. Just kissing. Needing.

Ethan raised his arms as Lincoln slowly slid the shirt over his head, and then Lincoln did the same for Ethan.

When Lincoln licked Ethan's nipple, they both

shuddered, the exquisite delicateness of the moment almost too much.

Ethan had wanted this for so long, he was afraid it was going to be a dream. Or that they would go too fast and he would miss it all.

But he just focused on the moment, lasered in on what was happening. And then leaned in for more.

Together, they stripped down, Ethan gently sliding his hand behind the waistband of Lincoln's boxer briefs. When he curled his fingers around Lincoln's hardness, his best friend sucked in a breath and groaned.

"Jesus, just one touch, and I'm ready to blow," Lincoln groaned out.

"You're not even touching my dick, and I already know I'm not going to last long. What does that tell you?"

"That I probably should have done this before. We should have met Holland before."

"Just imagining her on that park bench in that wedding dress, picturing lifting it up over her hips makes me hard, too."

Lincoln's eyes narrowed, even as heat filled them.

"You thought that, too?"

Ethan licked his lips. "I did. You, taking her from behind as she swallowed my cock. Or maybe me in her pussy with you in her ass. With all of that delicate lace around us. She was another man's, but right then, and right now, all I can do is picture her in that dress, just how we met her, and her being ours. And then she and I sharing you. Does that make me a horrible lech?" Ethan asked as Lincoln slowly slid Ethan's underwear down.

He shook them off, then got rid of Lincoln's until they were both naked, both pumping each other's dicks in their hands.

Ethan stood a little closer so their dicks rubbed against each other, and when Lincoln took them both in hand, Ethan groaned out and then reached around Lincoln's ass to play with his crack.

Ethan met Lincoln's gaze, and his best friend gave him a tiny nod, so Ethan began to play. Slowly at first, even while Lincoln moved his hands, jerking them both off.

"I need lube," Ethan growled and then pulled away.

"I'm sure you have some, right?" Lincoln asked, and Ethan just nodded.

"Of course, I do. I'm not a monster." He went to the dresser drawer and pulled out some lube, putting some on his fingers and then on his dick. He handed the bottle over to Lincoln, who did the same. Then Ethan went back into the drawer and pulled out condoms. "Just in case we go that far," he said.

Lincoln nodded. "Good. Because I really want to fuck that ass of yours," Lincoln growled.

Ethan's brows rose. "Oh, so you're going to top?"

"Top or bottom, depends on the mood. But when I dream this, you're usually on all fours."

Ethan closed his eyes and counted to ten. He would not come right then. He was not going to last much longer, though.

"Ah, well, I've had similar dreams. But, sometimes, I'm on all fours. And sometimes, you are. You want to flip a coin?"

Lincoln took a step forward, thrust his hand down, and squeezed the base of Ethan's dick. Ethan's eyes crossed, and he tried to count to ten again but he forgot what number came after three. Was it seven? Was it ten? Did it matter? Dear, God.

"How about I go first? Then, we'll take turns. When Holland's here? That'll be fun with figuring out who gets to top."

"It's her. The answer is always her." Ethan gasped. Lincoln laughed. "Pretty much. And that image almost just sent me right over the edge." Ethan growled, but he was laughing at the same time.

"Tell me about it. Now, fuck me."

They kissed, continued holding each other until they were finally on the bed, both of them grinding against one another as they added more lube, with Lincoln slowly and methodically working on Ethan's hole. He frowned as a curse word bubbled up, knowing he was going to come too soon. He just kept working, kept grinding their dick's together, then it was too late. He was coming on both of their stomachs, shouting Lincoln's name. Lincoln just leaned down and lapped it up, licking Ethan's cock in the process, both of them groaning.

"Jesus Christ. You weren't even inside me yet."

"Well, I guess we'd better get you hard again. Oh, look. Already halfway there."

And so, Lincoln began to work Ethan's cock again, this time hovering over Ethan as he slowly prodded at his entrance with the tip of his now condom-clad dick.

"Are you ready for me? I've been working you with my fingers, but if it's too much, we can stop."

Ethan spread his legs and gripped his dick.

"I'm ready for you. Just hurry, already."

Lincoln grinned, then there were no more words. He wasn't rough, was actually gentle. As if they had been waiting for this moment forever. And maybe they had.

Lincoln slowly worked his way in and out of him, carefully, reverently, as if he were afraid Ethan would break. Or maybe *he* would. That perhaps this would be too much. But it didn't matter. This was everything. It was so much.

When Lincoln finally came, Ethan joined him. After, they were both panting, connected in every way. Always.

And Ethan knew that this was one of the best moments of his life. Tomorrow, they would add their third. They would find Holland and make sure she knew that she could be a part of this, too.

Because Ethan knew that as much as he loved this, as much as he wanted this with Lincoln, something was missing. And he knew Lincoln felt it, too.

This was everything. But if they added Holland? It could be even more.

As he held his best friend, curled into him, he knew that this was just the start. Because with Holland, it could be so much more. It could be everything.

He just hoped to hell it was worth it.

CHAPTER EIGHT

Somehow, Holland was working. Somehow, she was functioning and smiling and thanking people for their purchases. She was dealing with budget and work orders and organizing her store. She was making sure her employee, Fiona, was doing what she needed to do and working at the cash register as well as helping to dust all the little collectibles.

Somehow, Holland was getting all of that done.

And she wasn't thinking about Ethan and Lincoln every second of every minute of every hour of every part of her day.

And the day before.

Okay, so it was every other second, but that had to count as progress, considering she'd been hungover the day before, trying to work and thinking about the guys so much it physically hurt.

There was something wrong with her. Something seriously wrong with her.

But there was nothing she could really do about it. Because she just knew deep down in her heart that she was never going to see them again. They were either going to think her a horrible person for what she did when she was drunk, or maybe they'd just fall for each other, and she would be left out.

And, honestly, that wouldn't be that bad, actually. Because they deserved each other. They were good together. And she had sensed the lingering tension between them. She just hadn't realized it would explode like it did.

But she was happy that it had.

Because they were so good together. So good in fact, it was making her hot just thinking about it.

She wasn't going to think about it at all.

She honestly couldn't.

"Are these the ones going on sale? Or is the other section?" Fiona asked, bringing Holland out of her thoughts.

Holland shook her head and then realized it likely looked as if she were saying, "No." She forced a smile as she made her way over to where Fiona was standing.

"This is the right shelf. You're going to need to mark each one, though, because we don't have it in the system what each thing is individually."

"That's not a problem, Holland. Do you want me to cover the barcode?"

Holland explained what needed to be done, liking the fact that Fiona asked so many questions. She learned quickly but also wanted to make sure that she was completing things correctly. Fiona was sixteen, and this was her first job. She only worked part-time and was saving up money to buy a car. But she worked hard, and Holland liked her.

She also liked Steven, her other part-time worker, who was in his thirties and was just finishing up being a stay-at-home dad. His husband worked full-time with pretty unreasonable hours—not that she would ever say that. Steven worked when the kids were in school for a little extra money for the family. And those college funds. Sometimes, he even brought the kids in so she could say hi and hold them and see how their days were.

She loved the kids. Had always thought she would have some of her own with Dustin.

Well, that wasn't going to happen, was it?

And it seemed as if a relationship with the two people she thought maybe she could have in the future wasn't going to work out either. She'd made things so awkward between them that it would be best if she wasn't part of it. No babies for her anytime soon. Or, ever for that matter. But it was fine. She didn't need that. All she needed was her job, and well...that was about it.

Because her friends had been Dustin's friends. And her little sister's for that matter. After her wedding day, they had all gone with Dustin and Dakota rather than her. It didn't matter that she had been the one slighted. Everyone thought that it was almost like Romeo and Juliet, the fact that Dustin and Dakota were finally together after so many years of being with the wrong people.

Well, fuck them. Fuck them hard. Holland didn't need them. She didn't need anyone. And, if she kept telling herself that, maybe someday, she wouldn't want to vomit every time she thought about it.

She wasn't sure how people made friends these days. Maybe she could hit up a bar and find some girls who needed one more member in their group. She could use some friends. She hated that she felt literally alone at this point.

And now, she sounded whiny. And she hated that even more.

She helped Fiona a bit longer and then went up to the front of the store to help a few lingering customers.

Her store did decent business, did even better business on the weekends, and she loved it.

She loved Boulder, Colorado. It was situated right up in the mountains so the views—no matter where you were—were spectacular. It was a college town, a hippie town, a crunchy granola town, and just...a weird one. But it was perfect for her.

People came into the shop all the time for little trinkets or for presents or just for something to say that they were in Boulder. She didn't overprice her merchandise so she made a decent profit, but the artists earned their wages, as well. She had one-of-a-kind pieces. Things you could only get in Boulder, from these local artisans.

Of course, thinking about art made her think about Lincoln. She had looked him up and almost wept at the art she had seen. He was famous. Maybe not outside of certain art circles, but people knew his name. And his work was breathtaking. She had seen it before even without knowing who he was, had fallen in love with his pieces, and had hoped, one day, to be able to own something of her own.

Not that she thought she'd ever be able to afford it now. His prices were starting to skyrocket. She was sure his agent was part of that, but Lincoln deserved to be paid for his work. If people wanted it, and he was in high demand, she understood. Sometimes, art got expensive.

She just wished she could afford it.

She said goodbye to a couple as they walked out, their bags full of gifts for their nieces and nephews and was just about to head to the back to nibble at her lunch when the door opened again. She froze. And before she could even turn to see who had entered, that familiar perfume hit her senses.

Why? Why today?

She had bags under her eyes. She hadn't slept well because all she had done all night was think about Ethan and Lincoln. She knew she looked like crap.

Of course, her mother would be here.

"Holland. This is enough."

"Hi, Mother, would you like to come to the back with me?"

"No, we are going to talk. Right here, right now."

Out of the corner of her eye, Holland noticed that Fiona was staring wide-eyed. Holland just sighed.

"This is my place of business, Mother. How about you come into the back with me and Fiona can watch the front? It's either that, or you walk right out, and we don't talk at all." She had been avoiding her family for a while now, with good reason, but when her mother got a burr up her butt like this, there was no avoiding her.

Holland didn't know how or when her parents had stopped loving her. Had stopped even *liking* her.

And she hated that she was jealous of her sister. Not because of Dustin, but because her parents loved her little sister so much. Dakota could do no wrong, and yet, it was always Holland who did the wrong thing.

But she couldn't dwell on that. She just had to focus. And try to get her mother out of her store before she lost business because of the woman.

Her mom rolled her eyes, looking like a teenager rather than a woman in her fifties. "Fine."

She stormed past Holland into the back. Holland just shrugged, giving a small smile to Fiona. "I'll be right back. Do you mind watching the front?"

"No problem. Are you going to be okay?"

"I'll be fine. If you need anything, let me know."

"You, too," Fiona said quickly. Holland just smiled before rolling her shoulders back to go and face the firing squad.

Or, you know...her mother.

She headed to the back where her mom surveyed Holland's inventory and desk, clicking her tongue at the stacks of paper.

Holland was neat, everything was in order, she'd even dusted that morning. Nothing was out of place.

But it wasn't exactly a doctor's office or a medical school like her mother wanted for Holland. They'd wanted lawyers and doctors and everything clichéd you could think of in the family. Holland just wanted happiness. And, she liked her shop. She knew that having her store in business was a blessing. She saved and scrimped and made sure that her place was the best it could possibly be so she didn't end up losing it.

Her mom didn't understand that. Didn't get that not everybody wanted to be a doctor or a lawyer.

"You need to apologize to your sister."

Holland just stood there, stunned.

"Excuse me?"

The woman who had raised her turned on Holland, her eyes narrowed into slits. "You have been declining her calls and ignoring her. And you haven't once congratulated her on her engagement. What kind of sister are you?"

"I honestly cannot believe you're even saying this. You do understand what she did, right?"

"You're the one who walked out on your wedding. You're the one suffering the consequences now because of it. You don't have to punish your sister because of your poor choices."

Holland rubbed her temples and knew that this shouldn't be a surprise to her. Her mother always misconstrued facts and twisted things into her own version following her own timeline. It never made any sense to her, and Holland would always end up in the wrong no matter what happened.

But she seriously couldn't believe the words coming out of her mother's mouth.

Because, dear God. Her mom was insane.

"Mom, I don't want to talk to her. I don't want to talk to Dustin. I don't want to talk to anybody who blames me for walking out."

"You were always such a selfish girl."

That was it.

"You need to go. I'm really tired of this. You know I'm not selfish. You know this is just..." Holland tried to ignore the hurt, but she couldn't breathe. She could not understand who this woman was. Didn't understand how she could have raised Holland.

"Just go," Holland repeated.

"I will not. You need to talk to your sister."

"No, I don't. I don't need to talk with any of you. Not anymore."

"It was an accident, Holland."

Holland just rolled her eyes, snorting. "So...she just slipped and swallowed?"

Holland didn't even register the slap until the sting made her eyes water.

"Did you just hit me?" Holland asked, her voice a gasp.

"How dare you talk like that? With that tone?"

"Leave. Before I call the cops."

"You are such an ungrateful, spoiled brat. Your sister needs you. She's getting married to the love of her life, and you are just jealous of her. You don't understand."

"You know what? Fuck you. Get out. Dakota's welcome to Dustin. But I'm done."

"You were never happy with what you had. No, you always wanted something different. Wanted more. You ignored who you had, what you could be, and now look where you are. Alone. In this trash heap. And with *nothing*."

"I have my own place. My own shop. I moved out. Moved on. I want nothing to do with him. I want nothing to do with you or my sister, either. And, if you ever hit me again, I'll press charges. Do you hear me? You are nothing to me. Do you get that?"

That seemed to register with her mother, but, like always, she had to have the last word. "You're dead to us."

Her mom stormed out as if she were in some

dramatic movie, but Holland didn't care. She went to the bathroom in the back, splashed some water on her face, dried it, and then quickly applied some powder so no one would see the red mark. It would fade soon. Her mother hadn't put much power behind the slap, but Holland still couldn't quite believe her mother had done it at all.

Never in her life would she have thought that would happen.

And yet, here she was. She couldn't even figure out what she was supposed to say. What she was supposed to do or feel. That was not the mother she *thought* she knew. Oh, her mom might have once been a little harsh on her and always seemed to prefer Dakota, but she had never been like *this* before. Not really. And it hurt.

Everything hurt.

Fiona came back to check on her, and she smiled, saying, "Don't worry, Steven will be in soon."

Fiona didn't look like she was convinced, but it didn't matter.

Holland would be off for the rest of the day since Steven was closing, and she just wanted to go home. And pretend like nothing had happened.

Her phone buzzed then. She hoped to hell it wasn't any member of her family.

She wasn't sure what she would do if that were the case.

She looked down and froze.

Lincoln: *Do you want to meet us for coffee? We're nearby.*

She swallowed hard, trying to formulate thoughts.

Us. As in both Lincoln and Ethan.

Maybe this was going to be the brush-off. Or perhaps they just wanted to continue as friends and pretend like nothing had happened.

Either way, it would be better than Holland going home and crying herself to sleep.

She didn't want them to know what her mother had just done, so, she wouldn't tell them. But she did want to see them. Even if it hurt, it would be better than dealing with her family.

Holland: *Okay, when and where?*

Lincoln told her the place. It was only a block away. He gave her a couple of time options. She chose the closest one and then quickly went back to the bathroom so she could make sure she looked at least somewhat presentable.

She still had those dark circles she loathed, still looked a little shell-shocked, but maybe by the time she had coffee, things would be better. Regardless, she needed to get out of here.

She really hated the fact that her mother had tarnished this place. A place she had put so much of her life into, so much of her soul.

She was done with her family. Completely done.

Her next step would be to make some friends. Find a new way to survive. Because she didn't know what she'd do if she couldn't.

Steven showed up ten minutes after the text from Lincoln, and Holland said her goodbyes, ignoring the worried look on Fiona's face. She would be fine. She wouldn't let what had happened, happen again. No matter what.

She didn't have time to go home and change, but it wasn't like she looked horrible. She just looked as if she had worked a long shift.

Hopefully, she didn't look as if her mother had come in, trying to ruin her day.

The guys were already there by the time she walked in. She swallowed hard, trying to remember the way they tasted, the way they had felt writhing against her.

She tried not to think about exactly what they look like naked, or how she had felt with both of their cocks in her hand as if it were just a normal, daily occurrence.

But as soon as they stood up, and she saw their eyes darken as they watched her move, she knew the guys were thinking something similar.

This was so not going to end well for any of them. But did it matter? Honestly, she didn't think so.

Her night with Lincoln and Ethan would be forever the best night of her life. Definitely the most erotic, sensual, and pleasurable.

And she wanted to do it again. Even though she knew she shouldn't.

"Hey there," Lincoln said, kissing her cheek and then giving her a hug. She squeezed him tightly, inhaling his spicy scent before taking a step back. Before she could say anything, Ethan had her in a bear hug, kissing her other cheek.

She blushed, remembering exactly what it had felt like to be pressed between them.

She knew this was probably a mistake, and she couldn't help but wonder what people were thinking. Were they wondering if they were just a group of friends? Or did they know that she had been between these two? Had felt them?

She didn't know what she wanted the answer to be, so she didn't let it bother her one way or the other.

"I'll go up and get our orders. Just let me know what you want," Ethan said, bouncing on his feet.

Holland met Lincoln's gaze. Her brows rose, and Lincoln just shook his head.

"He's always like this when he's nervous."

She swallowed hard. "Nervous?"

"Everything's fine, don't worry."

She quickly rattled off her order to Ethan before he bounced right out of his shoes, and he went to get them coffee—and probably a pastry or two, knowing Ethan. It was a little weird that she already knew him so well. But she couldn't help it. She liked him. Both of them. And she didn't want to leave them, even though if she wasn't careful, it wouldn't matter in the end. They'd find each other or someone else, leaving her behind. Which was fine. She just needed to live in the moment—something she'd forgotten to do before.

"Take a seat," Lincoln said, and she did, smiling while she tucked her chair back under the table.

"Hey," she whispered. "I didn't actually say hello earlier."

Lincoln smiled, and she wanted to reach out and caress his cheek. Seriously, her desire to touch them was getting a little insane.

"Hey, yourself. You look good."

Her brows rose again. "I don't...but thank you for saying so."

Lincoln just snorted.

"I always think you look good. You look a little tired, but then again, I haven't been getting much sleep either."

"And here I thought I'd worn enough makeup so I wouldn't look so bad."

"You don't look bad. I probably shouldn't have said anything. I'm not always good with my words."

"I think you're pretty good."

"Thank you for saying so."

Ethan was there in the next instant, a tray in his hands that made her laugh.

"Do you work here now?" she asked, getting up quickly to help him.

Lincoln was there, too, and the three of them set the coffees and three plates of pastries and sandwiches down.

"Are we feeding an army?" Lincoln asked.

"You know I get hungry when I'm nervous."

"Okay, you keep saying the word *nervous*. Should I know why? Should *I* be nervous?"

"No. Although now that I think about it, maybe we shouldn't be talking about this in a public space." Lincoln looked over his shoulder, and Holland tensed.

"Because you're afraid I'm going to start crying or screaming and run away?"

"No," Ethan said and reached out to grip her hand, giving it a squeeze. "Mostly because we don't want anyone to overhear. But we're safe in this booth area. It's pretty quiet back here, and no one's really around."

"Okay."

"Maybe we should just blurt it out?" Ethan asked, and Lincoln pinched the bridge of his nose, a smile playing on his lips.

"Maybe we should."

"Blurt out what?" She looked between them, definitely worried now.

"We'd like to ask you out on a date," Lincoln said, his voice soft.

She froze, trying to absorb exactly what he had just said. "Excuse me?"

Ethan rolled his eyes. "We like you. A lot. And...we'd like to ask you out on a date."

"Oh."

"Is *oh* good? Or bad?" Lincoln asked.

"You said *we*. I'm very confused. I seriously thought that I was coming here for you guys to tell me that everything was nice but that you either wanted to forget it all happened, or that you were just going to date each other." She said the words so quickly, she was afraid the guys weren't going to actually understand her, but they did, and she let out a shaky breath.

"That's not it, at all," Lincoln said. He reached out and gripped her hand again, then Ethan did the same with the other. They both squeezed and then let go, looking over their shoulders.

Going out on a date with one person was fine, but they should be careful when it came to public displays of affection between three people. Maybe. Or, perhaps she was wrong.

"We'd like to take you out. Both of us. All three of us."

She looked at Ethan as he spoke.

"Are you serious?"

"Of course, we are. We like you. And each other," Lincoln added, smiling over at Ethan.

That smile did things to her insides, and her toes curled in her shoes.

"We like you, and we want to spend time with you. And we'd like to see where this goes."

"The three of us," she reiterated.

"I know it's not exactly...usual. I don't want to say it's not normal. Because what *is* normal?" Ethan continued. "My cousin, Maya? She has two husbands. And the three of them worked things out. They go on dates in public, and they make things work. I'm not saying we should get married," Ethan said quickly, holding up his hands.

"Oh my God, you suck at this."

"I really do."

Holland just smiled, her mind going a thousand miles a minute as she tried to catch her breath.

"You want to date. The three of us. But, just the three of us? Or in pairs, as well?" Both guys blushed, and her brows rose. "Have you two already started dating?"

"Maybe," Lincoln said, clearing his throat.

Ethan was the one who answered the first part of her question. "Yes, think of all the math. Pairs and triples. All of it. Everything. We'd have to make this work, so that means open communication and telling each other exactly what we want and what we're comfortable with. Just like a real relationship is supposed to be."

"And if we ever get stuck, we can figure out what to do by asking my cousin." Ethan closed his eyes. "Or, maybe we can't. We can just figure it out between ourselves. One step at a time. But we like you."

Holland smiled. "I like you both, too. And I was really afraid I was never going to see you again."

"I was afraid you wouldn't want to go out with us, but I think this could work," Lincoln said quietly, gesturing between the three of them. "The three of us. We could try it. See if it works."

"And if it doesn't?" That worried her. But then again, she knew there was so much more to worry about.

"Well, if it doesn't, then we find a way to be friends. Because I'm selfish, and I want you in my life," Lincoln said. Then he looked over at Ethan. "Both of you."

"What do you think?" Ethan asked. She swallowed hard.

There were feelings there. Not just between them, but between her *and* them, as well. There were so many connections, and she wanted this. At least, she thought so. Because...why not? She didn't love her ex. Maybe she never had. But perhaps this could be good for her. The three of them together, figuring out who they were. At least having fun. And the two of them would always have each other if they got bored with her. But if they all went into this with eyes wide open, then it wouldn't be like before with her sister and her ex. It wouldn't be cheating. Because all three of them would be together. And if she wasn't enough for both of them, she could walk away. Because she liked them enough to at least want them to be happy.

She smiled. She knew this might be a mistake, but it was one worth making. "Yes, I think I'd like that."

When they smiled at her, their eyes bright and their hands outstretched to grip hers, she hoped she was making the right choice. Because she didn't want to mess this up. And she didn't think she could, at least not right then. Not with the way they were looking at her. Like they wanted her. It had been so long since she had been wanted. She held on.

She never wanted to let go.

CHAPTER NINE

"I still can't believe I said yes to going to this dinner," Lincoln said as he looked over at Ethan in the driver's seat.

Ethan raised a brow and turned down the next street. "You have been to how many Montgomery dinners now? This shouldn't be strange for you. You're family."

"Families don't do what we did to each other a few nights ago." Lincoln paused. "Well, I hope they don't. I mean, am I like joining the Montgomery *Deliverance* now?"

"You're lucky I don't kick your ass."

"You're driving. You'd only end up hurting yourself," Lincoln said, holding onto the oh-shit bar as Ethan took a turn a little too quickly.

"Okay. Maybe I should have driven."

"Hey, I'm not a bad driver. It's only in Mario Kart."

"I don't know, you're starting to act like that's real life, too."

"You know, I bet Holland wouldn't make fun of my driving."

Ethan just raised a brow.

"Okay, fine, she would be on the front lines making fun of me." He paused. "You know, you guys are just going to gang up on me, aren't you?"

"Yes, we are. But I kind of like it."

"And I'm sure we'll gang up on you, too. Right?"

"I hope so."

"But you and I won't gang up on her."

"Nope. Unless it has to do with sex. Then, that might be fun."

Ethan groaned and adjusted himself in his jeans right when they were parking.

"You really should not mention things like that right when I'm about to walk into my parents' house. I do not want a hard-on when all of my family's hugging me and saying hello."

"Sorry about that."

He wasn't the least bit sorry. He liked the fact that they could joke like this. As if they had moved on to a new phase of their relationship and things were working out.

He knew that the bottom would fall out at any moment, and this little happy phase of things being easy and not difficult at all wouldn't last long. He was going to breathe it in.

Because the more he thought about it, the more he was afraid that he was going to lose his shit, and everything would end up horrible.

Because that's what usually happened with him.

Things worked out great for a minute, and then they burned to the ground.

Just like with his art. He had slept with Ethan, had done some amazing things with Holland, had a date planned with her soon *with* Ethan, and he still couldn't paint.

It wasn't his best friend cock-blocking him. Or even Holland.

It was all him. He was the loser.

"What's up?" Ethan asked as they got out of the vehicle. "You can get right back in that car and drive off. I'll get a ride home with Liam or something. Are you okay?"

Lincoln shook his head, and Ethan took a step forward, frowning. "What's wrong?"

"I was shaking my head, saying I'm fine. That didn't

come out right. Sorry. I really am fine. Just thinking about work."

"Hey, I thought I was the workaholic." Ethan winked, and Lincoln shook his head again.

They weren't going to talk about that. Ethan had been doing well the past few days, but it was only two days. Work would likely get in their way again, Lincoln knew it. But, hopefully, they'd be able to work it out. They'd been friends for long enough. The change in their relationship couldn't ruin things. Right?

"You're right. Now, let's go inside and face the firing squad."

"It's not a firing squad." Ethan paused. "Okay, maybe it is. The Montgomery firing squad. We can at least make it branded."

Lincoln snorted and took Ethan's hand, giving it a squeeze before letting go quickly.

He wasn't exactly sure where they were with the public displays of affection, and he didn't want to mess things up by going too fast.

Plus, he kind of liked that they were still figuring each other out. This was the fun part of the relationship. Because he really didn't want to get to the next phase where things got screwed up and turned cold. Got broken.

"Are we telling them?" Ethan asked, and Lincoln barked out a laugh.

"This is when you're going to ask that question? Right when we're standing in front of the house, and you know someone's probably watching us right now?"

"What? I was trying to figure out how to ask before it got really hard, so I didn't do it at all."

"Great job."

"Shut up. What are we going to do?"

"Well, I'm pretty sure Bristol's going to figure out what's going on with one look."

"She can't see everything. She doesn't even know Holland."

"She's your sister. She'll figure it out. And so will Aaron. He's quiet, but he figures things out quicker than we give him credit for."

"I guess you're right."

"And then there's Liam. The guy who needs to fix everything. He's going to notice that something's different, and he's going to want to work at it. Because that's who he is."

"There's no hiding this."

Lincoln was pretty sure he hadn't hidden his feelings from the Montgomerys. They all probably knew that Lincoln had wanted Ethan all along. Ethan was likely the only one who hadn't noticed. Probably because he had been too busy hiding his own feelings.

Dear God, they really sucked at this whole communication thing. They needed to get better at it if they wanted to make their relationship work. But they *were* working on it. At least, he hoped so.

"We don't hide?" Ethan asked. Lincoln nodded. His throat closed, and he couldn't speak.

"Okay, good. Because I'm really not good at lying."

"I know. I remember the time you tried to pretend that the paisley shirt I was wearing looked good on me."

"I'm sorry about that. Because it really didn't look good. At all."

"Thanks," Lincoln said, snorting again.

They made their way from the car to the front steps.

Timothy Montgomery was at the door even before Ethan and Lincoln got there.

Ethan's dad was a big man with a big smile, and Lincoln loved him.

He was always there. Always helpful.

Lincoln knew that Timothy and Francine had been through a lot in their lives, but they had both come out stronger because of it. And Lincoln was proud of that. Nobody was perfect. People didn't need perfect lives or a perfect past with no mistakes. He didn't think that actually existed.

Lincoln liked that the couple owned up to their mistakes and had raised their children the best they could. Considering that the Montgomerys were some of his favorite people in the world, he figured they had done a pretty damn good job.

"Well, it's about damn time you showed up. Your mom was stressing out that you weren't coming, and then wondered what she was going to do with all this food." Timothy rolled his eyes and hugged his son hard before reaching out to do the same with Lincoln. Lincoln inhaled the man's scent. He smelled like home.

Lincoln loved his mom and dad, they were the best parents he could have ever hoped for. But he also loved the Montgomerys. They were his second home. Even with his first being amazing, he liked the fact that he had a second one.

A different place to call home when his other family had been pulled across the country because of a job.

"I'm sure we won't eat all the food. I mean, there's how many of you guys in there? And she's worried about us?" Lincoln asked, and Timothy just smiled.

"You know Francine. She wants all of her little baby chicks in a row."

"I thought it was ducks in a row. Or squirrels. I

never understood that saying because it's not like the ducks are always in a row. Sometimes, they go off on their own, and then the mama duck has to keep finding them." Francine just kept speaking as she hugged Lincoln tightly and then did the same with Ethan. "It's good to see my boys here. It's been forever since we had all the family together."

"It's been like three weeks," Liam said as he walked over.

Liam looked just like Francine, and had a wide grin on his face just like his dad.

Lincoln would have assumed that Liam was a Montgomery like the rest of them. They all looked so much alike. But, apparently, Francine's DNA had pulled him right out of the gene pool of whoever Liam's birth father was and had made him look exactly like a Montgomery, as well. The eyes were different, that much Lincoln knew, but it didn't matter. Liam was a Montgomery through and through, even if it wasn't full-blooded. Lincoln even felt like a Montgomery, and he was just the friend.

The friend currently dating Ethan, but they weren't going to mention that today.

"Oh good, you're here," Bristol said, pushing past Liam to throw her arms around Ethan. "I've missed you something fierce." She kissed her brother's cheeks and then came and did the same to Lincoln.

"Well, you kind of missed the last dinner. How was the performance?" Ethan asked. Bristol just shrugged, the light in her eyes dimming a bit.

Lincoln hated to see that, but as a fellow artist, he got it. Sometimes, work sucked. And when it was your literal soul being thrown onto the canvas—or in her case, through her fingers into her music—it felt like a double-edged sword in the chest rather than just the single blade.

"It was fine. You know, play a little cello, meet some royalty, laugh and dance and pretend that everything's okay." She looked over at her mother and smiled widely. "And everything *is* fine."

"Tell her what that duke did," Marcus growled from behind her.

Lincoln met the other man's gaze and raised a brow.

Marcus shook his head, his dark brows lowering as he glared at Bristol.

Lincoln knew that the two of them were best friends, but like he and Ethan, he wasn't sure if the two of them had ever dated. And he didn't know if they would ever take that plunge—or if they even wanted to.

Considering he was afraid that he was making a mistake with every push, he wasn't going to edge them in any particular direction. Even though Francine probably would have liked her little girl to be married off by now. But only because she would want Bristol to be happy. And Lincoln agreed with that. He liked Bristol, and he wanted her happy, too. He didn't know if it was going to be with Marcus, though. She had been dating someone for a while, but her ex-girlfriend was now getting married herself. Lincoln knew that Francine had even tried to get Bristol and him together, but that wasn't ever going to work.

Especially not when he was in love with another Montgomery.

"What did he do?" Liam asked at the same time as Ethan.

Aaron stood in the back, his arms folded over his chest as he glared at everybody.

"Yes, what did he do, dear sister? Do we have to kick his ass?"

Bristol looked over at Lincoln and pleaded.

"Please, please help."

Lincoln just held up his hands. "Oh, I want nothing to do with this. Unless I have to kick his ass. I will do that."

"You're going to have to stand in line," Marcus growled. She glared at her best friend and then at the rest of them.

"Why couldn't I have had sisters? Seriously. Why am I the only girl?"

"Because you're more than enough for me. I swear, another of you, and I wouldn't have made it," Francine said, smacking a kiss on her daughter's cheek. "And if that duke did anything too untoward, the boys won't have to do anything. Because I'll castrate him myself. You hear me, little girl?"

"You're scary sometimes, Mom."

"I know. And that's why you love me. Anyway, what did he do?"

"Nothing." A pause. "He tried to kiss me. I didn't want it. He tried again. I kicked him in the nuts. And...I will no longer be playing in that country."

The boys grumbled and growled, threatening things that would land all of them in jail, but it was Francine who hugged her daughter and then clapped her hands. "It settled?"

A nod.

"Good. We'll talk later. I promise. You're my baby." She looked at all of them. "Now, let's all actually go into the house and not just stand around in the foyer. We'll get you guys something to drink. And then you can tell me what's new in your lives. Because I feel like I've missed so much. I swear, none of my children call me. They never tell me what they're doing. I have to force you to come to my house."

Lincoln just laughed, shaking his head as he kissed the top of Francine's hair. "You know that you're full of it. You know that, right?"

Francine patted him on the chest. "Yes, but none of the others are allowed to tell me that. Only you, my darling."

"And why is that?" Ethan asked, coming up on the other side of his mom. "Why am I not allowed to say that you're full of it?"

"Because I will beat you, kid." She patted his chest and grinned. "Lincoln's allowed because, while I think of him as my son, I didn't push him out of me. Nor did I adopt him legally. Yet." She winked.

"Please don't adopt him legally," Ethan said, and Lincoln held back a grin.

"And why is that?" Francine asked as she went over to the wine and started pouring glasses for everyone. Suddenly, she slowly set down the bottle and stared at them.

"Really? Really?" She bounced on her feet.

"What?" Bristol asked, pushing through the crowd of men to get to Francine's side. "What?"

"Oh, I think I know," Arden said, and Lincoln looked over to the side.

"I didn't even know you were here," Ethan said, going over to kiss Arden's cheek.

"I was dealing with a work thing, but I'm here now. What did I miss?"

Bristol scowled. "I have no idea, but I don't like that I don't know."

"Shocker," all three Montgomery brothers said, then looked at each other before bursting out laughing.

Bristol threw up her hands in a mock huff. "You see? I should have had sisters. Sisters would have helped."

"You have me now, though," Arden said. "I'm just saying."

Bristol's eyes warmed, and she ran over to Arden, pulling her in for a hard hug. "Yes, I do. Now it's the two of us against the rest of them. This is good. Soon, we'll outnumber them."

"That's not how this works," Liam said, pulling his woman away from Bristol.

"Well, shush. Eventually, there'll be children, and if all of you are good to me, you'll make sure there are daughters."

"You know you're going to end up with like six boys, right?" Aaron said to Bristol, and she flipped him off.

"Now, children. Act your ages," Timothy murmured from the doorway.

"We are," Aaron and Bristol said at the same time and then grinned at each other.

Lincoln just leaned against the counter, folding his arms over his chest. This was family, and he missed it. Oh, he had his cousin, and he and Madison were close and were honestly pretty much like this when they were together, but it wasn't the same. Mostly because he didn't have the amount of people the Montgomerys did. All of the extended Montgomerys were wonderful. At least, the ones he had met so far. None of them were truly evil people or any shit like that—like his uncle. And they all seemed to care about each other, even if they were growly and kind of rude about it.

"Now, wait, we've gone off-topic," Bristol said, sliding back into the conversation. "What do you know, Mom?"

Francine looked between Lincoln and Ethan, but it was so quick, he was sure that no one had even noticed. She was giving them an out. A way for them to be secret about it. And he was grateful. Just because she had seen the changes between him and Ethan, didn't mean she wanted to ruin their surprise. Or their secret. He knew he liked that woman for a reason. But he also knew that secrets weren't good for family. He reached out and punched Ethan in the shoulder.

See? Caring.

"Well," Ethan said, clearing his throat.

Bristol looked between them and then bounced on her feet. She jumped so high, Marcus had to put his hands on her shoulders to calm her.

"Use your words. Stop making that high-pitched sound that only dogs can hear."

"Sorry, Marc."

"Hate that name."

"I know. But I also hate when you compare me to a dog."

"Enough," Timothy said. "Stop leaving us in suspense. What's going on?"

"I know! I know!" Aaron said.

"What do you know?" Ethan glared.

Ah, brothers. Lincoln was kind of glad he didn't have them. However, he had the Montgomerys. He really hoped he didn't lose them.

"What Dad said. Stop leaving us in suspense." Liam grinned.

"We're dating," Ethan said.

And then there was pandemonium. That high-pitched squeal from Bristol grew into one that was echoed by Francine and Arden. They bounced on their feet, and the men in the room just looked at each other and then laughed, both Aaron and Liam handing over cash to Marcus, who slid it into his pocket.

"Wait, did you bet on us?" Lincoln asked, a little annoyed.

"I bet that you would be together by this year," Marcus said. "Sorry, it's really hard not to bet when Aaron starts to sneer about it."

"I was thinking by next year." Aaron shrugged.

"And I thought the two of you wouldn't actually have the guts to do it," Liam said.

"Liam!" Arden admonished, and Liam blushed.

"What? I didn't think everybody could be as lucky as I was."

"Aww," Bristol said as she leaned into Marcus's hold. He hugged her tightly, and she wiggled into his side.

Marcus grinned. "He's probably just sucking up because he did something wrong."

Bristol scowled. "Oh, you're such a hard-ass and not a romantic at all."

"You're enough of a romantic for both of us," he said, and she just rolled her eyes at him.

"Yay. I'm so excited," Francine said, clapping her

hands as her husband held her. "How long have you guys been together?"

Lincoln looked at Ethan, and Ethan shrugged. "Not that long, it's still new. But we knew we couldn't hide it from you, mainly because I suck at it."

"Yes, you do," Aaron quipped. Ethan flipped him off.

"And it's not just us," Lincoln said into the void.

Ethan grinned, and Lincoln was happy to see that he didn't mind that he wanted to tell them about Holland, as well.

Because there would be no hiding her. She wasn't going to be only a third in their relationship. Wasn't going to be an afterthought. She was an equal part, and she wasn't there. Therefore, they had to make sure that the world knew she was important. That she could have been invited. But meeting the parents before an actual first date probably wasn't the best thing. Even though it didn't feel as if they hadn't been on a full date yet. After all, game night and near sex and heavy petting should really count.

And maybe it did.

"Oh?" Francine leaned closer.

"Yes, her name is Holland," Ethan said.

"Runaway bride?" Aaron asked, grinning. "I love it."

"The runaway bride?" Francine asked, a frown on her face. "She's married?"

"No. Remember, we told you that we found that woman after running out on her wedding day because her family's an asshole and the jerk cheated on her?" Ethan said, and Francine put her hand to her mouth.

"Oh, that poor woman. And, yes, I knew you were becoming friends with her, but now there's more? How exciting. This is amazing. And it means more chances for babies!"

Everyone went silent, and then Bristol cleared her throat. "Um, you know that's not actually how it works, but...okay, Mom. Glad to know you're so focused on babies."

Aaron grinned. "I told you she was a Regency mom. It's a truth universally acknowledged that a single Montgomery in possession of our last name, must be in want of a wife—or a husband. Or both."

Lincoln just blinked at the man. "Did you just sort of quote *Pride and Prejudice*?"

"I did. It's my favorite movie. Well, one of them. Though I think Macfayden is a far superior Darcy than Colin Firth. And I will die on that hill."

"I cannot believe you just said that," Arden said. "It is Firth Darcy all the way."

"I don't know. I kind of have to go with Aaron on this," Marcus said, surprising all of them.

"Really?" Lincoln asked.

"What? That one scene where he's walking away and has to stretch his hand because he touched her? Damn hot."

Bristol just blinked at him. "How did I not know this?"

"You made me watch that movie like forty times. And then the miniseries, as well. Of course, I'm going to have opinions on *Pride and Prejudice*."

"I just assumed you did it because you were my friend."

"They're good. And, anyway, I'm allowed to have an opinion on my favorite Darcy."

"Oh, you're welcome to it, it just surprised me."

Everybody started talking at once about their favorite Darcy, and Ethan sidled up to Lincoln and leaned against him. "That went pretty well."

"Yes, it did."

Francine cleared her throat again and then looked between the two of them. "I just wanted to say I'm very happy for you two. Lincoln, you're like a son to me already, and now I'm kind of glad that I never adopted you because that would be weird."

They all laughed. "But, really, it's fine if there are no babies. It's just fun to make you smile when I say it." She reached out and squeezed Arden's shoulders, and Arden looked at the other woman, a small smile on her face.

"I just like making you guys laugh and pretend like I'm that Regency mom Aaron always thinks I am anyway. I want you guys to be happy. In any way that happens. And, if anybody gives you shit about being in a throuple or whatever they're calling it these days, they're going to have to come through me. And I'm sure if I talk to my sister-in-law, she'll be able to tell me exactly what she does if someone dares to talk about her daughter's relationship. Now let's have some wine and celebrate the fact that there is happiness in the world. I cannot wait to meet this Holland."

Lincoln cleared his throat and then opened his arms as Francine slid into them. "You're a good mom," he whispered.

"I'm the best."

Then she wiped tears from her eyes and went over to hug Ethan.

Lincoln loved this family. Adored that even when things were tough, and they were fighting, they were still always there for each other.

He just really hoped to hell he didn't fuck this up. Because he couldn't lose them. And he just might if he wasn't careful. Because if things with Ethan didn't work out, he would lose the Montgomerys, too.

But as he looked at Ethan chasing his sister around

the room, laughing when she jumped over an ottoman and protected her hands since those were insured thanks to her work, he knew he didn't want to mess this up. He couldn't. Because this could be his future. And all of them were already part of his past.

He needed to find a way to make this work. He *had* to.

CHAPTER TEN

Ethan wanted to count this as their second date. However, he knew that Lincoln was counting it as their first. If this went past two nights, and turned into something more, and if they actually ended up celebrating anniversaries—something he knew he wasn't very good at—they really should settle on a date that they'd started this thing.

And also a date with the three of them.

Not just when he and Lincoln got together, or the first time he'd kissed Holland. They needed an actual time. He figured Mario Kart with lots of orgasms should count as date one.

But, apparently, he wasn't right.

At least, according to Lincoln. And from how nervous Holland looked on her front porch, maybe according to her, as well. But even though she looked anxious, she looked sexy as hell.

She had pulled her hair back and to the side a bit so it curled around her face on one side and did this complicated twisting thing on the other. Ethan had no idea how girls were so good at that kind of stuff, but he knew his sister could do an updo in like five minutes and look as if she had been at the salon for hours. Of course, her ex-girlfriend had been the one to teach her all that stuff, and now Bristol wanted to make sure that everybody in the family knew how to do it, as well.

Ethan was inept, so even when his hair was long like Lincoln's, he wasn't able to actually do anything with it other than hopefully remember to brush it. He really sucked at the day-to-day things. Have him do work? He could totally do that. Have him organize what he needed to do to get things done for the day? He could probably get that done, too. Remember something important when he had other things on his mind?

No, he wasn't good at that.

That's why he really needed to settle on an actual day so he could put it in his calendar and hope it reminded him enough that he would remember.

But, seriously, all of that flew from his mind as soon as he looked at Holland.

She wore a black dress that went out in a cute little

wave of some sort over her knees and hugged her breasts perfectly. She had on a coat, but the dress itself had sleeves that covered her shoulders, at least from what he could tell. Were those called cap sleeves? Bristol or Lincoln would know. Ethan? Not so much.

Ethan had driven, but Lincoln was the one moving quicker, so he reached Holland first and took her hands, kissing her knuckles.

Well, wasn't that smooth? He hadn't kissed Ethan's knuckles. Ethan might have to try it on Lincoln one day just to make the other man blush.

Holland did indeed blush, and then she giggled, something he hadn't really heard her do before.

"Look at you, acting like a knight in shining armor," she said and then looked over at Ethan. "Hi there," she said, a smile on her face.

Ethan couldn't help but smile back, and then he leaned down and kissed her cheek. He looked over at Lincoln, who rolled his eyes.

"So not a competition, bro," Lincoln said, and Ethan just grinned.

"Not in the slightest. I don't want to constantly do the same thing as you and feel like I'm messing up. Plus, I really don't think I can pull off the whole knuckle kissing thing as well as you do."

"Well, I'm a fan of both. Even though this is super

weird." Holland winced. "Not that it's strange to be with you guys, just going on a date with two people is weird. I never in my life thought I'd be doing this. And when this is over, I'll look fondly upon it I'm sure. And it's always fun to try something new.

Ethan's brows rose. "Well, if you want to try something new..." His voice trailed off as Lincoln punched him in the arm.

"Hey, stop thinking dirty thoughts. We're going out on a nice date, going to eat some pasta and then call it a night. Got it?"

Holland and I looked at him, and he shrugged. "Okay, we'll just eat some pasta, and then we'll see what happens. But, no pressure. Just a fun night. We'll figure out exactly how dating two people at once works."

"Oh, good. So I'm not the only one who has no idea what they're doing?" Holland asked.

Ethan turned and helped Holland into the passenger seat as Lincoln slid into the back.

"No, you're right, we have no idea what we're doing either, other than making sure we always ask each other if we're okay."

Holland looked at him and just smiled. "And that won't get annoying?"

"Oh, it's going to get totally annoying if we keep

asking over and over, but it'll probably be worse if we try to read each other's minds." He quickly closed the door and ran around the front of the car so he could slide into the driver's seat.

Lincoln and Holland were already talking about what they planned to have for dinner, so Ethan started up the car and then pulled out of the driveway.

"You know, I've never really liked gnocchi," he said as he pulled up to a stop sign.

"I only like it in some soups, but it's not always my favorite thing. It's probably because I haven't had *good* gnocchi," Holland said.

"I think the only gnocchi Ethan's ever had was from Olive Garden." Lincoln grinned.

"Hey, do not knock Olive Garden. Their breadsticks used to be amazing."

Holland frowned. "Their breadsticks aren't amazing now?"

"No, they changed them like a decade ago or something. I'm still a little resentful."

"Interesting." She looked over her shoulder at Lincoln as Ethan turned to get onto the highway.

"Well, he's a little resentful about a lot of things that changed. Don't even get him started on the McRib."

"The McRib is disgusting, and I have no idea why people line up for it."

"Because it's fun to say that they like something that's new and limited." Lincoln leaned forward as he spoke, and Ethan could feel the heat of him at his side. This was going to be a hell of a long night.

"Plus, some people like it. Just like I like gnocchi."

"You only like it because you were actually in Italy and had some little Italian grandmother make it right in front of you."

Holland twisted in her seat. Her eyes bright. "You've been to Italy?"

Lincoln nodded. At least, that's what Ethan could tell from the rearview mirror. It was kind of hard to drive and have a conversation with both of them, so he let them be.

"I studied there for a bit. I jumped around Europe right after college and was grateful that I found friends from art school who were able to keep me on their couches so I didn't go into complete debt."

"That sounds amazing," Holland said, her voice a little breathy. "I've never actually been to Europe. But I've always wanted to go. The big cities and the ones that you can say are out of the way that the tourists go to now. I just want to visit. I mean, I also want to leave

Boulder and go to some different places in the United States. Just travel. You know?"

"We've done a few road trips around America, but I haven't been out of the U.S. either," Ethan said as he got off the highway.

"I've been lucky in my job. I sometimes get to visit other artists or do art shows around the country and the world. But I'm more of a homebody than Ethan here."

"Really?" Holland asked.

"Yep," Ethan said as he pulled into the parking lot of the restaurant. "Even though it would seem like I'm more of the homebody, sometimes, I get on a tear and want to take a road trip while Lincoln only wants to hang out at home and be comfortable. But then, other times, we switch, and it works."

"It's kind of nice that you guys have so much history between you. And now you're taking it to the next level. I'm glad I'm here for it."

Ethan met Lincoln's eyes through the rearview mirror, and he knew that there was worry in his gaze, as well.

Did she think this was just temporary? That she was just a fling before they moved on? He sure as hell hoped not, so he was going to have to make sure that she understood that this was the three of them. Not just two. Three. And even if he had no idea what the fuck he was doing, he needed to figure out how to make sure she knew she was wanted.

He knew Lincoln was good at that. Because all throughout their friendship, he had always known that Lincoln wanted him as a friend.

He might not have been able to see that Lincoln wanted him as more before, but he had likely been blind to that because he was scared. He understood that now, and he wasn't afraid anymore.

No, he was terrified. But that was a whole different matter.

Lincoln got out of the car first to help Holland out of her seat, and Ethan made sure that the doors were locked behind them. The three of them had reservations at this little Italian place that he and Lincoln liked.

Ethan knew that the owners were gay and had friends of all sexual orientations. It was a safe place for their first date. At least, he hoped so. For all he knew, he would end up screwing this up, and it would be awkward as hell.

But they were going to try and make this work. After all, if his cousin could make it work down in Denver, they could try and make it work up here in Boulder. Boulder was weird, everybody was crunchy and did strange things. At least, that's what people said. Having a threesome and a permanent ménage shouldn't be weird.

But if anyone said anything, he was prepared to fight.

Not that he wanted to, but he would.

And he knew Lincoln would, too. Just as long as Lincoln didn't hurt his hands.

Ethan didn't want Lincoln to hurt himself. He didn't want *anyone* to get hurt. Hopefully, everything would be fine, and he was just overreacting.

"Montgomery, party of three," Ethan said as they made their way to the hostess stand.

The guy smiled at him and then looked at the three of them, gave them a nod, and then walked them to their table. "Right this way."

"You know, I've never been here," Holland said. "I've driven by a lot, but Dustin didn't eat carbs."

"Some people are gluten sensitive, and some people don't like to eat a lot of carbs with their diet." Ethan was trying not to hate the guy. Plus, he couldn't really fault the man for not wanting to eat too many carbs.

"No, he just refused. Didn't even like to eat some fruit. And it wasn't like he was dieting or anything. He just read somewhere once that carbs were the devil. Therefore, anyone who ate them must be evil. I should have seen it then. I used to hide my love of cupcakes. Not that I needed the sugar, because...hello, too much processed sugar isn't good for you. But it's okay to have a cupcake every once in a while. Or a whole plate of pasta if you want it."

"You can eat whatever you want. We promise we won't judge." He paused. "Okay. We might judge if you just eat like a side salad or something and then snack off our plates. Because that's just wrong. You want pasta, you get it yourself."

Lincoln snorted as they took their seats in a corner booth. They placed Holland between them, and it was nice. The way the U-shaped benches worked, meant that they were all somewhat together and yet out of the way.

Not that they were going to do anything in the restaurant, but a whole bunch of fantasies came to mind.

Not on the first date. And not in a restaurant that he wanted to come back to.

"Okay, now I'm starving," Ethan said, looking over the menu.

"You want to share a bottle of wine?" Lincoln asked, perusing the drink menu. "There's a good bottle of pinot noir that I love here."

"Oh, that's my favorite," Holland said, looking over the menu with Lincoln.

He liked the way they looked next to each other. And he couldn't help but want to either move closer or take a step back, so it was just the two of them. That was a good sign, right? An indication that they were doing this right?

There were so many potholes in the way, and he knew that if they weren't careful, he'd fuck it up. But he was going to try. That's all he could do.

"I don't mind sharing. I'll only have half a glass, though since I'm driving."

"Are you sure? I can drive."

Ethan shook his head at Lincoln's words. "No, you can drive next time."

"Or I can," Holland said, and Ethan smiled.

"You going to go on another date with us?"

"Maybe. Or maybe just with you. Or Lincoln. We're trying to figure this out, right?"

"Right," Lincoln said, staring at her with such intensity that even Ethan swallowed hard.

They ordered their drinks, and then their food, starting with an antipasto and then each of them getting pasta and a salad. When it came to dessert, they gorged themselves on tiramisu, but it was worth it. Ethan was stuffed, happy, and had had probably the best date of his entire life. He just never thought he would have it with two people.

Yes, sometimes, it was a little awkward, trying to figure out exactly what needed to be said, or making sure everybody's needs were being met. They would work it out, though. It was no different than a date between two people. Figuring out what the other person needed or wanted or was thinking was a whole territory unto itself. Adding another person just complicated things. But they could and would form a plan.

Ethan worked with math and complicated equations that contained way more than three. He could definitely find a solution.

Or, Lincoln could, and Ethan would follow along. That was probably the better bet.

"Where to next?" Lincoln asked casually from the back seat.

They'd only shared a single bottle of wine, which meant that it was less than two glasses each, and so Ethan knew it wasn't a buzz making Lincoln's cheeks red. No, it was probably the high of just being together. The three of them. And that made Ethan hard.

Damn it. He didn't know if they were ready for this next step, even though they had pretty much already taken it.

"Well..." Holland said, her voice trailing off.

"Well?" Ethan asked, tapping his finger on the steering wheel. He hadn't started the car, was afraid to do so. Would that pop this perfect bubble of theirs and ruin the moment? Or was he, once again, thinking too hard?

"I'm still having a fun time. Why don't we go back to my place for coffee?"

Ethan looked at Holland, and he knew there wouldn't be any coffee. Not the way she was staring at him and Lincoln. Not with the way her eyes had darkened, and her lips had parted.

"You're going to have to be a little more specific. Because I don't want to think the wrong thing," Ethan said, swallowing hard.

"I think I want your mouth on me. And your hands. And if that's too forward, then I'm sorry."

Lincoln crawled up a bit between the seats, cupped her face, and kissed her hard right on the mouth, sending a shocked moan through her—and Ethan.

And then Lincoln turned and kissed Ethan right there, their tongues tangling, the taste of tiramisu and wine on his best friend's tongue.

"Hey there," Ethan said, clearing his throat. "Well, I think we know what your answer is," he said, laughing a bit.

"My answer is whatever you want it to be. But, yes, let's go to Holland's place. See what happens."

"You say 'see what happens,' but I have a feeling that we're going to get naked and sweaty. Just want to make sure that's what everyone wants."

Holland laughed and then leaned forward. "If this never happens again, I know I'll die happy."

Lincoln slid under Ethan just a bit as the other man pulled back and kissed Holland softly, a gentle caress of lips that was just as hot as the hard and powerful kiss Lincoln had given him earlier.

"Okay, your place, Holland," Ethan said, clearing his throat. "And then we'll see what happens."

She looked at both him and Lincoln and swallowed hard before reaching out and gripping Ethan's hand. Lincoln slid his hand over both of theirs, giving each a squeeze.

"I feel like I should say 'all for one and one for all' or something, but let's just see what happens," Holland said, and they all laughed before Ethan quickly started the car and did his best not to speed his way to Holland's house.

Because he knew, just *knew* that there'd be no coffee. No talking.

It'd just be them.

And he—and his dick—couldn't fucking wait.

CHAPTER ELEVEN

Holland could barely catch her breath, but maybe that was the whole point of this.

She stood in her bedroom, still wearing her clothes, standing between two of the most handsome, generous, and wonderful men she had ever met. She was afraid if she pinched herself, she would wake up, and this dream would be over. Then she'd have to figure out exactly what she was going to do with her life. But for the moment, she could revel in this fantasy of hers. She could pretend it wasn't real, that it was just the best her imagination could conjure. Because if she thought it was real, then it would likely fall apart.

As Ethan had voiced, they hadn't had coffee. She hadn't even started the pot. Instead, they had kissed just slightly, only a little to start, and then had walked to her bedroom.

Now, she stood between them, Ethan running his fingers gently down her arm while Lincoln did the same to her cheek. She sucked in a shuddering breath, afraid —so damn afraid—that all of this would end.

She really didn't want it to end.

"You're so beautiful," Ethan whispered, kissing her throat.

She leaned into Lincoln as Ethan stood behind her, keeping his hands on her arms as he massaged her. She couldn't catch her breath, couldn't even pretend that she wanted to. She didn't want to lose this, any of this. Didn't want to wake up and realize it was a dream, even though she wasn't sure she wanted it to be real either.

"Tell us when to stop, if you want us to stop," Ethan whispered, gently biting down on her ear.

Holland stood there, sandwiched between them, as Ethan kissed her neck and bit down on her ear again, while Lincoln slowly took off her clothes until she stood naked between them. Her nipples were hard pebbles pressed against Lincoln's chest, her core was tight and already slick between her legs.

If she weren't careful, she would come right there without them even touching her where she ached.

She was about to combust just by their voices alone.

And even though she knew that couldn't actually happen, this fantasy of hers told her there would be surprises. "I've never been with two men before, so while I want to say just keep going, I'm going to have to ask exactly what that entails."

"It can mean anything you want it to mean," Lincoln said, slowly cupping her breasts. He gently plucked her nipples, squeezing, caressing. She arched her back, wanting more.

He grinned at her, giving his attention to her chest even as he gazed into her eyes.

Ethan slowly slid his hands down her belly and over her mound, cupping her heat and making her gasp.

Then he used his other arm to slide around and run the back of his hand down Lincoln's jean-clad dick.

They both gasped, and she leaned back into Ethan's caress, rubbing her butt against his erection.

All three of them groaned, and she just smiled, loving the feelings bursting inside of her. Seriously, how could this honestly be real?

"What have you done before?" Lincoln asked. She tried to focus on exactly what he was asking, her brain cells slowly fading away with each caress, with each touch from the men.

"I've never been with two men. I've never done that." Lincoln raised a brow at her, and she swallowed hard. "Anal. I...I've never done that either. I don't know if I'll ever be ready for that."

The guys chuckled before giving her a kiss—first Lincoln, and then she tilted her head so Ethan could kiss her, as well.

"No pressure at all. We can do a lot of things without doing that."

"Are you sure?"

"I'm very sure. There are lots of places to touch, to lick. And I have this guy, too," Lincoln said, reaching around to cup the back of Ethan's neck before kissing him hard over her head. She shivered between them, her hands around Lincoln's back, digging her nails into his flesh.

"I get to watch," she whispered.

"Oh, I have a feeling you're going to be doing more than watching. I think you'll be underneath," Ethan said, winking.

"However, it's still my turn," Lincoln said, and Ethan snorted.

Her brows rose. "You guys, uh...take turns?"

"Apparently." Lincoln growled, but there was heat in his eyes.

"Just so I can picture it correctly," she said, closing her eyes and smiling for just a moment before raising her lids so she could look between them. "Lincoln, you've taken Ethan before. That means he gets to take you?"

"Yes, so it seems. That means I get to be inside you when he does, though," Lincoln said, kissing her hard. And then she was lost.

She could barely catch her breath, hardly focus with his mouth on hers, Ethan's hands on her body. He slowly slid his fingers between her folds so they danced along her clit and against her core.

She arched, wanting him to go deeper and not just play, and then Lincoln's mouth was on her breast, and she was shivering, needing, wanting.

Ethan continued working her, slowly teasing her entrance and then sliding a single finger inside her. She gasped, tightening around his finger as he growled against her neck.

And then he was kissing Lincoln above her again, both guys still paying attention to her even as they touched each other. And then they were both touching her, and she came on Ethan's fingers. She couldn't even gasp for breath because Lincoln's mouth was on hers. Then, they were suddenly taking her to the bed, both of them shedding their clothes so quickly, she was afraid they were going to trip in their haste.

"Dear God," she whispered. "I swore I knew how good you guys both looked."

Ethan grinned. "We we were all a little too drunk to really get to know one another before," Lincoln said, slowly sliding his hand down his belly to grip the base of his dick.

Her eyes went straight to that movement, and then she turned to look at Ethan, swallowing hard.

"Is that a Kraken tattoo on your stomach?" she asked, smiling.

Ethan blushed all the way down his chest and arms, and it was seriously the cutest and hottest thing she had ever seen.

"I got drunk and, somehow, the tattoo artist still did it, even though they probably shouldn't have. I bled all over the place since my blood was so thin thanks to the booze in my system, but now I can say 'release the Kraken' when I look at my dick."

Naked and somewhat curled into a ball at the end of the bed, she put her hand over her mouth and started laughing.

"That makes me so happy," Holland said, wiping a tear from her eye.

"My dick makes you happy?" Ethan asked, grinning.

"Well, that, too. But the story more so. And you weren't there to help him?" She looked over at Lincoln and licked her lips. Her skin felt flushed yet still pebbled as if her body didn't know what was happening but wanted to be involved no matter what.

"No, I was out of the country."

"You probably would have ended up with a matching tattoo because once we get drunk, things happen." Ethan grinned.

She blushed, looking between them. "Things do."

Then the men looked at her and took a step forward at the same time. She let out a little squeal, and then Lincoln was on her in the next second, covering her body and kissing down her neck, her chest, and all the way to between her thighs. She gripped the bedsheets, her knuckles turning white as she arched into him when he went down on her.

There was movement on the bed, and then Ethan was kneeling by her face, his dick in his hand.

She licked her lips and opened wide. Without another word, he slowly slid the tip of his cock into her mouth. She lapped, sucking hard, loving the way he groaned, the same way Lincoln did.

Everything was almost too much. So much sensation, so much touching. And she loved it. Wanted more.

Ethan slowly worked his dick in and out of her mouth, and she freed one hand so she could grab his thigh, keeping them both steady. Lincoln kept eating her out, licking and sucking and spreading her legs wide so he could dive deeper, using his hands and his tongue in a way that she never thought possible. And when she came again, she called out, shaking. Ethan pulled back, grunting.

"Don't want to go too early," he said and lay on his stomach so he could kiss her hard, playing with her nipples as he did.

She moaned, wanting more, but then the guys were adjusting her on the bed so her head was on the pillows, and Lincoln positioned himself above her, a condom over his dick, and he was between her thighs again.

"Ready, love?" he asked. Her heart clutched at the word, but she pushed that away. This was only for a little time. Just fun before everything ended, and the guys realized what they were to each other and how they *only* needed each other. Not her. But she could at least be part of this magic moment. Be a part of them just for a little bit.

And everything would be okay. Because everything was fine.

She nodded, holding out her hands so she could bring Lincoln closer. And then he was inside her—one deep thrust that stretched her to the max. Both of them groaned.

It had been far too long since she'd had anyone

inside her, and Lincoln was bigger than the average man. But then again, so was Ethan.

Lincoln groaned, sliding in and out of her, once, then twice, going slowly at first as he pushed her to the top of the hill. But she never crested it. It was as if they were making love, but she knew that wasn't the case. It couldn't be.

And then Lincoln groaned, going still inside her. She knew Ethan was working him. She angled to the side so she could watch, and Ethan gave her a wink, his eyes dark as he slowly slid inside Lincoln.

He groaned, and Lincoln arched for him, which pushed him deeper inside her. She spread her legs wide and wrapped one around Ethan, and one around Lincoln. Her foot could barely touch Ethan since she wasn't that tall, but she wanted to touch them both, somehow. Needed to be with them both. And then Ethan was hovering over Lincoln's back, and all three of them were connected as one. She couldn't breathe.

Every time Ethan moved, Lincoln would move the same. It felt as if she were with both of them, and she wanted that.

She arched, kissing Lincoln and then running her hands over Ethan so she could be with him, too.

And when she came again, Lincoln followed, groaning.

She clung onto him tightly, feeling him pulsate inside her. And then there was the sound of another condom being opened, and then Ethan was inside her in an instant.

She didn't even know how it had happened. It was as if they had orchestrated it. There were just tongues, touches, skin, and need. Lincoln's mouth was on hers and then it was on Ethan's. And Ethan was still inside her. He came, but she was too spent to do anything other than scream his name, even though it came out as a whisper. Somehow, they all crested the rise, panting, sweaty, and just needing to touch each other. She was still groaning as the two men moved her to her side, Ethan remained inside her as he shifted her. And then Lincoln was behind her, his now fully erect cock sliding between her cheeks, but only to rest. Despite his renewed arousal, she knew they were all spent, and she still wasn't sure she wanted that, but she realized that if she could, she would do this all again. And again. And again. And again.

As the night went on, they just kept touching, continued kissing. And then they moved her so they could look at each other, and then at her, and when they did it again and again, she didn't even know who was whom, except for the fact that she knew their individual touches, knew their tastes. She didn't have to ask for what she wanted because they just knew. They made sure she got everything she needed.

She couldn't focus, couldn't breathe. But that was fine. Because she had Lincoln and Ethan, if only for the moment.

In the morning, when she woke up, if they were still there, she would know it wasn't a dream. But she knew it also wasn't reality. Not really. And that was fine.

Because she had never felt like this before in her life, and she knew she never would again. But she reminded herself that she had this moment. And that's all that mattered. At least, right now.

T he next day she was sore, and still thinking about the night before. In fact, every time she did, she blushed from head to toe, and she knew that her coworkers probably thought she was insane.

But that was fine with her. They didn't ask, and she was never going to tell. Because she had this moment, and that was all that mattered.

She would remember what had happened between the three of them until the end of her days, even if it never happened again.

She had seen the way they looked at each other. Perhaps at one point, she thought *maybe* they'd looked at her too, but she didn't think so. It must have been just passing glances between them where she was caught in the crossfire. But what a way to burn.

Somehow, she had gone to work and had tried to be fully functional on about an hour of sleep, though she wasn't sure she'd even gotten that hour. The guys had left early in the morning because they had jobs, too. And that was fine by her because it let them avoid conversation. Sure, she knew about their lives and had gotten to know them as people. But they hadn't actually talked about what they were doing with each other. And, honestly, that was fine. Because she didn't have the answer. Wasn't sure she wanted to know right then what their answer would be.

They had left, and she had gone to work. She went through the motions and even made some really good sales for the day. In fact, the whole week had been great, and that meant that she would be able to put more into savings than usual for the month. Of course, she knocked on wood as soon as she said that because something was bound to break or flood or do...something. That's what happened with small businesses.

Thankfully, she wasn't closing today, and that meant maybe she could get a nap in after she finished some paperwork. Or, she could do nothing and just try and enjoy her afternoon off at home. Not that she was really good at that. But the guys had been helping, at least recently. She at least knew what it meant to take a day off and have a little fun with it.

Of course, as soon as she thought that, she remembered exactly what they had done to have fun, and then she blushed again.

Part of her wanted to call them or text, just to see what they were up to, to find out if they were thinking about her. But she firmly put that out of her mind because there was no way she was going to do that. She'd put herself out there enough already. If they wanted more, she'd be there. But she wasn't going to be the one who made the next move. She didn't want to get hurt, not again. And if that made her a coward, then so be it. Honestly, she was used to it.

Now that she was at home, she wanted to try and relax.

Only, she couldn't. Not really.

She kept thinking about her bedroom and how that's where she had seen the guys the last time, and then she thought about the fact that, at one point, after the first time, she had held the base of Lincoln's cock as he slowly slid into Ethan, and she had to moan at just the memory.

Dear God, she was going to hell—and she was going to love every moment of it.

Before she could let herself go too far down into the depths of the pit, the doorbell rang. She frowned.

Then her phone buzzed. She looked down at it. It was a text from Ethan.

Ethan: *I'm so sorry. She somehow got it out of me.*

Holland had no idea what that meant, but then the doorbell rang again. She went to the front door to look through the peephole, only to see three women standing out there, things in their hands, and smiles on their faces.

Odd.

Holland opened the door, careful to keep the chain on as she smiled.

"Hi, how can I help you?"

"Did Ethan text?" one woman asked, the smile on her face wider now.

Holland frowned, a little worried about why three women would be at her house asking about Ethan.

Holland looked down at the text on her phone and nodded. "He apologized. But I hadn't gotten to the part about why before I answered the door."

"Well, yes, sorry. I'm kind of evil that way."

"And who are you?" Holland asked, a little worried now. Should she be calling 911?

The woman behind the one speaking mouthed the words *I'm sorry*, and Holland was actually really ready to call the police at that point.

"I'm Ethan's sister, Bristol."

Holland relaxed a little. Only somewhat, though.

"And this is my future sister-in-law, Arden. She's with Liam. And this over here is Lincoln's cousin, Madison."

Holland just blinked, remembering the dark circles under her eyes because she hadn't slept, and the fact that she had a coffee stain on her shirt. She swallowed hard.

This was the guys' family. At least, some of them. Here. At her house.

With no warning.

Oh, Ethan was *so* going to be in trouble later.

The woman named Arden once again said that she was sorry, and Madison blushed, wincing a bit. Bristol looked as if she had done nothing wrong. And maybe she hadn't. But this was all still really weird.

"We're here just to say hi. Ethan mentioned that you didn't have a lot of friends right now because your ex is an asshole, and so is your sister."

"Dear God, Bristol," Arden growled, closing her eyes. "You did almost this exact thing to me. I still don't know how we ended up friends."

"I'm not sure how I was dragged into this at all." Madison groaned.

"What exactly is *this*?" Holland asked.

"This is us saying hi. We wanted to get to know you." Bristol smiled as she said it, yet Holland was still almost ready to call the cops.

"You don't have to let us in," Bristol added quickly, and Holland was grateful. Regardless, she still had her phone at the ready.

"Okay."

Holland didn't move.

But Bristol continued.

"We were talking to the guys about you, mostly because we're Montgomerys, or at least I am. Arden will be, and since Lincoln is an honorary Montgomery, that means Madison is one of us, too. And, anyway, the Montgomerys are the kind of people who want to make sure everyone knows that they're always invited to things and needed and loved and part of the family, even if only in friendship."

"I didn't sign up for this," Madison said, her eyes filled with laughter—and a little horror. Holland liked her.

"You never sign up for these things, it just happens. And it's usually because of Bristol," Arden mumbled under her breath, and Holland held back a smile.

"I'm not that bad," Bristol mumbled.

"Yes, you are. But we love you anyway." Arden moved forward, a bag full of tequila and triple sec in one hand, and a bag of limes in her other. "Anyway, the guys mentioned you. When they said that you were dating, everybody got really excited."

Holland swallowed.

Dating? Oh, God.

"You know that the three of us, uh..." She couldn't even finish the sentence, and her face turned so hot, she knew she was blushing.

"Yes, we're excited. The guys are great, and if they chose you to be a part of what they have, that means you must be great, too," Madison said, and Holland just smiled at the other woman.

"Anyway, we're here because we wanted to get to know you before my mother finds you."

Holland froze.

"Your mother?"

"She loves her kids and wants to make sure that whoever's in their lives knows that they are loved. And she wants to know when babies are coming."

"Dear God," Holland said at the same time as Arden.

"But, don't worry. No pressure. She just jokes about things like that."

"Don't jest about things like that," Madison said.

"I know, I know. She only does that in front of family who realize that it's not real, and when she knows it won't actually hurt anyone. But this is a very long way of saying...hi, we are in Ethan's and Lincoln's lives, and we know that you've been through a rough spot, and we'd like to just get to know you. If you'd like us to leave, we will. But we want to welcome you to the madness that is the Montgomery family. At least being with a Montgomery, or being near one."

"One second," Holland said quickly, then looked down at her phone.

Holland: *Your sister, Arden, and Madison are here. With tequila.*

Ethan: *Dear God. They are good people, but I will murder Bristol for you if needed.*

Holland: *Don't spill blood because of me...but should I let them in?*

Ethan: *They are some of the best people I know, and if you want them in your life, they'll have your back. They're amazing women. I have to go, but you don't have to let them in if you don't want to. But if you want a chance at new friends, then do so.*

Holland: *I trust you, but you owe me.*

Ethan: *Always, babe.*

Holland just shook her head, slid her phone into

her pocket, and then said the only thing she could. After all, she was trying to live in the moment. "Margaritas?" she asked, and the other three women grinned widely.

"I knew we were going to like you."

She opened the door and let them in, quickly sending another text to Ethan, saying that they would talk about this later.

She hadn't realized that she was in the group text until Lincoln replied with:

Lincoln: *What the hell did you do, Montgomery?*

Ethan: *The girls found her. But it's fine, right?*

Holland looked at the women in her living room, all of them appearing a little nervous. But then again, so was she.

Holland: *It'll be fine. But you're going to have to make it up to me.*

She grinned as she typed it, and the girls laughed.

Holland looked up, blushing again. "What?"

"Talking to the guys?" Arden asked, setting down the bag on the coffee table.

"Sorry."

"Don't be sorry. You look happy," Arden said.

Holland just kept smiling. And she was happy. But she didn't know how long it would last.

"Anyway," Bristol said quickly in the silence of that

statement. "Finish your text, and we'll make some margaritas. I brought chips and guac, too."

Bristol shook the other bag, and Holland's stomach growled.

"I skipped lunch, so that sounds great. As long as you don't poison me."

Madison let out a nervous giggle, and Holland's eyes widened.

"No, no. No poison. It's just, I don't know how I always end up in these schemes with Bristol."

"You weren't there when she showed up at my house the first time," Arden put in.

"She really did this to you?"

"Wanted to make sure that I had a girl to talk to since, apparently, dating a Montgomery is a big thing." Arden rolled her eyes, and Holland couldn't help but smile.

"But dating a Montgomery *and* a McClard is even bigger."

"Well, the McClards might not be as vast as the Montgomerys, but we come with our own issues. And I know all Lincoln's childhood stories." Madison grinned.

"Oh?" Holland asked.

"And I have all the childhood stories of Ethan," Bristol added.

"I don't have any of those, but I can tell you how great they are now. Or I can just listen to you if you don't actually like them and you want out. If you do, we'll find a way." Arden smiled widely.

Holland just laughed as Bristol went kind of pale, shaking her head. "We're not going to do that." She paused. "Okay, if you need to, we will. Though you sound like things are going amazing, and you're with two of the most incredible people in my life. And since you apparently don't have any girlfriends anymore thanks to that evil sister of yours and your ex, we're here for you."

Tears filled Holland's eyes, and she shook her head quickly to keep them at bay.

"I didn't mean to make you cry!"

"You're not. Not really. I just...thank you. It's been a weird few months. I'd love to get to know you guys. Even if I feel like I have no idea what I'm doing."

"Well, I don't think you're supposed to know what you're doing with things like this. But that's fine. Now, let's have some margaritas, and you can tell us all about how you met Ethan and Lincoln."

"You don't know the story?"

"We know what the guys told us, but we want to know everything, and we want to hear it from you."

Arden just held out her hand. Holland looked at it before taking it. "Okay. Let's do this."

The girls smiled, and Holland knew that, yes, this was probably a mistake. But she'd been making them over and over again lately it seemed, so why not keep going? She did need someone to talk to, and even though these three were probably the worst women to talk to because of their connections to the guys, she didn't have anyone else to confide in, and she could just tell that she was going to like them. She was trying to trust her judgment more than she had in the past, so maybe it was time to listen to her gut. And perhaps she could be okay with that. At least a little.

CHAPTER TWELVE

Lincoln hovered over his sketchbook, flipping from page to page, working on one angle and then the next. Ideas were flowing, sliding through his body and out of his fingers as if his gift had a mind of its own. It wasn't what he needed to be working on. It wasn't part of the plan for this commission. But it was something. And considering that he hadn't sketched or painted anything in over two weeks, he was going to take this as it came.

He closed his eyes and rolled his head over his shoulders before getting back to it. His back ached, and his hand was starting to cramp, but he didn't want to stop.

He just kept sketching over and over again.

The strong line of Ethan's jaw. The long line of

Holland's neck. Her curves. The way she looked when she hovered over Ethan, the dark look in her eyes. The way Ethan parted his lips when he came. The way Holland gasped, her mouth parted just like Ethan's as he sucked on her nipples.

Lincoln grew hard and groaned as he kept drawing, knowing nobody but he would ever see these.

They would never sell, he didn't want them to, and he would burn them if he had to. But he couldn't get the images out of his head. Mostly because he couldn't get Ethan and Holland out of his head. And he was going to see them again tonight.

It had been four days since he'd been with them. Almost a week since he had touched them. But they all had things to do, and he had work to complete. Not that he was actually doing any of it. But he was drawing again. And if he worked through this block, maybe he would be able to get what he needed to done.

He hated the fact that he wasn't actually working. He wasn't a nine-to-five-jobber.

He'd work on what he had been commissioned for later. But first, he needed to get this out. Lincoln worked when he could, sometimes twenty-four hours straight, even though he didn't do that as much nowadays as he had when he was younger. His body couldn't handle it anymore. But sometimes that was all his brain wanted. That's what he did.

Right now, though, he just kept drawing. And then he blindly searched for a colored pencil, something that wasn't just black or gray. He looked down and picked the perfect shade for the red of Holland's hair.

A smile curved his lips, and he added some of that color to one of the sketches. The one where she was bent over Ethan, and he smiled up at her.

Lincoln was aware that he wasn't part of any of these images. Rather he was the voyeur, the one watching, standing off to the side so Holland and Ethan could be together.

He didn't know if that's what would actually happen in real life, but he could see it. Because for all that Lincoln wanted to imagine that this could be permanent between the three of them, that this could work, he knew that they were just a stack of cards. A house that could fall with a brush of wind, or a bad decision.

And he was really good at making those.

He didn't know what would happen between them, but he didn't want to think about that right now. Because if what they had right now shattered, he'd lose Ethan, lose his connection to the Montgomerys. He'd lose Holland. He'd lose that spark that they'd found together. All of them.

And he didn't want to do that.

Lincoln added more red to her hair with a little bit of brown, and then layered a deeper shade of red. She had so many facets to her, so many different colors in her hair, and nuances to the expressions on her face. He could never tell exactly what she was thinking, and he liked that. He loved the fact that he had to dig deeper to try and figure it out. Ethan was the same way, even though Lincoln knew him inside and out. He hadn't been able to see all of Ethan, and he adored that he was learning something new about his best friend. And he liked that he sometimes worked as a team with Ethan to figure out what Holland wanted.

Lincoln couldn't wait to discover more.

He just needed to protect himself. Because he didn't know what he would do if he lost them. Even after such a short time together, he didn't know what he'd do.

Ethan had been in his heart for what seemed like forever. He knew he'd break if he lost him. But now with Holland? It'd be too much. And he knew that.

He let out a breath and set his sketchbook down, rubbing his temples. He needed to paint, needed to do something. It felt good to create, felt like it had been far too long since he had done anything like this.

And then he looked down at his phone and cursed.

It beeped again. He had missed it the first time, but now he saw the text.

Damien: *Art show is tonight. I got you that extra ticket, better bring someone good. I'm sure you still want to bring your little friend, though.*

Lincoln growled and wanted to throw his phone against the wall, but that would just be a waste.

He really needed a new agent, or at the very least, he needed to have another come-to-Jesus moment with the man. Because he really hated Damien's attitude. But he had been there when Lincoln had nothing. When all he had was an idea of talent and not even the full scope of it.

Lincoln had been the typical starving artist who had worked two full-time jobs while painting just to get some of his art out there. And then, as Damien liked to put it, he had been *discovered.*

Lincoln hated to think about it like that because that put way too much power in Damien's hands, even if it was all metaphorical. But Lincoln had to remember where he had come from, too, and the fact that Damien had been there since day one. But then again, so had Ethan, and Ethan never hung it over Lincoln's head like his agent did.

Lincoln: *I'll be there. Same with Ethan and Holland.*

Fuck. He hadn't meant to mention her, had just asked for an extra ticket for a guest, not even putting her name down because he hadn't wanted to deal with Damien's questions.

Damien: *Who's Holland?*

Lincoln: *A friend.*

As was made evident by the fact that the girls had stopped by Holland's place a few days prior, and Ethan's family and most of Lincoln's knew that Holland existed, they weren't hiding their relationship.

However, he still didn't want to get into it with Damien. Telling the man about it almost made it feel cheap. And Lincoln didn't know why. Maybe because Damien made him feel cheap. And…now was not the time to get into that.

Lincoln looked back down at his screen.

Damien: *What kind of friend? Are you finally getting over your little friend?*

That was it.

Lincoln: *Call him that again, and we're going to have words. More words. Thanks for the tickets. However, this is the last show I'm doing for you. Now, I have work to do.*

Damien: *So you're actually working? Going to have it done on time? I should alert the media.*

What an asshole.

Lincoln didn't answer. Instead, he just closed his

eyes and set his phone down. He needed to get ready to meet with Holland and Ethan, and he didn't want to be late. However, he was not feeling very happy at the moment. He had a headache now, thanks to his agent, and that was just one more nail in the coffin of that relationship.

He did his best to get Damien out of his head, and then really looked at the time.

"Fuck."

He'd promised Holland that he'd pick her up. Ethan was going to meet them at the show.

He'd have preferred to have Ethan with him the whole time, but the other man was working late on a project. Lincoln didn't know much else. Ethan couldn't really talk about some of the software because it was need-to-know and private, so he was sort of wishy-washy with some of the details.

That was fine with Lincoln, as long as Ethan made it tonight. He really didn't want Ethan to back out again.

Lincoln pinched the bridge of his nose, telling himself that it would be fine. Ethan hadn't backed out of a date with either of them yet. He'd been late, but he'd shown up. Just because his best friend was really good about backing out of other things didn't mean it would happen now with them.

Ethan was doing his best, and had been doing well for...what? A week? That had to count for something. Even if it might be a record.

And now Lincoln was acting like an ass because of his agent, and more than likely his art.

He needed to get over his internal struggles when it came to whatever was blocking him and just try to live in the moment.

Easier said than done, apparently.

He quickly showered, tried to fix his hair in some sense of fashion even though he probably should just shear it off. However, he couldn't help but remember the way Holland had looked at his hair. The way she'd run her fingers through it. Therefore, he decided to keep it long. Maybe he'd get a trim, at least. Or perhaps figure out how to style it.

It wasn't that bad. After all, this wasn't the first or the last time that he'd be at an art show that wasn't his or even one where he had to look good. He would forever be that guy who had paint in his hair and under his fingernails and looked as if he had just gotten out of bed.

That was the guy he knew and liked. The one he knew Ethan liked.

He smiled at the thought, remembering the first time he had taken Ethan to a show. The other man had been so lost. But he had tried. He didn't mock, didn't pretend like he knew what he was doing, but he did seem genuinely interested.

It just wasn't his thing. Sort of like some of the things that Ethan liked weren't Lincoln's things. But that was fine. They were allowed to have different hobbies and interests because so many other parts of their lives intersected.

That's what made them who they were. That was evolving with the addition of Holland and figuring out what all three of them liked.

Doing this thing that was part of Lincoln's world with the two of them? It was big.

His mouth dried up at the thought, his heart rate increasing. He swallowed hard, trying to create some saliva.

Probably shouldn't think about how momentous this occasion could be. Not when he had to try and think of things in the now, rather than things in the future.

Because he wasn't sure there would be a future for them.

With that thought, he quickly got his stuff and made sure his suit looked okay. He'd gone with the navy blue one with no tie since he didn't really have to show off too much. But he liked sporting a suit, and he really liked the way Ethan's eyes sometimes trained on him while wearing one. Now that he could look back on all of their interactions, he realized that maybe he'd been missing some cues. He'd always brushed it off as just Ethan liking guys and appreciating the male form, but maybe there was something more. Yes...he'd been blind.

Then he remembered that Holland had seen him in suit pants before, too, and her eyes had gotten just as dark.

He was glad that he was wearing the ones that made his ass look great tonight. Add in the fact that it looked just like that suit Chris Evans wore when he ushered Betty White up on stage that one time? He'd had totally bought it because of that. Not that Lincoln had a crush on Chris Evans. Okay, he had a massive crush on Chris Evans. Who didn't? America's ass and all that.

With thoughts of Captain on his drive, he was just pulling into Holland's driveway when he got a text.

Ethan: *The boss called us in for another meeting. I'm so fucking sorry. I want to be there. I don't want to be here. But I can't go. We're apparently near some breakthrough and everything's just getting fucked up. I'm so sorry.*

Lincoln looked down at his phone and shook his head, irrational rage filling his veins. Somehow, he had known this would happen. Work was important, and he got it. But he hated that Ethan wasn't going to be there for him. For Holland. Hated that, once again, Ethan was letting him down.

Lincoln: *No problem. I get it.*

Ethan: *It is a problem. Can you tell Holland? I got to go.*

Lincoln just snorted, shaking his head.

Lincoln: *Fine.*

And then he put his phone on silent and stuffed it into his pocket. It vibrated again, but he didn't care.

Ethan didn't tell Holland. He didn't even go to their group chat. He wanted Lincoln to handle it.

And he got it. Because Lincoln would be able to explain to Holland that Ethan's job sucked sometimes, lay out that Ethan was a workaholic. She might already know, but he'd be able to smooth things over. And Lincoln would make sure that everything was fine. He and Holland could have a nice date, just the two of them.

Lincoln didn't want Holland to feel the ache he was currently feeling. But it didn't matter. Because he had known that something like this would happen. And beyond tonight, he had a feeling they were going to fuck things up.

Well, maybe not Holland. Though she might run

away first. After all, he knew she was doing her best to try and keep some distance between them. He saw it in her eyes and in the way she never set plans. And she always looked surprised to be asked when either Ethan or he did. And tonight? What happened tonight certainly wasn't going to help things.

No, fuck that. He would fix this. They both had to figure out Ethan at some point, but for now, Lincoln would make sure his date with Holland was good. Just the two of them. Because they were one pair in the three. He'd work on that, and he'd make sure that what they had was solid so she didn't run. And then they'd work on Ethan together. Because he sure as hell didn't know how to do it by himself.

Instead of focusing on what hurt, on what he couldn't fix at the moment, he got out of the car and pushed those thoughts away as he made his way to Holland's door. He only knocked once before she was there. His tongue stuck to the roof of his mouth at the first sight of her, his breath gone.

She wore a black wrap dress that did amazing things for her waist and her breasts, so much that he was having a hard time focusing.

She had on bright red fuck-me heels that matched pieces of her hair, that same color he had used earlier with his colored pencils. Lincoln knew right then and there he needed to draw her. Even if it was just for himself. He wanted to paint her.

His hands itched for a paintbrush, but then that feeling was gone, and there was just nothingness. Because reality intruded. He wasn't supposed to be here alone. He was supposed to be here with Ethan. But work came first with his best friend.

And he knew that was a cop-out, knew that wasn't always the case. But sometimes it was hard to actually think about what Ethan *could* do versus what he *had been* doing.

"You look amazing," Lincoln said to Holland, clearing his throat. "Actually, *amazing* isn't a good enough word. Spectacular. Stunning. Beautiful. So fucking good, that I really don't want to go to this art show at all. I just want to fuck you against this wall."

He said the words so quickly that her eyes widened, and then she threw her head back and laughed. She had such an interesting, tinkling laugh. It started off high and then went deep and throaty. It made him even harder for her.

"I didn't know what color suit you were wearing, and sometimes, it's really hard to find outfits that don't clash with this." She tugged at her hair, and he just took a step forward, slid his hand around the back of her neck, and brought her in for a kiss.

She moaned, and he grinned.

"You with that hair? Pretty fucking amazing. You in this dress? Just tops it off. Don't do anything with this hair. Okay? I have dreams about this hair."

She just shook her head and slid her hands down his suit. "You look pretty damn fine yourself. I like this color blue on you. Makes your eyes pop."

"Now, you're going to make me blush." He kissed her cheek, careful not to touch her lips just in case her makeup wore off.

"I'm wearing a long-lasting matte," she said, fluttering her eyelashes. "You're welcome to kiss me hard, it's not going to come off." She paused. "At least, I hope not."

He raised a brow and grinned. "Now that sounds like a challenge."

He moved forward to kiss her, but she put her fingers on his lips, so he kissed those instead. "We're about to go out into public. Maybe not go for conquering that challenge right away."

"Okay, sounds like a plan."

She looked around him and frowned, that little line between her brows deepening. He had been dreading this part.

"He had to stay at work," Lincoln said, his voice gruff.

Holland shrugged and grabbed her bag. "He said that might happen. Are you okay?"

"Just a little pissed off. I was going to try and make it sound as if I wasn't, and that everything was fine, but I hate it when he does this."

"He does it often?" she asked as he helped her with her wrap, and they walked to his car.

"Often enough. But then I get stuck in my head with work, too. Though he cancels more than I do."

"Well, you're here, so let's make the most of it. We'll just have to tell Ethan what he missed."

Lincoln leaned down and kissed her softly so he wouldn't smear her makeup, even though he had taken that challenge earlier. He helped her inside the car and tried to smile, attempted to let the bad stuff go. "You and me. It's a date." He kissed her, then closed the door and went around to his side of the car, sliding into the driver's seat.

They were going to make this work. Even if it was just the two of them for the night. But he'd be damned if it would only be the two of them forever. Because Ethan was part of this. It was the three of them. And while now felt right, like this was important, he knew they both understood that they were missing someone tonight.

Neither of them was going to be a replacement for

Ethan. They were going to be who they needed to be for each other, knowing that Ethan was another cog in what they had.

By the time that they made it to the art show, it was well underway, and Lincoln was grateful.

"I hate being early to these things," he said as he helped Holland through the door and got her a glass of champagne.

"So you like being fashionably late?" she asked, and he just shrugged.

"No, I just don't like to be early because then people ask me for things or pretend like I'm their best friend because they want my art or for me to do something for them."

He hadn't actually meant to be that honest, but no one was really around to overhear, so it was fine.

"I'm sorry. Well, I'm not going to ask you to paint me something for my shop."

"But I would, though."

She looked at him, her eyes wide. "I sell amazing and unique art in my store. But it's nowhere near your caliber."

"And because you said that, I'm going to paint something for you."

If he could ever paint again. It wasn't as if he was actually having luck with that recently, after all.

"Lincoln."

"What?"

"I can't charge what your stuff's worth."

"Then we won't charge that much." He winked, and she just frowned.

"Don't do that. Don't make it weird."

"It's not weird."

"Well, it makes me feel like I'm using myself to get cheaper art."

He cursed under his breath as someone came by, nodding at him and waving. He didn't know who they were, but they clearly knew who he was. In fact, most of the people walking by nodded, whispering to each other or themselves.

He was an artist.

Lincoln McClard: up-and-coming artist. They couldn't wait to get his paintings. Couldn't wait to get a piece of him. And he didn't have a chance to say anything about that with Holland because person after person came up to talk to him. They recognized him, knew his art, and wanted to talk about the artist.

"Who's this?" Damien asked as he slithered up to them, his eyes narrowed and focused on Holland.

Lincoln froze before tightening his grip on Holland's hip. "Damien. I didn't know you would be here. You never actually said before."

"I'm your agent. I'm always by your side." He leaned forward and held out a hand. "And, you?"

Holland looked up at Lincoln, and he cleared his throat. "This is Holland." No need for more explanation than that since Damien was acting strangely tonight—weirder than usual. Holland seemed to understand that and didn't say anything more. Instead, she just took his hand and smiled.

"Ah." Damien looked between them, his eyes now slits. "Good to see you. Ethan bail again?"

Lincoln ignored the barb. "He was busy, but no worries. Excuse me, Holland and I have to head over and meet some people."

Damien just smiled and nodded as Lincoln pulled Holland to the side.

"Sorry about that," he whispered.

"No problem. Thanks for getting me away from him, though."

He leaned down and kissed the top of her head, hoping to salvage some of their night, but he wasn't sure they could do it here. By the time they left, Lincoln was exhausted and grateful that he hadn't worn a tie because he likely would have torn it off by then.

Holland slid her hand into his and gave it a squeeze as he shifted gears.

"You had a terrible time tonight," she said as they pulled up to her house.

"What do you mean? You were there."

"I was. And you smiled, and you were great to me. You introduced me to so many people that I will never be able to remember their names. And we saw some awesome art. Exquisite pieces that I never would have been able to see without you."

"I love the painter. She really figures out exactly what emotion she wants to convey and doesn't care if you don't see or feel the same one she does."

"You're the same."

"I try. Sometimes, I want you to see what I do."

"And that's fine. You're the artist. It's what you do. However, everybody was vying your time tonight, including your agent. But I get it. I'm just glad I can be part of this while I can."

Lincoln ground his teeth as he helped Holland out of the car. "I didn't know Damien would be there for sure. And I definitely didn't know he would act like that."

"Thankfully, we were too busy to deal with him. He's kind of an asshole. And he kept looking at my boobs."

"If I tell you that your boobs are pretty nice and that I can understand, will you hit me?"

She shoved at his chest, and he grinned, taking her hand in his.

"I shouldn't have said what I did."

He frowned at her words.

"What do you mean?

"About the whole selling myself for art thing. You were trying to do a nice thing, and I got weird about it."

"I didn't want you to feel weird about it, and I didn't know how to fix it. But everyone was there, and I didn't really know what to say with others around."

"I understand. And don't worry about it. Really. It was just something on my mind. But I'm figuring it out."

"Holland?"

"Ever since Dustin—which doesn't seem like long ago in retrospect—it's been hard for me to take things at face value. Even when we were still dating. Because no one really understood what I wanted. And I didn't realize that until it was too late. I'm not very good at accepting things, or more so, not comfortable with people being nice anymore. I'm working on it, but it's not easy."

"I get that. But you can feel whatever you need to feel. I'm not going to judge you for that."

"I know you won't. And it makes me feel amazing. If you want to paint something small—notice I said the word *small*, not extravagant—for my shop, I would lovingly take it. But only when and if you want to, and only so long as it doesn't actually interfere with the rest of your work. And if Damien doesn't get a cut."

She raised her chin at that and grinned.

"I knew I liked you."

He stopped and kissed her as they stood in her foyer, but he didn't stop after the first kiss. Or even the second.

Instead, he let her drop her bag to the floor, her wrap right along with it, and gripped her hair in one hand, tugging. She moaned, and he lapped at her mouth, her tongue, biting gently at her lips.

"I guess that lipstick is pretty long-lasting.

"I don't think it was meant for this," she panted into his mouth. He kissed her again. And again.

"What do you say I take you against the door like I talked about?" he asked, his voice a growl.

"I'd say I'm really glad this dress comes off so easily."

He licked his lips as he took a step back and then tugged at the bow on her side.

The dress fell off as she rolled her shoulders back, leaving her in her hot, red stilettos and matching red lace panties and a bra that barely covered anything.

Lincoln groaned and gripped his cock through his

pants, willing himself not to come right then in his slacks.

"Jesus Christ."

"I wasn't sure if red was the color to go with my hair, so I wanted you to see. You're the artist. What do you think?" she asked, cupping her breasts.

"I think you're going to be the death of me. And I can't fucking wait to see exactly what you look like all blushed and red under that color."

And then she did blush for him, that pretty pink color slamming over her skin in a wave.

And when she moaned at just a gentle touch, a soft caress, he could almost feel her ache. It was the same one he had.

She tugged at his suit jacket, and he let it fall to the floor along with his shirt, and then his shoes and pants.

Soon, he was standing naked while she stood in her bra and panties and heels, and he wanted to fuck her right there. But, first, he needed to taste. To touch.

"You in these heels makes you just tall enough that I can do this," he growled and then dropped to his knees.

Her side was next to her front table, and she let out a gasp as she gripped the edge of it. He knelt, huffing out warm breaths between her thighs, over her panties.

"So pretty and pink and flushed under all this red."

"Lincoln," she gasped.

He lowered his head, kissing and shoving the lace to the side. And when he twisted his lips, sucking hard, she moaned, her legs shaking.

"Jesus Christ," he growled, and then he was up on his feet, gripping her ass in his hands.

She wrapped her legs around his waist, and he kissed her, rocking himself against her core, her panties still shoved out of the way.

"I could do this all night, but I know I won't last."

"There's a condom in my purse," she growled.

"I like a woman who's prepared. And, thankfully, I have a condom in my wallet, too."

"We're okay doing this without Ethan?" she asked, her words serious. He agreed.

"Like you and Ethan can. Like Ethan and I can. We just need to keep talking. The three of us. Is that okay?"

"I like you, Lincoln. And I like Ethan, only in different ways. I like when it's the three of us, or just two of us. But I want you inside me right now. And then I want to talk to Ethan later so he can see what he missed." She winked, and he groaned, quickly going for her bag since it was closer than his pants. He sheathed himself and then quickly undid the clasp of her bra.

"I need your breasts in my mouth."

"Deal."

He licked and sucked, loving the way she arched into him.

And when he twisted her around so her breasts were against the front door, he grinned.

"Hold on tight, baby, I've got you."

"I know, Lincoln. I know."

The seriousness of that tone hit him like a shot, and he swallowed hard, then gripped the base of himself, and her hip before sliding in.

Since she was wearing heels, they were able to utilize this position. And she was so tight at this angle, he could get even deeper than before. She pressed against the door, pushing back on his cock, and he rode her.

He had one hand on her hip, the other on her breasts, moving back and forth so he could hold her, touch her.

When she came again, he followed, calling out her name as he did and biting down gently on her shoulder. She threw back her head, reaching around to hold him even as her body shook.

And then they ended up on the floor, laughing as they held each other, the strength in both of their legs having gone out.

Lincoln loved having sex with Holland. Loved touching her. Loved being with her. Loved the way she smiled as if she didn't have a care in the world even though, sometimes, he knew she felt as if the world were on her shoulders.

He wanted more of this. Even if he didn't feel like he deserved it.

Even if he knew that she would likely run.

Even though Ethan wasn't there because he had chosen work over them.

Lincoln held Holland and pushed those thoughts out of his mind. This was okay.

This was what he wanted. What they both needed.

And then they made love again on her floor, gently, face-to-face, with eyes just for each other.

This is what he had been missing.

And he was afraid he would break when she left.

So he told himself right then and there that he wasn't going to let her leave.

He had to show her what she'd be missing if she did.

But first, they needed to make sure that Ethan would be here, too.

Because this wouldn't work without the three of them. Lincoln knew it. He and Holland were only two-thirds of a whole. And, eventually, they'd have to figure out how to fit everything together. In every way that mattered.

CHAPTER THIRTEEN

"Ethan, have you worked on this one yet?" Maximilian asked as he walked into Ethan's office.

Ethan rubbed his temples and looked down at the tablets that Maximilian handed over.

And, yes, his boss's name was Maximilian. Not Max, not Ian, but always Maximilian.

He liked his full name, and even though it was a mouthful, Ethan went with it.

However, he didn't want to be here. He wanted to be at home or, preferably, on his fucking date with Holland and Lincoln.

It had been over a month of dating, over a month of them figuring out who each of them was and how they could make things work.

And this was the third date he'd missed in that month.

He knew that Lincoln and Holland had been together on their own, and that was fine with him. He wanted that. He liked that it wasn't just the three of them, that they mixed it up and figured out who they were as couples within this triad of theirs.

But he hadn't been with Holland alone. And not only sex-wise. He literally hadn't been in a room alone with her in so long, it was getting ridiculous.

Let alone with his best friend, who he rarely saw these days because Lincoln was working too—except for when they had dates. Then, Lincoln actually showed up.

As for Ethan? No, he was stuck here.

He liked his damn job, and he was good at it. But, sometimes, it took a lot out of him.

And he apparently didn't know how to say no.

He would have to figure it out, though, because he was really fucking afraid that he was going to lose the two most important people in his life if he didn't.

He just didn't know how to walk away from this place.

As Julia walked into the room behind Maximilian and gave Ethan a look, he knew he wasn't the only one.

He thought Julia had someone at home, but he

didn't know for sure. Because they didn't really talk about their personal lives here. Who had time for that?

Even their lunch breaks were spent on the computer, trying to figure out how to get some program to work, writing code, or researching the actual science they were working on.

He wasn't just someone who coded, he also learned the science and the background parts. He constantly read and wrote papers.

It was be published or die here, and he felt like he was the only one sinking.

"I've got it written down for later," Ethan said as he finally looked over what Maximilian wanted.

"Well, it was supposed to be done three days ago."

Ethan shook his head. He didn't look at Julia because he knew that she was rolling her eyes, and he didn't want to smile right then.

"No, you *mentioned* it three days ago and said to put it on the list. There are about a hundred other things that we need to do beforehand. We only have so much computational space."

"You need to get it done. We have that paper that we need to finish, and it's not just you who has to answer to your bosses. I do, too."

Maximilian huffed, nodded at Julia, and then went off to his office, slamming the door behind him.

It was seven o'clock on a Friday evening, and they were still here.

Because one of their servers had blown, and they were trying to catch up.

It wasn't always like this, and Ethan kept telling himself that, reminding himself. But he was terrified that it was going to be like this for far too long.

"Why are we still here?" Julia asked, taking the chair next to Ethan. She had her tablet out, as well as a notebook and pen, taking notes that had nothing to do with what she was saying. He had no idea how she could do that, but she was brilliant.

"Because we need to get this done...yesterday?"

"I don't think that's a good enough reason. We've already put in more than forty hours for the week. We should go."

"And lose our jobs?" Ethan asked.

He met her gaze then, and she sighed. "I'm afraid we're going to lose something more important if we keep staying here like this."

"You want to talk about it?" Ethan asked. Julia just shook her head.

"No, but I have a feeling that my guy is going to start thinking I'm having an affair."

Ethan's brow shot up, and he rolled his chair a couple of inches away from her.

She noticed the action and snorted. "I meant with my job, not with you. But thanks for thinking so highly of yourself."

"Hey, I can't help it. I worry."

"Let's just go. We'll tell him what time it is because you know he hasn't noticed. And then we'll all go home. There's nothing we can do right now anyway. We're waiting for more space."

"We need another server."

"And he's not going to spend the money for it because he never has to deal with it."

"I know," Ethan grumbled and then went back to work for another hour.

The fact that Julia was by his side told him how much she was worried about her job, as well. It didn't matter that they both had two PhDs and worked their asses off every week. The economy was tough right now, and people wanted into their company. And that meant if they didn't work hard, didn't produce results once the quarterly reviews came in, they could easily lose their jobs. There was no tenure here, they had to work their asses off every single day.

But Ethan was afraid that he was going to work to the point where there would be nothing left but an empty shell.

He looked down at his phone and noticed there were no texts.

Other than the single message from Lincoln saying *okay* after Ethan had canceled another date, Holland and Lincoln hadn't said a word.

This was all on him.

He wished he could fix it all, but he didn't know how. He couldn't lose this job. There weren't a lot of places in Boulder where he could do what he did best. He'd have to change his field of study, and he would if he had to, but he was doing good work here.

But, at the same time, it was the *only* thing he was doing.

He pulled into his driveway and noticed that Lincoln's car was there.

"Great," he mumbled under his breath. No, this *could* be great. He could fix this. He could apologize. He could get this done.

But the fact that he had no idea what to say was kind of scary.

He lugged himself out of the car, his joints aching. He hadn't run in a month either, and he could feel his body slowing as if it needed better food, more exercise, and being outside of the four walls of his office. He was burning the candle at both ends, but he didn't know how to fix it.

Not until they finished this project, at least.

He made his way inside and saw Lincoln on the couch, drinking a bottle of sparkling water and looking at the TV that wasn't on.

There were only a couple of lights on in the house, and Ethan could tell that Lincoln was alone. Holland wasn't here.

"Hey," Ethan said, setting his stuff down on the table.

"Hey," Lincoln said back, his voice gruff.

"I'm sorry. Soon as we get this project done—"

"No, no," Lincoln interrupted, shaking his head. He stood up, went to the kitchen, and put the bottled water back into the fridge. That was Lincoln's bottle, one that he re-used all the time; it always had a place there.

It should have warmed Ethan's heart to see that, but he was so damn afraid that the bottle wouldn't be there anymore. That he would just take it and leave, never to return. And it would be all his fault.

Ethan didn't know what to do. His job sucked right then, but it didn't always. He just needed to figure out how to make things better.

"I'm sorry."

"No, you always do this." Lincoln turned on him and slid his hands through his hair.

That's when Ethan noticed that Lincoln was wearing a suit again, the shirt unbuttoned at the collar. He looked damn sexy. Ethan wanted to reach out, needed to touch Lincoln. He wanted to kiss him and slide his lips over Lincoln's just to make things better. Hold him and say that he *would* make things better.

He wanted to be held and to know that while this month sucked, it wouldn't always be like this.

But he didn't move from his spot. He was afraid to. Because what if Lincoln didn't want that? What if he walked away, what if he shunned Ethan's touch?

Before they'd kissed, before they'd become who they were now, Ethan wouldn't have thought twice about it. He would have gone to his best friend and hugged him tightly, complained about his job. And they would've been okay.

But things were different now.

He should have realized that. He'd known that things would be different as soon as they had sex, but he hadn't thought it would be like this. He hadn't been able to put two and two together to realize that if they fucked this up completely, there was no going back. If he didn't fix this, he was going to lose Lincoln forever. He was going to lose Holland, and he had just met her.

He didn't know what to say.

He just swallowed hard and stuffed his hands into

his pockets, without words. He knew that was probably the wrong thing to do.

It was confirmed when Lincoln just stared at him and shook his head.

"You always do this," Lincoln repeated. "I know your job is amazing and important, and I get it. I work long hours, too. And I lose myself in my art sometimes." There was something in Lincoln's eyes, but he didn't say anything. Ethan wanted to ask if painting was going well. Inquire if Lincoln was actually producing anything. But he couldn't. He felt like he didn't have the right.

When the hell had that happened?

He was such a fucking idiot, and he didn't think he could fix this.

There were no words to fix it. It had to be actions. But what could he do other than change his entire life? And maybe that was the answer. He just couldn't do it right then, especially on no sleep and with no caffeine in his system.

He needed to talk, but he didn't know what to say. And for a man who was usually better with words, he felt as if he were living in his mind right now, not able to even string two words together.

"Holland and I are good, but I don't even feel like you're a part of this anymore."

Ethan blinked. "I am. It's the three of us. It's always been. I've been here. I only missed a couple of dates."

"Three. You've missed three. And considering it's really hard to get the three of us together, that's a big deal. And you've yet to go out on a date with Holland by yourself. And you and I have yet to actually spend time by *ourselves*.

"And considering that we used to be together all the time as best friends, it's a little concerning. I don't feel like you're a part of this. Holland's not saying much, and that worries me, too. Because you know she's hiding as it is. You see it just like I do."

Ethan got it. She always looked ready to bolt, even with a smile on her face and that attitude she had, the one where she was willing to try anything. Still, he knew she was ready to run. Then again, he was partly ready for *any* of them to do that.

"It's like she's waiting for the other shoe to drop and for us to leave her like her ex did. Oh, she might have been the one to walk away that day, but he cheated. He left the relationship emotionally long before she did. But it's not her, Ethan. It's not me. You're the one pulling away. You are so damn brilliant, but you never stay *here*. You always get in your head and forget what's waiting for you. Don't fuck this up."

Ethan swallowed hard and just stared. He didn't know what to say.

"Because I can't lose you. But I will let you go. If we don't fix this, if *you* don't fix this, I'm going to lose you. And so will Holland. This wasn't supposed to be like this. You were supposed to be here. For me. For us. We were supposed to figure out how to help Holland together. But you're not here. It seems like you're never here. I don't know what to do anymore." And then Lincoln walked past him, his hands outstretched for a minute as if he wanted to touch Ethan but didn't. And that may have hurt worse than anything. Ethan watched his best friend, his lover, walk out the door, leaving Ethan standing in the kitchen with his mouth dry, wondering what the fuck he was going to do.

Instead of running after Lincoln, he just looked down at his hands and quickly pulled out his phone.

He shot an email to Maximilian, saying that he wasn't going to be there the next day. That he had enough hours for the week already, and he didn't need to come in on the weekend, too.

He needed to fix this, he just didn't know how. But maybe he could figure it out step by step. The first change: he wasn't going to work weekends anymore. He couldn't.

He grabbed his keys and went out to his car.

Lincoln needed space, Ethan got that. He knew his best friend well enough to figure that out.

But while Lincoln needed space, Ethan wasn't sure about Holland.

He had to fix this. It couldn't be like this. First, Ethan would go to Holland and he would talk to her.

He just hoped to hell he didn't fuck things up more than he already had.

CHAPTER FOURTEEN

Holland had already washed her face, had taken off her date outfit for the night, and had just slid into her pajama shorts and a tank top when the doorbell rang. She looked down at the clock to check the time. Her brows rose.

"Well, either it's a serial killer or one of my men."

She paused, a coy smile playing on her face. *My men.* She liked that.

Of course, she had to remind herself that this was temporary. It was just fun. Because if she let herself feel, yeah...that wouldn't be good for anybody.

She looked through the peephole, and her heart clutched a bit. She'd missed him. She was a little annoyed, but she'd missed him. She opened the door and leaned against the doorjamb.

"Hey there, stranger," she said, looking at Ethan as he stuffed his hands into his pockets.

"Hey." He wore a rumpled button-up shirt with the sleeves rolled up to his elbows. It showcased his forearms, and she had to swallow hard. She loved those arms of his.

Just like she loved his mind.

He was brilliant and consistently thought of little ways to make annoying routines easier.

He was good at what he did, but it made her sad that she didn't get to see him as often as she wanted to.

Though maybe that was a good thing. Perhaps it let her focus on what they were rather than what her damn, treacherous heart *wanted* them to be.

He had on gray slacks that she knew hugged his ass because she had seen them before. She loved those pants on him. If she remembered right, they were some European cut that Lincoln had given him. Ethan had said that he didn't even know there was a difference between these and the other pants he wore.

But she noticed. She took in the way they tapered at his waist, showcasing the fact that it was slightly narrow. And she saw how they hugged his ass and his thick thighs perfectly. They made him look sexier than he had any right to. Especially since she was supposed to be mad at him just then.

But how could she be mad when he was the one who was helping her keep her emotions in check?

She'd already had her heart broken once in her life, all for someone that she realized she never truly loved. Someone who hadn't understood her.

Honestly, she didn't want to think about what would happen if she fell for one of these guys. Or worse, both of them. Because she could see herself falling for them. Falling so hard, she wouldn't be able to find her way back out of that crevice.

Watching her sister cheat on her with her fiancé—on their wedding day, no less—had been heartbreaking enough. There wouldn't be enough wine in paper bags or enough park benches for her to get over what would happen if she fell for Ethan and Lincoln, and something happened.

She wasn't going to think about that. Instead, she'd let Ethan in.

Into her home, but not her heart. She couldn't let the latter happen.

Ever.

"Hi," she whispered. Ethan looked up, his eyes sullen.

"Can I come in?"

She nodded and took a step back. He brushed by her.

She felt a moment of disappointment that he didn't touch her on the way in, but then she closed the door, and he leaned forward and placed his mouth over hers.

She leaned into him and moaned, and then he pulled back, licking his lips.

"Hi."

"Hi," she said again.

"I'm sorry. I suck."

She raised a brow.

"Really, I do. I'm sorry for canceling again. I would say it's just this work project and that I need to figure out what to do to get through it so I can get back to normal, but I'm starting to see that maybe this *is* my normal, and I'm an asshole."

"Okay? You're going to need to back up a step. Where is this coming from?"

"I canceled on our date tonight."

"I know. Because of work. And I know it's not the first time you've done it to us. And from the way Lincoln was acting earlier, I can guess it's not the first time you've canceled plans with him either."

"It's not." He started to pace the room, sliding his hands through his hair.

She was not going to comment on the fact that him being all disgruntled and grumpy just made him look sexier.

No, that wouldn't be good for either of them.

"This job is taking so much out of me. I love it, but I don't like what it's doing to everything else."

"Okay, that makes sense. Sometimes, our jobs do that to us. I work really long hours because I own my place. And Lincoln does the same with his art." When he was working, but she wasn't going to mention that. Ethan had to know that Lincoln wasn't painting as much as he used to. They'd even talked about it in hushed tones, but they didn't want to make it a thing. Lincoln was stressed enough.

"I...just...I..." Ethan started to pace again, and she shook her head and then took a few steps forward. When she put her hands on his forearms, he paused and looked at her.

"What?"

"I'm screwing this up. I was the one who was so urgent with *this*, and I'm screwing it all up."

She swallowed hard. "Screwing what up?"

"Us."

Her pulse raced, but she tried to look as if she weren't feeling anything. That everything was fine, and she wasn't panicking. "I don't know what you're talking about. You can't screw us up when we're only starting to figure things out. We'll find a balance."

He shook his head and then stared right into her

eyes. It made her feel like he was trying to search deep into her soul, to burrow beneath the layers until she couldn't even breathe.

She didn't want that. Because if he did, he'd see. He'd see that she wanted this. That she wanted all of this with him and with Lincoln. With the three of them together. And she couldn't let him see that. Couldn't want that. Because she didn't want to end up lying broken on the floor, wanting something that she couldn't have.

Because she saw the way the two of them looked at each other. They were so perfect for one another. They had all that history and beauty between them.

She didn't want to get in the way of that. But she could admit that she wanted to be a part of it, if only for the moment. But all of that meant that he couldn't see her. She couldn't let him. Even if it broke her into a thousand pieces just thinking about it.

"You need to know. You need to not feel like you're not part of this. I'm the one who needs to do better."

She paused, wondering if he had seen into her thoughts, but that couldn't be.

She shook her head. "Okay, back up. What?"

"Lincoln said—"

She interrupted him. "You saw Lincoln tonight?"

"He was at my place when I got home. And he tore me a new one. Something I rightly deserved."

She sucked in a breath. "Okay. But I wasn't there for that. So I don't know what you're talking about. There might be three of us in this relationship, but you have to communicate with *both* of us. I can't actually read your mind." Since she'd turned the tables on him, they wouldn't talk about the fact that he thought she didn't want to be a part of this. Because she did...so much that it hurt. She couldn't. She needed to keep those boundaries, even though it was getting harder and harder to figure out what they were.

"I'm really bad at this." She moved forward so she was encircled in his arms, and he leaned his forehead against hers. When she inhaled his scent, her toes curled, but she also felt as if she were coming home.

Warning. Danger. All the wrong moves.

But she didn't move away. She sank into his hold. She knew this was just one more mistake in a long list of many. But she didn't care. Not then.

"I'm going to try to do better."

"I hope you do. You missed out on that really amazing art show, and then you missed out on dim sum. And, tonight, you missed out on sushi and ramen."

"I forgot tonight was sushi." He grumbled, and she smiled.

"Lincoln was telling me each of your favorites while we were eating them."

He grumbled again.

"I kind of liked learning about you through him. But, Ethan?"

"Yes?"

"I want to learn about you through you, as well. And maybe learn a little bit about Lincoln through you, too. I love the fact that you guys have so much history. I guess that means that Lincoln knows that maybe you've been working too much. Or putting work before him."

"I know. That means I'm putting work in front of you, too."

She ignored that clutch in her belly again. Because she wasn't allowed to think of them as a true relationship. If she did, she'd break.

"I know how you can make it up to me," she whispered. There, she'd use sex to make herself okay. Because that was all this was. Right?

She'd use her body, not her soul.

But only with them.

Because, honestly, she didn't think she'd ever be the same when this ended. When they found each other, and she was left to walk away. Because she would. For them.

But she was so afraid that she was going to fall in love with them. Or worse, that she'd *already fallen*.

Ethan lowered his head and brushed his lips along hers once, twice. Then his hands slid down her back and gripped her ass.

She ground against him, grinning.

"Stop making it so easy for me."

She looked up at him then and bit his chin. "Stop hurting yourself because you're making mistakes."

She ignored the fact that she'd just said that because she was not going to listen to her own advice in this case.

"I don't know what I did to deserve you. Or Lincoln. But I'm going to try to actually make it worth it."

"All you have to do is be yourself, Ethan." Holland reached up and trailed her fingers under the dark circles shadowing his eyes. "You look so tired. Like you're not getting enough sleep and putting so much pressure on yourself. It's not just Lincoln you're hurting."

"I know. It's you, too."

She shook her head. "No, I'm talking about you. You need some time for yourself."

"I'd rather just spend it with you."

"Well, you've come to the right place, then. I was

just about to put on a face mask and take a bath with some candles. What do you say? Want to join me?"

He raised a brow. "I don't know about the face mask. Probably not good to ingest if I'm going to kiss you all over."

She knew she was blushing from her head to her toes, and she didn't care.

"Okay, well, my house is pretty small, but the bathroom was remodeled."

"I like what I've seen of your place."

"I like it, too. But, it's not my dream home yet. However, as I was saying, the bathroom was completely remodeled. And that means I have a tub that can easily fit two."

His brows rose, and once again, her toes curled.

"Oh, really?"

"Oh, yes. Now, let me get you comfortable. You look like you deserve a little relaxation."

She pulled away from him slightly but held his hand in hers as she led him to the bathroom.

He looked around her house as they made their way, and then she remembered he hadn't really seen much of it. But there really wasn't much to show him. This was the place she was trying to make hers after moving out of the house she had bought with Dustin. There were pictures on the walls and furniture that was her, but pieces were missing. She didn't like the flow of the house yet. This place wasn't *hers* yet. Not entirely. Maybe one day it would be, but for now, the bathtub was what she wanted.

That was her oasis. Whoever had owned the house before her had put in a huge, sunken tub. It was obscenely large, and if they worked at it, it could probably fit the three of them. Maybe not entirely comfortably, and it would be way too small for sex with all three of them, but she could easily ride Ethan in this bathtub.

Not that she thought about it. Often, at least.

"Wow," Ethan said with a whistle. "I forgot how huge this thing is."

"Aww, are you talking about your dick?" she said, laughing when he turned around and slapped her on the ass.

"Hey," she said, grinning.

"What? I couldn't help it. And, yes, I'm also talking about my dick."

"Okay, strip down. I'm going to run you the perfect bath."

"Really? You're not going to strip me?"

She tapped her foot on the tile as she folded her hands over her chest. "Don't be rude. Get naked, and then maybe I'll touch your dick."

"You say the sweetest things." He winked, then slowly undid the buttons of his shirt, sliding it off his shoulders before undoing his belt buckle. She swallowed hard, watching his forearms and wrists work as he shucked off his pants and shoes. And then he stripped off his undershirt and his boxer briefs. That left him naked, standing in her bathroom, and she hadn't even turned on the water yet.

The damn man knew. He'd been watching her the entire time.

"I thought you were going to turn on the water," Ethan said, his tongue in his cheek.

She shook herself and then flipped him off before bending over to turn on the taps. She added a little bit of lavender bubbles and a touch of effervescent salts to help with his sore muscles—but not so much that it overflowed.

But as she was bent over, Ethan came up behind her and gripped her hips, slowly rubbing his very erect cock against her ass.

She moaned and leaned back, rubbing herself against him before standing up. That left her back completely pressed to his chest, and she grinned at him over her shoulder.

"Soak first, maybe sex later," she whispered.

"Are you going to get in with me?"

"Only if you're good."

"You know I'm never good."

"Ethan? You're one of the sweetest, nicest guys I know. Same with Lincoln. You're very good."

When he looked as if he were ready to pout, she grinned. "But I love it when you're bad." And then she kissed him hard right on the lips but pushed away when he tried for more.

"Get in that tub. I'll be in in a minute." And then she sauntered off, knowing his gaze was glued to her ass.

Oh, yes, she knew exactly what she was doing to him. But he was doing the same to her.

When she heard him get into the water, she looked into the mirror and met his gaze. Then she pulled off her top, her breasts falling free of their confinement. Then she bent over, loving the way Ethan whistled again as she pulled her shorts down.

And when she turned, she watched as he slowly slid his hand over his dick, pumping once, then again.

She moaned, gripping her breasts as he continued jacking himself off.

And as he soaked in the tub, she moved closer so she could turn off the tap.

"Jesus Christ," he groaned.

"Pretty much."

She quickly turned around again and went to the

cabinet as he grumbled behind her. She pulled out a condom and held it up.

"Sorry, I forgot this part."

He licked his lips, and she handed it over. When he was fully sheathed—thankfully out of the water somewhat because she hadn't filled the tub completely—he gripped her hands and helped her in. She straddled him and then slowly began to lower herself on top of him. He kept one hand on hers, the other on her hip as he helped to guide her over him.

She probably could have used a little more foreplay, but then again, she was wet just watching him. And she couldn't help it, she wanted him. But when he slowly slid his hand over her clit, she moaned and knew she was wet enough. And then she slid down even farther, the tip of his dick penetrating her with ease. And then she lowered herself completely. They both moaned, the water sloshing around them, and then she just rocked. Having him fully seated inside her as she tried to catch her breath made her feel whole. Like this could be *it*. Even if she was afraid to want that.

"You're so beautiful," he whispered, sliding his hand through her hair. He pulled her closer for a deep kiss, and she undulated again.

They moved together, her rocking as he slid in and out of her softly.

He was already so deep that she knew she could come easily. And when she squeezed her inner muscles, he groaned and kept kissing her. They worked as one, slowly, sensually, the sound of the water sloshing around them filling the space. When he pinched her nipples and bit down on her lip, she moaned and then came.

He followed her, slamming into her one last time with a hard thrust that sent water over the edge of the tub. She shivered, calling his name even as he kissed her, hard.

And then she leaned over him, holding him close as he slowly slid his wet, slick hands over her back, holding her as if she were the most precious thing in the world.

She was so afraid that he actually thought so.

She didn't want to let go. She didn't want to leave this at all. Ever. But she was so afraid she would have to once they found something better—like Dustin had.

She wanted this. Wanted it more than anything. And as Ethan held her, as he whispered sweet nothings in her ear that told her she was important, she knew she couldn't have this. Because this wasn't hers.

But for now, she could live the lie. She could pretend. She could hold on.

L incoln lay in bed, wondering when he should get up, or *if* he should get up at all. Maybe today would be the day that he sat lazily and tried to get his head in the game or work a little bit on his painting. But he was still so pissed off from the night before, he just wanted to stay in bed and try to think about what he was going to do.

Because he wasn't only angry at Ethan, he was angry at himself. He'd gone off on Ethan when he'd done nothing more than what he usually did. Ethan always made things up, Lincoln knew that. But Lincoln had flown off the handle because he was afraid of losing Holland. He knew the way she constantly took that tiny step back. As if she were waiting for them to run away with each other rather than staying with her. He didn't know how to fix that. That's why he needed Ethan. But Ethan wasn't helping matters. And, hell, maybe Lincoln wasn't doing well. Maybe this was his fault. Perhaps if he weren't so focused on what he wasn't doing with work, he'd be able to fix what was important between them.

Maybe he just needed to get out of bed and go find Ethan and apologize. And then he'd go find Holland and chain her to them or something.

Lincoln was working just as many hours as Ethan had been lately, but they were both working far too hard at this point. Because Lincoln hadn't missed the dark circles under Ethan's eyes. Hadn't missed the fact that his best friend and lover looked exhausted.

And Lincoln needed Ethan to make sure that Holland didn't run.

After all, he'd first met her while on the run, even if it hadn't been her fault that she'd fled. He'd likely always be worried. Until she said that she wanted to stay. Until this wasn't just a moment or a little bit of time and fun while they were together. He was going to worry.

Maybe that was on him and not her, but he couldn't help it. That's what he did, he worried.

His phone rang, and he frowned. It'd better not be Damien. Lincoln really didn't want to deal with the asshole right then.

He needed a new agent. Maybe even a new studio. Something to push him into drawing. He hadn't sketched again since that one time with Holland's and Ethan's faces. He kept wanting to, thought about Holland's curves and the way she smiled, the way Ethan looked at her, but every time he tried to put it down on paper, he just couldn't. Or Damien showed up, and Lincoln lost the inspiration.

He was done. So fucking done.

But he looked down and let out a sigh.

He slid his finger to accept the call, and Ethan's face popped up on the screen. But he wasn't alone.

"Hey, you two," Lincoln said, clearing his throat.

Ethan sat shirtless—probably naked—on Holland's bed, his back against the headrest while Holland lay over his chest, her red hair splayed over Ethan's skin.

It was hot as fuck, and Lincoln wanted to draw it.

He almost reached for a pencil but couldn't grab it without showing off the fact that he was sleeping naked.

He didn't think naked FaceTiming was something they did. Right?

"Just wanted to see what you were doing," Ethan said.

"Hey there," Holland said, and Lincoln grinned.

"Well, I was sleeping, but then I woke up and was just lying here."

"We didn't wake you?" Holland asked.

"No, babe. You didn't wake me."

She grinned at him, and his cock went hard. Jesus Christ, that smile could do things to him. Just like Ethan's. This felt right, the three of them. But he was so afraid that he was going to fuck it up somehow. They really needed to figure out what to do because he did not want to lose this.

"I came over here after talking with you last night," Ethan began.

Lincoln nodded. "I can see that."

"I wanted to apologize." He paused. "Apologize for a lot. And, one thing led to another."

Lincoln laughed. "I get that. How's our girl?"

"Your girl is lying right here, and she's doing just fine." Holland stretched, arching her back so the sheet slid down to her waist. Lincoln groaned.

Her beautiful, pink nipples were pert and hard on those voluptuous breasts of hers. He wanted to reach through the phone and take a lick, but he couldn't. However, Ethan groaned as well and reached around to cup one breast, rolling her nipple between his fingers.

"Jesus Christ. Is this how you're going to wake me up in the morning now?" Lincoln asked.

"I'm okay with that," Holland breathed.

"Well, before we get to the fun part," Ethan said with a wink, "I wanted to apologize again."

Lincoln shook his head, palming his dick in his hand under the sheet. They couldn't see, but given the way his biceps bunched just a bit, he knew they would notice that part, at least. "No need to apologize. You said you're going to try and fix it. *We're* going to fix it."

"That's why I'm not working today."

It was a Saturday, so Ethan shouldn't be working at all. But considering what his boss had been making him do recently, Lincoln counted this as a win. Ethan was trying. He had been trying. Lincoln would, too.

"Okay, we're all going to do better," Holland said, arching into Ethan as he played with her breast. "But it's really hard to concentrate with your hand there."

Ethan looked down at her and then into the screen.

The camera shook a bit, and Lincoln swallowed hard.

"What exactly are we doing?" he asked, and Ethan licked his lips. He wanted that tongue on his mouth, his dick, everywhere.

But they were at Holland's, and he was here. But he was still going to make the most of it.

"I have an idea, you naked under there?"

"Yes," Lincoln answered, a little wary. He wanted whatever they were willing to give him, but this was new for him.

"Well, since it's just the three of us. How about we have a little fun this morning?"

"I'm in if you are. But this is just us, right? You're not streaming it anywhere?" Holland asked.

"I promise you. Just us." Ethan kissed her hard, and

Lincoln increased the speed of his hand on his dick. "We can stop this right now," he growled.

"Anything you want, I'm yours," Holland said, and Lincoln met Ethan's gaze. Ethan gave a tight nod, and Lincoln knew he was thinking the same thing that he was. They weren't going to lose her. They would fight for her. But for now, they could have a little fun.

Ethan moved the camera around, and all Lincoln saw was a bit of flesh. Then he heard a giggle, and the sheets rustling and all he could do was shake his head. But then Ethan put the phone somewhere close—on the nightstand, most likely, leaning against the lamp from what he could tell—and Lincoln got a full view of Holland spread out on the bed, her hands on her breasts as she looked directly at the camera. From this angle, he could also see Ethan's head between Holland's legs, a wry smile on his face, and his eyes dark.

"Angle that camera so we can see what you're working with, big boy," Ethan said, and Lincoln barked out a laugh before doing as he was told. Well, this was going to be a fun way to start the day.

Lincoln slowly worked his hand up and down his shaft, cupping his balls as Holland played with her tits, her gaze on his. Her eyes darkened, her mouth parted as

Ethan started to lick, sending spasms of pleasure through him as if Ethan were licking down his cock.

He tried to keep his eyes open, did his best not to come right then and there, but he couldn't help it. All he could do was imagine Holland's mouth on his cock, Ethan's dick in his mouth, and try not to blow right then.

Holland gasped, arching her back as Ethan moved, growling against her core. Lincoln's hands increased their friction, and his balls tightened, the base of his spine tingling. And then he was shooting his load on his stomach, growling out their names as Holland arched her back again, her eyes closed, her mouth parted in an O as she came. But Ethan didn't let up. Instead, his hands dug into her hips as he licked and sucked. All the noises hit Lincoln so hard, he almost came again, his dick nearly as rock-hard as before. He kept touching himself, holding out his orgasm so he could see Ethan move again. When Ethan finally lifted his head from Holland, his mouth wet, his tongue darting out to lick the juices from his chin, Lincoln held everything back since just watching, needing made it impossible. And then Holland was suddenly on her knees, swallowing Ethan whole, her ass, and her wet pussy right in front of the camera.

Lincoln grinned, looked up at Ethan as Ethan growled, tugging on Holland's hair as he fucked her mouth, hard.

Lincoln wanted to be there, wanted to be part of this wake-up call, but he couldn't.

Though he was part of this. They'd made him part of this.

This had to work.

When Ethan finally came, Lincoln just sat there holding the phone, waiting for his lovers to quit panting so they could look at him.

"Coffee?" he asked, and both of them nodded.

"I have to work today, but I want coffee," Holland said.

"Well, make sure you get to work on time." Lincoln paused. "Thank you for waking me up."

"Anytime, big boy," Holland said. Her laughter was the last thing he heard before Ethan waved and hung up.

Lincoln just shook his head and set his phone on the nightstand. He had work to do, and he would get to it. But first, he would remember what was important. Maybe then he'd figure out what inspiration he needed in order to be able to draw again. Because his hands itched for a pencil, but he also knew that nothing was going to come to him right then in terms of his art.

He'd focus on what could, on what might work for him. On who mattered. The rest would come eventually. At least, he hoped.

CHAPTER FIFTEEN

E than rolled his shoulders back and looked at the clock, grinning. He had twenty minutes left, and then he was going home. Finally.

He planned to work his actual hours, and considering he had already finished what he wanted to do from his to-do list, he was happy with that.

Maximilian probably wouldn't be too ecstatic about him leaving, but he didn't care. His boss needed to understand that, yes, he would put in the hours and get shit done, but he also needed a break.

Or at least he *hoped* his boss would understand. If not, Ethan would be looking for a new job. And that scared the shit out of him. But he was going to figure this life of his out. And he was going home. Home to Lincoln. Lincoln had said that he'd be cooking dinner for the three of them tonight after he finished with work.

Ethan had offered to actually do the cooking, but Lincoln had scoffed, saying that it was his turn.

Maybe it was. But Ethan wanted to be able to take care of Lincoln, just like Lincoln constantly took care of him. Call him sentimental and all that shit.

There was a knock at his office door, and he tensed, afraid it was going to be his boss wanting another project from him. He was almost done for the day, even though he still had a little bit of work to do to get ahead for the next day. Unfortunately, he couldn't really hide. He turned and frowned.

"Liam? What are you doing here?"

His big brother walked in, looked around, and smiled. "This place looks great."

Ethan frowned and took the place in, as well. Four walls, a window with a set of blinds, and one big desk that took over two walls. He had filing cabinets and another table that had stuff piled on it, as well as two whiteboards that covered one wall. Not too much.

Ethan just looked at his brother.

"Hey, you're doing amazing. You have your own place, your own little office."

"Are you here for a reason?" Worry swamped Ethan, and he stood up quickly, his chair almost toppling over and falling to the floor. "What's wrong? Is it Mom?"

Liam held out his hands and shook his head. "No, everything's fine. I just wanted to check on you. And I know you have plans with Lincoln and Holland tonight, so I didn't want to interrupt that."

Ethan nodded, his pulse finally calming down.

"I'm almost done. You want to take a walk or something?"

Liam shook his head and leaned against the door-frame before looking over his shoulder.

"Can I close the door?"

Ethan nodded, a little worried again. "What is it?"

"Nothing. I just want to make sure you know that the family loves you and we're here for you."

"Well, doesn't that sound like something bad's happening?" He swallowed hard, dread filling his gut. "What's the real reason you're here?"

Liam scowled and ran his hand through his hair before he started pacing the little area in front of the door. "I suck at this. I don't know why Aaron and Bristol had me come here."

"The siblings wanted you here?"

"We're worried about you."

"You're worried. About me. Why the hell are you worried about me? I'm fine."

"You are. We just want you to stay that way. We love Lincoln. He's like a fucking brother to us, you know that. And I'm *really* glad that he was never a brother to you." Liam laughed a bit.

"Yes, that joke will never get old," Ethan deadpanned.

"Well, I don't know how to say this without sounding like an asshole."

"Why don't you just say it, and I will deal with it?" Liam was the overprotective brother, just like Aaron was the one who was always there and funny. Bristol got you where you needed to be. And Ethan? Well, Ethan organized things behind everyone's back. Except he really wasn't that person right now because he had been so focused on work. It was just another thing he'd fucked up on. He needed to step up, but he was doing his best. And as he looked at the clock, he realized he only had a few more minutes before he needed to head out and get to Lincoln and Holland.

"Okay, anyway, we love Lincoln. And we really like Holland."

"Oh?" Ethan asked, his stomach settling a bit.

"Yes. She is amazing for you two. She's quirky, funny, and she makes you laugh."

"You don't really know her," Ethan said wryly.

"No, but Arden met her. And Bristol and Madison.

They love her. And the fact that you haven't brought her to a Montgomery dinner tells me you're trying to protect her."

"Or it could be that it's not serious," he added.

"No, you wouldn't risk Lincoln for something that wasn't serious."

"True." Ethan paused. "We're happy. I don't know what's going to happen, but we're finally getting happy."

"Does that mean you're going to stop working so fucking much?"

Ethan took a step back, rubbing at the place over his heart. "Just dig a little deeper next time."

"What? You always work hard. And you always miss family things because of it."

"I get it, I'm a workaholic. The fact that you had to come to my place of work to tell me that is probably evidence enough."

"I just want to make sure that you know we love you. And to tell you that you need to bring Holland to the house."

"I know. But we need to make sure she doesn't want to run first."

"Kind of figured that since you guys are keeping her so close. Don't want the Montgomerys to scare her off." Liam laughed.

"If she can deal with the fact that Bristol came to her house out of the blue after somehow getting the address out of me, so...I'm pretty sure she can handle anything."

"Oh? Good. Then make sure she can handle us. Because we want the best for you. And the fact that even with those dark circles under your eyes, you look happy? It seems like those two are exactly what you need."

"Thanks, but I could really do without people mentioning the dark circles under my eyes. Maybe I need to start using those eye patches."

"Hey, Arden has me using them sometimes. And a scrub that helps with the beard and everything."

"You're a celebrity now, with your face all over the backs of books and on websites and shit. You have to be fancy."

"And on that note, fuck you. Anyway, you're coming to dinner at the house on Saturday. Mom's already planned it, and I'm just going to call Holland myself if you don't agree."

Ethan scrubbed his hands over his face. "Fine."

"And give her flowers or something. You haven't seen her in a bit."

"Holland? I saw her yesterday."

"Haha. Come on. Seriously, get Mom flowers or something."

"I will. Though Lincoln will probably already think of that. And Holland."

"See? That's why you have two loves in your life. They're going to help you make sure that you have your head on straight. Because you're always so busy making sure everyone else is where they need to be that sometimes you forget yourself."

While that was true, Ethan got caught on one word. "We haven't said the big *L* word yet," he mumbled.

"That's fine. You've got time. Take it slow, you have a lot of feelings to deal with. And a lot of limbs." Ethan snorted while Liam scrubbed at his eyes. "Never mind. I never, ever want you to say that phrase again. Or even think it."

"Hey, I'm sure Lincoln could draw you a diagram if you get confused."

"I hate you. I really hate you. Now, sorry for interrupting the end of your workday. I'm off to pick up Jasper from the vet, and then I'm headed home to my girl."

"Is Jasper okay?" Jasper was Arden and Liam's white Siberian Husky, and he hadn't been sick as far as Ethan knew.

"Yes, he ate a fricking sock because he was nervous.

He's fine. Apparently, it passed while he was there. Arden and I have been in and out of the vet with him to make sure he doesn't need surgery."

"Why didn't you call me?"

"Because we were doing just fine. But if I had any news other than what I had earlier today? Then I would have called you. And, Ethan, I bet you Holland would have been there, too. And Lincoln. Because you're good people. And you love those good people."

"Liam."

"Sorry. I'll stop saying the L-word. But see you Saturday. Don't disappoint Mom."

"I'm doing my best to stop disappointing everyone."

Liam smiled and then hugged his brother tightly before walking out.

Ethan looked up at the clock, saw that it was five minutes after his scheduled end time, and picked up his stuff, making sure he had everything on his checklist that he needed. He had a couple of programs that were going to run overnight, and he could check on them from his work computer at home if he needed to. Nobody would hold that against him since he did need to work on the data that would run overnight. However, he didn't need to sit in his office to do it.

His boss didn't say a thing as he waved on his way out, Julia right on his tail.

"Hey, you're fleeing the coop?"

"No, I'm taking a stand with you. Maximilian never yells. He just gives you that shaming look. And I hate that look. However, if we start following the rules and set ourselves within the purview of this job, maybe he'll get it, too."

"I like you, Julia."

She grinned. "I like you, too, Ethan. Say hi to Lincoln and Holland for me."

"Will do." He waved as she got into her car, and he walked a little farther to the back where he usually parked. He liked parking under this one tree since it shielded him, even though sometimes he had to deal with bird shit more than he wanted to.

He made it about four steps from his car when something slammed into the back of his head. He let out a sharp cry, reaching up to determine what the fuck had just happened, and tried to turn, but someone's fist hit his jaw instead. He hit the ground, spitting out blood as he blinked.

The sun shone behind the man in front of him, so Ethan couldn't see his face, only shadows. His ears rang, and he felt as if he were going to throw up. He couldn't make a move, couldn't figure out what the hell was going on.

Was he being attacked? Mugged?

He didn't even have his computer with him. He'd left it at home in his office there. All he had was his wallet, but he couldn't even open his mouth to say that. Instead, the man straddled him and punched him again. Ethan held up one hand, blocking his face, and used his other fist to swing at the guy. The attacker cursed, and as soon as he did so, Ethan knew exactly who it was. "Damien?" he spat, blood filling his mouth once more.

"He gives the best hugs, doesn't he? And I had that. Before...you," Damien snapped and tried to punch him again.

Ethan attempted to move, but whatever had hit him had almost knocked him out. Bile filled his mouth, and he couldn't see straight. His eyes narrowed as his vision went wonky. He was pretty sure he had a fucking concussion, and he couldn't even focus. Instead, he tried to push Damien off him again, but it wasn't enough.

Damien picked something up that made a grating sound on the gravel. A metal pipe? A crowbar? Jesus Christ. Was Damien going to kill him?

"He was mine. All mine. And you ruined everything." Damien tried to hit him again, but Ethan rolled to the side. The piece of metal or whatever it was slammed into the side of his shoulder, the corner of it catching his eyebrow. He screamed and pushed Damien off, trying to crawl away, but then Damien stood up and kicked him in the gut.

Ethan reached for his phone, trying to call 911, attempting to get away, knowing that with whatever had just happened to his head, he couldn't fight back like he needed to. He had to run. Why didn't anyone hear him? Why wasn't anyone there?

He couldn't focus enough to call the police, so he called the first person he could, the last person he had called that day, just to hear her voice. But when Damien hit him again, there was nothing.

Holland stretched her back as she walked into her house, grateful that Steven was going to close for the evening. They'd had a good day, even though her mother and her sister had called. She had ignored the calls, though she knew that they might show up again. Or, they wouldn't. She didn't care either way. And she honestly didn't know how to feel about that. The fact that she didn't care that her parents had written her off? That her father hadn't even talked to her since the wedding? She honestly didn't care. And it really had nothing to do with her anymore.

Her phone rang, and she looked down, smiling. Ethan. She was supposed to meet him at his house later, and she really hoped that he wasn't going to cancel. She didn't think he would, though. He was trying. And she shouldn't immediately go to the negative, either.

"Hello?"

"He was mine. All mine."

Holland blinked, looked down at the phone, and then pulled it back as she heard a man screaming, shouting. There were more shouts and moans and groans. The sound of flesh against flesh, and then the terrifying sound of what sounded like metal against something soft.

When the phone went silent, she looked down at it, tears streaming from her eyes, and her hands shaking.

"Ethan? Ethan!" she called out to the phone, but there was no answer.

Just dead air.

Shaking, she looked down at the screen, hoping like hell that Ethan was okay. That had to have been him, right? It was his number. She hadn't recognized the other voice on the line. Who had that been? Was Ethan hurt?

She tried to call back, but it just rang and rang. With each tone, her heart raced, and her palms went damp.

She didn't know what to do. Could she call 911? But where was Ethan? Was he at work, or was he on his way home? He should have been on his way home by now. But with Ethan, you never knew. She didn't know who she should call, but she had one number in her phone for a person she knew might have answers. She called Liam, hoping to hell that Ethan's brother might know what to do.

"Holland? What's wrong?"

"I just got a call from Ethan, and it sounds like he's hurt. But I don't know. He won't answer now. But it's still ringing, so I know his cell has to be on. He said that you guys were on the same family plan, right? Can you like...do that find your phone thing or something? I don't know. He's never done this. I can't... I can't." She started to hyperventilate, and Liam cursed into the phone.

"Okay, tell me what happened again."

"Ethan called, but it wasn't his voice I heard. There was some man there, yelling, and then it sounded like there was fighting. And it sounded really bad, Liam.

And then Ethan didn't answer his phone when I called back. I don't know what to do."

"Okay, fuck. Hang up, call Lincoln. Tell him to get to you or something. I'm going to try and find the phone. We'll make this work, okay? He's going to be fine. He probably just dropped it or something."

"It didn't sound like that."

"Call Lincoln. And answer right away if I call back, okay?"

"Okay."

She hung up, her hands shaking as she called Lincoln. But he didn't pick up right away either. Oh, God, what if he'd been with Ethan? What was going on?

Liam called back, even before she could leave a message for Lincoln, so she just hung up. "What is it?"

"He's not answering his phone, like you said. But I found his location. I'm going to call 911. It looks like he's at work. I'm going to his building. I'm in my car right now. I just left there, so I'm close. Jesus Christ, I was just there."

"Oh my God. Okay, where do I go?"

"I don't know. Did you get ahold of Lincoln?"

"No. I don't know what to do."

"We'll figure it out. Okay? You're not alone in this. We're going to figure this out."

Liam hung up, and then Lincoln called, and Holland

almost threw up. "Oh my God, you're okay. Right? You're okay?"

"Yes, why wouldn't I be? What the hell, Holland? What's wrong?"

"I don't know. Can you come get me? I think we're going to need to go to the hospital."

There was a single pause and then the sound of movement. "I'm running out to my car right now. What the hell? Are you okay? What's wrong?"

"I don't know." She relayed what had happened with Ethan and then Liam, tears falling down her cheeks as she tried to figure out what to do. She knew she could not drive right then. She hadn't realized how much she loved Ethan until just now. Until she had heard that shout. Until she couldn't reach him. And the fact that Lincoln was already running to his car to come and get her? Dear God, it hit her like a two-ton brick. This was it. *They* were it. And now she was going to lose them.

Dear God, she loved them so fucking much. She couldn't lose them.

But it seemed like she wasn't going to get a choice in that.

"I'm on my way. Okay? Be strong, baby. I'm almost there."

"Drive safe. Don't get hurt."

"Be waiting for me."

"Always."

Liam texted with a group text that had to be with the rest of the Montgomerys.

Liam: *Ethan in ambulance. On the way to the hospital. Meet us at Mercy.*

And that was it. Holland's hand shook, but she knew that Lincoln would be there soon. She wouldn't be alone. She could figure out what to do as soon as he arrived.

Oh God, what had happened to Ethan?

His family would be there. She didn't want this to be the first time she met the rest of them. But it didn't matter. She had to get there.

She heard tires squeal, and she grabbed her purse and ran out the door, thankfully remembering to lock it on her way out.

Lincoln looked pale as a ghost, his eyes wide as he got out of the car and ran to her, crushing her to his body. He kissed her hard and then gripped her shoulders.

"I got the text. Let's go."

"Are you okay to drive?" she asked, being truly honest right then because he was shaking as much as she was.

"Yes, I just need to take a couple deep breaths, and

I'll get you there safely. Both of us. He's going to be okay, baby, we know this."

"Do they know what happened?"

"I got the same text as you, babe. But he called you, he got to you. We're going to figure this out, okay? You did good, baby."

He kissed her again, and she fell into him, wanting those words to be true. She just didn't know if they were.

They pulled away from each other and dashed to the car, not bothering to speak as Lincoln got them to the hospital, following every single traffic law, but only barely.

When they pulled into the parking lot, she saw that there were other Montgomerys getting out of their vehicles, all of them just as pale as Lincoln—and probably her.

Bristol saw her over one of the cars and did a quick wave as she grabbed Marcus's hand. But Holland couldn't speak, couldn't even formulate words. She just clung to Lincoln's hand as they made their way into the emergency room. Liam was already there, his hair looking as if he'd run his hands through it a few times. She only recognized him from photos since she hadn't actually met the man yet.

But Arden was there too, and she ran over, giving

Holland a hug and then hugging Lincoln. "We don't know anything."

"Okay, because that was my question," Lincoln said.

Holland couldn't speak.

Instead, they just stood there as the others walked in.

Francine and Timothy Montgomery gave her sad smiles and held her close and then hugged Lincoln hard before going to their seats. She hadn't met them before this, and she had no idea what to feel. They were in so much pain because of what had happened to their son, and yet they'd opened their arms to her as if she were part of this. After, they just looked at each other, and then their children before sitting down and holding hands.

Aaron paced in front of Liam and Arden, while Bristol and Marcus stood off in a corner, mumbling to each other, looking as if they were going to fight.

She didn't know what that was about, but she couldn't focus on it.

"Liam Montgomery?" an officer asked as he walked in. "We're here to take your statement."

Everyone rose, but Liam nodded.

"Okay, we can do that."

"Is one of you Holland?"

She started forward. "Yes, that's me. He called me."

"Okay, we're going to need to take your statement, too."

"But what about news? What if we hear something about Ethan?"

"We'll find you, baby. You want me to come with you?"

"We would really rather she be alone," one of the officers said.

But Lincoln gripped her hand and shook her head. "I'll be there for support. Nothing else. One of Ethan's siblings can come in and get us if he hears anything. That okay?"

The officers looked at each other and then nodded, but Holland just swallowed hard, wondering what the hell was going on. What had happened?

"We got some of your statement at the scene, Mr. Montgomery, but we're going to need to hear a little bit more," one of the officers said.

"All I know is that I got there right when the squad car arrived. Ethan was on the ground, coughing up blood and saying, 'Damien did it. Damien did it. Find Lincoln and make sure he's okay.' That's all he kept saying." Lincoln stiffened by her side, and Holland just blinked over at Liam as the words crashed down on her.

Lincoln's agent?

Oh my God.

"He was attacked?" Holland asked, her body shaking.

Lincoln didn't say a word.

"I take it you're Lincoln?" the officer asked, not bothering to answer her question.

"I am. Damien's my agent. I'm an artist. What do you need to know?"

"Do you know why your agent would want to harm Mr. Montgomery?"

Lincoln just shook his head and then froze. Holland wanted to hold him and let him know that everything was going to be okay. But she didn't know if that was true, how could it be?

They answered the officers' questions, trying to get to the bottom of everything that had happened.

The police were kind, but she didn't want to be there with them. She wanted to be near Ethan. To make sure he was all right. But she couldn't think. Couldn't do anything. She didn't miss the looks the officers gave each other when they found out she was in a ménage with both Lincoln and Ethan. She didn't miss the glances from the nurses when they came in to tell Liam they had no news.

What seemed like hours later, they finally let her go

so she could go into the waiting room and wait with the others.

They'd put a BOLO out for Damien. They still wanted to talk to the rest of the family more about why this had happened, but first, they needed to find Damien. And they needed to know exactly what to charge him with.

What type of injuries did Ethan have?

When the doctors finally came in, she sat still in her chair, her fingers entwined with Lincoln's as the rest of the Montgomerys moved as one to listen.

She met Marcus's gaze as he sat down, as well, letting Bristol get up with her family. He shook his head, and she understood.

This was for them, the family. They would find out more when the time was right. But it wasn't like they couldn't hear the doctor anyway. They were just giving the Montgomerys space.

"He'll be okay," Francine Montgomery whispered and then broke down in tears as her husband held her. Holland let the tears fall, as well.

Ethan had a concussion, some bruised ribs, and would need stitches over his eye. He also had some contusions, and probably more, less severe cuts elsewhere.

But he would be okay. He was awake, even with the

concussion, and they were dealing with that protocol. But he would be all right.

And as Holland wept in Lincoln's arms, she couldn't help but notice that he hadn't moved. He hadn't said a word. He hadn't cried.

She knew he likely blamed himself. And she would have to fix that. Somehow. Because it wasn't his fault. It was Damien's.

She had no idea what to do. Because she loved these two men. Loved them so much, she was breaking inside.

It hurt. It hurt so damn much.

Because she'd almost lost Ethan. And she didn't know what to do about that. Didn't know if there *was* anything to do about it. She sat, and she waited, and she knew she would see Ethan eventually. She had to. But after that?

She didn't know.

CHAPTER SIXTEEN

Ethan lay motionless in the hospital bed. Lincoln could only stand there, wondering what the fuck he was supposed to do. What should he say?

This was all his fault. All his fucking fault.

If he had just gotten Damien out of his life before this, maybe the attack wouldn't have happened. Perhaps he should've stayed away from Ethan. Maybe Damien wouldn't have gotten jealous, then, wouldn't have claimed Lincoln.

He didn't know what had happened exactly, what had snapped inside that brain of Damien's, but Lincoln knew *he* was to blame.

And they couldn't find the asshole.

He wasn't at his place, wasn't at his office. The cops were still looking for him.

The officers didn't let up on the questioning, though. They wanted answers, and Lincoln really didn't have any to give.

Yes, he had slept with Damien. But years ago.

No, he hadn't led the man on, hadn't given him any inclination that he wanted to be with him.

No, he hadn't slept with Damien since.

No, he didn't know where Damien was.

No, he hadn't asked Damien to do this.

Yes, Ethan was his, just like Holland was.

No, he wasn't in a sadomasochistic relationship where he was grooming Holland and Ethan.

No, he wasn't also seeing Damien while sleeping with Holland and Ethan.

No, they were not a quartet.

Yes, he was in a relationship with two people.

No, it wasn't any of their business.

On and on the questions went. He had just stood there, answering as best he could. He hadn't gotten a lawyer, didn't need one. Even though the first thing a lawyer friend would say was that you always needed a lawyer while talking to a cop.

But Lincoln just wanted it over.

Wanted Ethan to be okay.

He was sleeping now, finally. He'd been up, hadn't said anything, but had reached out, and Lincoln had grabbed his hand for a moment. And then when Ethan turned to Holland, she had taken his other hand. When Ethan finally went to sleep, the nurses letting him do so for a while thanks to the drugs in his system even with a concussion, Lincoln let go of Ethan's hand, needing to pace.

Holland hadn't said anything, and he knew she was pulling away. Maybe that was a good thing. Because it seemed like everything Lincoln touched lately just got fucked up. Because art, Damien, and now Ethan. Of course, Holland would want to stay away.

He hated himself. Hated all of this. But he didn't know what to do.

He couldn't do anything.

Fine. "I got to go," he whispered to himself, as Holland looked over at him.

"I know some of the Montgomerys went home, mostly because Liam forced them out. But Aaron's still in the waiting room. Do you need to switch with him?"

She made to stand, and Lincoln shook his head. "No, I'm going home. I need a break."

"Oh. Do you want company?"

He looked at her and knew he was going to lose it, knew he would probably say something he shouldn't, so he didn't say anything. Instead, he just shook his head and walked out of the room without touching her, without saying goodbye, without kissing her. Without doing anything to her or Ethan.

He simply left, unable to say anything.

When Lincoln walked out, Aaron was in the waiting room as Holland had said, playing with his phone.

"The rest of the fam's going to take turns, but we figured you two should stay with him. They letting you stay overnight?"

"You can go in there with Holland. I'm going home."

"Really?" Aaron asked and raised his brows. "You're just going to leave?"

"Yes, I am. I need to think."

"Don't do anything stupid, Lincoln."

Lincoln just shook his head and left, knowing he had already done something stupid. He'd had hope. He'd hoped that maybe this could work out between him and Ethan. Between him and Holland. Between the three of them. That nobody would comment on the fact that he was in a relationship with two people. That it wouldn't matter in this day and age. But he had seen the way some of the nurses had looked at the three of them. He had seen the way the cops had acted as if he'd had something to do with the attack because...why not?

Because he'd had sex with two different people at the same time? And even though they were in a caring relationship and committed, they must be deviants.

He'd seen the way some people at restaurants looked at them when they went out. Or the fact that they didn't actually hold hands or touch each other as a threesome in public to avoid the stares.

Yes, he knew all of that. He had known that going in, and yet he had hoped that maybe they could make it work.

But it hadn't. It was all fucked up.

And now Ethan was in a hospital bed and hurt because of him. Because of his past and his inability to let Damien go because he felt as if he *owed* him something for his work.

He just needed to get home. Needed to think about what the hell he was going to do. This wasn't the end of it, but he needed to at least make sure that he wasn't the one who caused any more hurt.

Ethan was making strides, or at least he *had* been. He was trying to make things work. And Holland hadn't run yet. That was good, right?

But everything Lincoln did seemed to break down. He couldn't paint right now, couldn't draw, could only think about doing that.

And now Damien.

He drove home on autopilot, wishing that he actually had a car that could do that for him so he didn't have to think at all.

He honestly didn't even know how he got home. His mind was whirling, his head pounding.

He staggered to his apartment, closed the door, locked up behind him, and made his way to his kitchen. He poured himself two fingers of whiskey and downed it even though it was supposed to be a sipping bourbon.

Then he poured another two fingers and figured he could sip on that.

Jesus Christ. He didn't know what he'd have done if Ethan had died. He could barely breathe thinking about it. But when Ethan was healthy again and realized that it was all Lincoln's fault? He'd lose him no matter what.

Ethan was his best friend, and he loved him down to the very depths of his soul. And Lincoln had almost lost him. Because of Damien.

That fucking jealous asshole.

And there was nothing he could do about it. He hadn't been there when Ethan needed him. No, Ethan had left work when he did because Lincoln had yelled at him to work less. He had been in that parking lot right then because he wanted to please Lincoln.

Bile filled Lincoln's throat as he thought over everything that had happened, and he set down his glass, gripping the edge of the counter for support. He took a deep breath and tried to count to ten, but he couldn't.

He couldn't breathe, couldn't think. All he wanted to do was punch something.

He looked over at the other end of the studio where his canvases were located, where the blue and gray canvas sat that he was supposed to be working on. He saw nothing. There was nothing inside him—no spark, no art.

All that was left was rage.

And the realization of the fact that he couldn't do a damn thing.

He staggered over to the painting and just stared at it, wondering if something would come to him. He let his fingers trail across the blank parts of the canvas, wondering if maybe he should just use finger paints. Maybe that would help. He opened up one of the tubes, put it on his pallet, and slid his fingers through it. The feel of it almost numbed his fingertips. It wasn't supposed to do that, but maybe *he* was just numb.

He slid his hand along the blank part of the canvas, wishing something would happen, but it didn't. There was nothing. This wasn't art, this was just him trying to figure out how to become who he once was. And there was nothing of that left.

A key slipped into the lock, and he froze.

There was only one person with a key now, and that person was in a hospital bed.

Maybe Holland had taken it. Or Aaron. Perhaps one of the other Montgomerys. But when he turned, he froze in place

Damien stood there, a key in his hand, and a smirk on his face. His hair was slicked down with sweat sticking to his forehead. His suit was disheveled as if he'd been running and hiding—which he likely had been—and Lincoln could smell the booze coming off the other man in waves from where he stood. Lincoln wiped his hands on his pants, not caring about the cops.

"Damien." He tried to keep his voice steady, as if his pulse weren't racing in his ears. His phone was right in his pocket. He could probably reach for it, but he didn't know if Damien had a weapon. He didn't know anything.

Jesus Christ, this couldn't be happening.

"Lincoln."

There was nothing in that tone, no emotion, no mania, no depression. Nothing. And that scared Lincoln more than anything.

"I didn't know you still had a key," Lincoln said as calmly as possible.

"You think I didn't make a copy? You really should

have changed your locks. But you've always been complacent. And that's fine. That's why I've always been here for you. And I will always be here for you."

Lincoln swallowed hard and hoped to hell he knew what to say next. Because he had a feeling even one wrong move wouldn't end well for anyone.

"How are you doing, Damien?"

"How am I doing?" Damien just laughed. It was a high-pitched comic laugh, and Lincoln barely held back a cringe.

"How am I doing? Well, I tried to help you. I tried to help, and now there are cops at my place. How could you do that to me? How could you send them after me when all I want to do is help?"

"You hurt Ethan."

"So what? He was never good for you. He doesn't understand you like I do. All he ever does is make fun of your art and never shows up. But you know who's always been there? Me. I was always there. I've always been here for you."

"You were," Lincoln said, trying not to anger Damien any more than necessary.

"You're right, I've always been here for you." Damien moved forward and got so close to Lincoln that he could smell the liquor wafting off his agent. Lincoln wanted to throw up.

"You're mine, you've always been mine. It just took a while to see it. But now that Ethan's out of the way, I can be here for you. And that bitch? Holland? No. You don't need her. I don't know why you think you do. You don't. You only need me. I'll help you get her out of the way, too."

Fear clawed at Lincoln's belly, and he shook his head. "Don't hurt her."

Fire slid into Damien's eyes.

"You care about her, too? She's standing in the way? She shouldn't be. She's nothing. She's only new. You just fell for tits and ass, but that's because you miss me. You miss me, and you pushed me away for so long. I'm not going to stand back any longer. Because I'm yours. And you're mine."

Rage slammed into Lincoln like a fist, and he shook his head. "I've never been yours, Damien."

"Yes, you have. I remember that night."

"That night was a long time ago, and we were both drunk. We haven't done it again since."

"You're lying. You care. You always think about me. Just like I think about you. We've always been in this together. I helped to put you on the map. You'd be nothing if not for me. And now you're trying to push me away? No." Damien leapt at Lincoln, fists flying. Lincoln took the first blow while standing, and then bent down and elbowed Damien in the gut. Damien kept kicking, clawing, punching, doing everything that he could to try and reach Lincoln, but Lincoln was bigger and faster. And even though he had whiskey in his system, he clearly hadn't had as much alcohol as the other man.

Lincoln shoved at Damien and punched him hard in the face. Damien spat out blood and grinned, as if he hadn't even felt the blow. Lincoln kept hitting and kicking, but Damien wasn't going to stop. Damien lashed out, hit and jabbed at Lincoln. This time, Lincoln was the one who spit out blood. It streamed down his face from a cut on his forehead, but he ignored it. He just needed to stop this.

Needed to stop Damien.

Because this was for Ethan, for Holland. Because no one was going to hurt those he loved. No more than he had already hurt them himself anyway.

And then Damien was on the floor, passed out. Lincoln loomed over him, his chest heaving as he sucked in breaths and tried to breathe, attempted to calm himself.

But he couldn't. He couldn't do anything. He quickly went to the drawer next to a bunch of his supplies and found some rope he had used for one of his mixed-media things and tied Damien up.

He wasn't good at knots, but hopefully, it would be enough. And then he called the cops.

Because he had no one left to call. He didn't know what to do. But he had to figure it out. He couldn't even process that the man who had been his friend, who had been with him throughout all of his art, had become... *this*.

Because this Damien wasn't the man Lincoln had been friends with for so long through. And then Lincoln looked over at his commission canvas, at the smear and mess he'd made with his fingers and let out a hushed laugh.

He couldn't do anything. Nothing he did was right. Because everything he touched seemed to turn to ash. People got hurt. And what he thought he was, what he imagined he had to offer, wasn't much.

Though maybe it was *too* much. Perhaps this had been a wakeup call, and Ethan and Holland were better off without Lincoln. He didn't know. He didn't have the answers.

He sat there on his stool, the one he'd used for so long to help him figure out what he needed to do with work, and he just waited.

Waited...with nothing.

CHAPTER SEVENTEEN

When the Montgomerys came to wish you well and tried to make you feel better, they tended to come in force. Ethan lay back on the corner of his sectional and wanted to scream. Not because he wasn't grateful. Because, dear God, he was so grateful.

He didn't have to lift a finger in this house, and his family was there for him. Everybody was there to make sure that he had everything he needed. Well, what he didn't have was time to think. Time to be with the two people he loved the most. Because they were avoiding him.

Oh, they might think they were getting away with it, but he knew when someone was avoiding him. And that's exactly why Lincoln had only been by twice in the last week since Ethan got home, claiming work and other things related to what had happened with Damien. And while Ethan wanted to believe him, he couldn't quite get there.

But he hadn't been able to sit down, alone, to actually talk with Lincoln. Tell him he didn't blame him.

That this was Damien's fault, no one else's.

But, Jesus Christ, just the idea that Lincoln could have been hurt as well when Damien showed up at his studio made Ethan want to scream. Or hurt *more* anyway. It made him want to rip at the blankets that were currently covering his lap because nobody would let him stand up.

But he couldn't do that. Everyone was staring at him, waiting for him to start bleeding again or something.

The bruises on his ribs were so bad that his doctor had mentioned that having them broken might have been better.

That wasn't something he ever wanted to hear.

He was taped up, wrapped up, and every time he coughed or laughed, he groaned.

But he was allowed to walk around, at least according to his doctor—not that his mother actually let him do so.

He hadn't been to work for a week. And, surprisingly, Maximilian had been fine with that.

Ethan's boss had been so overcome with the idea that someone had been hurt in his parking lot, that he had installed more security equipment outside so they could watch what was going on. And nobody was allowed to walk alone to their cars now.

On the second day, Julia had come by to see Ethan to explain that, and she had said that Maximilian was really stressed out, even thinking about stationing guards at the office.

Ethan wasn't sure how that would help, considering it had been a one-off thing, but whatever Maximilian needed to do to keep himself and his workers safe, Ethan would go along with it. That was if he were ever allowed to go back to work.

Oh, his doctor had said he could return the next week, but his mother might actually tie him down—gently—so he couldn't leave.

Currently, the entire Montgomery family was in Ethan's living room and kitchen, talking amongst themselves and ignoring him. Holland was sitting next to him, her legs crossed as she looked down at her tablet, working on inventory.

She wasn't even looking at him or talking to him, but the fact that she was there, warmed him.

If only Lincoln would stop glaring at him from the corner and come over to sit with them both.

Everyone was there to make sure that Ethan was doing okay on his last day of confinement. At least, that's what he kept calling it.

Aaron had brought up the word, probably thanks to one of the many historical romances he read, and now that's what everybody went with.

"Are you sure there isn't anything else we can get you before we go?" his mother asked, plumping his pillows behind him.

Ethan looked over at Holland, who smiled at him, one of the first ones he'd seen on her in a long while. He swallowed hard.

Dear God, he missed that smile. And he missed Lincoln. Physically, they were both right here, but it wasn't enough. He wanted them mentally there, too.

"I'm fine. Dinner was amazing. You know how much I love chicken and dumplings."

"And did she tell you that she made the bread from scratch?" Arden asked, kissing her future mother-in-law's cheek.

Francine patted Arden's shoulder and looked over at her son.

"I did, but that's because I need to have my hands

busy. I get really stressed out when one of my babies is hurt."

"I'm fine." His mom just looked at him. "Okay. I'm *going* to be fine. But I'm starting work again next week, and that means I should probably get used to walking around."

"I know. I know."

"Leave him be, Francine. Now, son, your freezer and fridge are full of food you can heat up. And I'm pretty sure Holland and Lincoln can help you with that. I'm going to drag your siblings and their significant others out and leave you three in peace. I'm pretty sure you guys haven't had a moment to yourselves since the hospital."

"Thanks, Dad."

"Hey, you don't have to drag us," Bristol said, literally dragging Marcus into the room. Marcus just rolled his eyes, though he didn't seem to mind being called a significant other.

Not that Ethan was going to touch on that subject with a ten-foot pole. He was far too busy worrying about his own issues to deal with his sister's.

"Thank you for being here."

Bristol teared up and then kissed his cheek.

"I love you, brother. Never do that again."

"I'll do my best not to have a crowbar-wielding

maniac hit me upside the head." He tried to sound funny, but he caught the way Lincoln's jaw clenched.

Jesus Christ, he sucked at this.

He needed to talk to his best friend. Had to fix this. And he needed to see what the fuck was up with Holland.

"Just don't do it again," Bristol whispered before kissing him and letting Marcus pull her away.

Marcus lifted his chin, and Ethan just grinned.

"Thanks for being here."

"Always. You know that."

The two left, and Arden and Liam did the same after they hugged him tightly.

Well, as tight as they could without hurting him. Which wasn't that tight at all.

His parents left next after kissing all three of them and patting Ethan's cheeks. His dad had to literally drag his mother out of the room, but that was fine.

When they were gone, that left Aaron with the three of them. His brother cleared his throat before looking between them.

"Well, I didn't actually mean to be the last person here. But if you need me, let me know. Don't do anything stupid, okay?"

Ethan wasn't sure who Aaron was talking to at that moment, and then Aaron left. Lincoln still stood in the corner. He hadn't moved for the past ten minutes. Holland finally set her tablet down and shifted on the couch, so carefully, he knew that she was trying not to hurt him.

He reached out and gripped her knee, giving it a squeeze.

"Hey, you." She smiled then, her eyes filling.

"Don't cry."

"Sorry. Hormones."

"Maybe you should be the one sitting in the corner with a hot water bottle."

"No, I'm fine. Though I did steal some of your chocolate earlier."

"What's mine, is yours. You know that."

"Yes, I do. I guess I should head home soon. I have to do a couple of things at the shop anyway. And I know you probably want some time alone." Ethan wanted to curse, wondering what the hell was wrong with everybody.

"No, I want you to be here. You *and* Lincoln. And why are you over there, man? Come here. Let's talk."

"Okay, I need to talk anyway." Dread settled in Ethan's belly, and Holland froze before turning to Lincoln.

"What's wrong?"

Lincoln looked between the two of them, and Ethan

reached out to grab Holland's hand. She slid it away before he could make contact, and he felt as if he were lost. Standing on an abyss with a vast ocean all around him with no one there to keep him steady.

What the fuck was going on?

"This isn't working."

Lincoln said the words, but Ethan could barely hear them over the buzzing in his head.

"What?"

His best friend and lover shook his head and stuffed his hands into his pockets. "I shouldn't have let it go this far. But this isn't working. I'd say it's not you, it's me, but that's just cliché, and I don't even know what it means. But it's not working. And I think it'd be best for everybody if I just left."

Ethan tried to get up, winced at the pain in his side, and then Holland was there, holding his knee down.

"Don't move, you'll hurt yourself."

"Well, I might just have to hurt myself if somebody doesn't tell me what the fuck is going on. What the hell, Lincoln?"

"I'm just...it's not going to work out. Okay? I'm not good at this. I've got to go."

Holland didn't say a damn word, and Ethan wasn't even sure he *could* speak as Lincoln walked away, leaving Ethan sitting there like an idiot.

"You can't just go. We need to talk about this. I got hurt, but it's fine. I'm fine. You don't get to just walk away like this."

"It's not only about that. I've been thinking about this for a while. It would be better if the two of you moved on without me. You'll understand eventually."

"No, I won't. Help me figure it out right the fuck now."

Lincoln stood frozen. Still, Holland didn't say a word.

Lincoln was breaking up with both of them, and she didn't say anything. Why was this happening? It was like he was getting hit in the head with a fucking crowbar all over again. "Talk to me."

Lincoln just shook his head.

"I can't."

And then Lincoln pulled himself off the wall he leaned against and was gone. Gone. The door slamming behind him.

Ethan couldn't breathe, and it wasn't just because his ribs were pressing into his lungs. No, it was because everything was wrong. Yes, he had gotten hurt, but it wasn't that serious, and it wasn't Lincoln's fault. Why the hell was Lincoln leaving them both? That's not how this worked.

He turned to Holland. He saw tears slowly sliding down her face, but she still didn't say a word.

"What the hell?"

———

Holland knew she should probably say something. But how could she speak when she was shattering inside? She should have known this would happen. She should have known, and she should have walked away long before this.

But now she was going to have to do it anyway. Because Lincoln was gone. He had walked out, and he hadn't even given a good excuse.

"Holland? Talk to me."

"I...I need to go."

Ethan's eyes widened, and he leaned forward, pain in his expression. She knew that it was because he was moving far too much for those bruised ribs.

He had stitches over his eyebrow, and she wanted to kiss them better, but that wouldn't help. He would have to deal with possible concussion issues for the rest of his life, and he was so fucking lucky that Damien hadn't shattered his skull.

The bruises all over his body were now a different shade of green and yellow with some purple still mixed in, and she couldn't even touch him. Because what happened if she touched him and she hurt him? She would never be able to forgive herself. But how was she supposed to forgive herself for what had just happened?

"I never meant to come between you two."

"What? Are you fucking kidding me?" Ethan grabbed her shoulders, and she knew he wanted to shake her, but he didn't. He didn't hurt her, and she didn't do anything. But she needed to go.

Lincoln was gone, and Ethan was hurting. If she hadn't been there, maybe they would've worked this out. But it was all too much for Damien apparently, and now for Lincoln. After all, Damien hadn't snapped until she'd been in the mix. And now Lincoln was gone, too.

If she weren't part of this, it would have been easier for everyone.

"I should go. You need to work things out with Lincoln. He's your best friend. Even if your relationship can't work the way it has been, I know you love each other. I should go. Because you can't lose him."

"I can't lose *you*."

Tears slid down her cheeks, and she wiped them away, refusing to cry over this. Because this was her fault. She'd told herself she should have left long before this. She shouldn't have taken this chance in the first place.

"I was only supposed to be a distraction." She scrambled off the couch, and Ethan reached for her again, but he couldn't move to do so. Couldn't get off the couch because he was hurt.

Because some monster hadn't wanted him in Lincoln's life.

"Work it out with him, please. The two of you are perfect for each other."

"Not without you," Ethan growled out.

"I'm not meant for this. I don't want to be another obstacle in your way. Fix it. I know you can. But I need to go."

And just like before with her last relationship, she ran. She ran out the door and to her car. She didn't let the tears fall. She couldn't. She'd kept her eyes dry except for those first few tears at the beginning. She drove to her house, hoping to hell she got there in time. Before the dam burst. Because she was going to break down, and she needed to do it in private. Because if she looked at Ethan, if she even thought about him, she would go back and make sure he was okay. Instead, she left him alone and in pain, and that was on her.

But she was scared. So scared of losing him, just like she had almost lost him when he got hurt. She ran.

Because if she ran first, then it wouldn't hurt as badly later—not that she actually believed that anymore. But she did know one thing: Lincoln and Ethan were made for each other. And she would just get in the way.

She left.

She had left while Ethan was hurting, but so had Lincoln. She had been trying to figure out exactly what to do once Ethan was healthy, and she hadn't thought things through. Because she had gotten between them. She knew, just *knew*, that Lincoln and Ethan would have been able to figure things out if she hadn't been there. And maybe if she hadn't been so selfish, Lincoln wouldn't have walked away at all.

She hated that she was hurting. Loathed the fact that she resented that Lincoln had left her, too. But she couldn't focus on that, she could only focus on Ethan. Because he was the one who was actually hurting physically, and he could fix things with Lincoln. They had so much history. They had been through so much together. She was only the hanger-on.

She pulled into her driveway, and it took her a moment to realize that there was another car parked in front of her house.

She looked at it, her mouth going dry. But she figured...why the fuck not? Why the fuck wouldn't this be happening right now?

She got out of her car and closed the door gently, mostly because she wanted to slam it. She wanted to scream at the world and ask the universe why this was happening, but there was no point in that.

"Holland," her sister said as she got out of her car.

Holland hadn't seen her sister since she was down on her knees, sucking off Holland's fiancé on Holland's wedding day.

Because...why the fuck not?

It seemed like so long ago. She felt like a different person.

She had thought she was going to be married and happy with Dustin until the end of her days. But, in reality, she had just been in stasis, doing what she thought she needed to do. Dustin wasn't it for her. She didn't even think about him anymore.

Oh, she was still smarting from the hurt of knowing that he had cheated on her with her sister, but he wasn't her be-all-end-all.

And as Holland looked at Dakota now, at those wide eyes and her sibling's look of complete innocence, Holland couldn't hate her sister either.

Because without everything happening, she wouldn't have met Ethan and Lincoln.

She wouldn't have been on that park bench, feeling sorry for herself because her world had fallen apart. But she had been wrong about what real pain felt like. Because watching her sister go down on Dustin was only the tip of the iceberg of what pain could actually be. The idea that Ethan could have died hurt more. The idea that Lincoln was gone, had walked out on them without a true explanation, hurt more.

The fact that she had done the same to Ethan because she was scared? That hurt the worst.

She didn't turn her back, didn't walk away from Dakota.

Because she knew what true pain felt like. And what Dakota and Dustin had done to her paled in comparison.

"Hey," she said again.

"You never answered my calls." Her little sister looked down at her hands, and Holland tried to remember the last time she had really spoken to Dakota about anything important. High school maybe? Middle school? She wasn't sure, and perhaps that was on her. But then again, her family had never really understood her. Hadn't kept her close. Her entire life had been about making Dakota happy. And once she attempted to find some happiness of her own, Dakota had tried to take it. Holland's family didn't know about Ethan and Lincoln. Didn't know how much her job meant to her. But that was fine. She had been doing just fine on her own. But then she had tried to find happiness again, and figured out too late that it wasn't for her.

"I didn't really know we had anything to say," Holland said honestly.

"I wanted to say I'm sorry."

The snarky comeback that had surged to her tongue before didn't come this time. Because Holland honestly didn't feel anything.

"Okay. I believe you. Is there anything else?"

"Oh," Dakota said, her eyes widening even more. She looked like a little cartoon deer caught in head-lights. But Holland didn't care.

She was better off alone. It was something she had learned long ago.

She shouldn't have tried to change that.

"You guys are probably better suited for each other anyway, Dakota." Her little sister's eyes widened at Holland's honesty, but she shrugged. "Seriously. I just wish you would've come to me. I really wish he would have broken up with me so you could have found each other another way. I hate the fact that I had to find out the way that I did, but it's over and done with. And I honestly don't care anymore."

"I'm so sorry. I knew I should've figured out some-thing else, but I just didn't know any other way to tell you."

Holland wasn't even surprised that Dakota had done what she did on purpose. Oh, yes, she had wanted her big sister to find them exactly as she had, because why have an actual discussion when you could make a big dramatic splash about it instead?

Considering she had run from the wedding in a dramatic way, and had just run from Ethan in a very similar fashion, it apparently ran in the family.

"I'm never going to trust you," Holland said honestly, and her sister gave a tight nod. "And I'm not going to the wedding. I don't even know if I want to be a part of the family the same way I was. But that's mostly because of Mom."

"Well, Dad's not much better."

Holland nodded. "No, he's really not. Just be happy. Be happy because, once you find it, it's really hard to hold on to."

"You're talking about Dustin, right?"

Holland just shrugged, not wanting to talk about Ethan or Lincoln with her sister. She didn't want to talk about them with anyone.

And while Holland stood there not saying anything else, Dakota nodded a bit and then got back into her car, started it, and drove off.

Her sister had gotten the forgiveness she'd come searching for. In a way that was needed. She'd be able to move on with her life, and once again, Holland would be left alone.

She wouldn't have family, and she wouldn't have her friends either. Because the friendships she had started to make with Bristol and Arden and Madison couldn't last. The three would stay with the men. As they should.

And Holland would be alone. Again. But that's what she deserved. She couldn't figure out what she wanted. She had trouble allowing herself to be safe enough to be loved. But she had to be all right on her own.

And that was fine. She had her job, and she could call Steven a friend. She had that much. And Steven's husband was really sweet, too. She could find new friends eventually, ones she didn't make through people she dated.

She would be just fine.

She walked back into her house, closed the door behind her, and sat on the bench near her front door. She put her hands on her face and finally let the tears out.

She'd left the guys before they could leave her. She understood that. Or at least she had with Ethan. Because Lincoln had left *her*. He'd left before she could, and that hurt. More tears stung her eyes. It felt as if she were going to throw up, her heart was racing, and her body shook.

Why wasn't she good enough? Why didn't anyone think she was good enough?

And as she cried, and wished she could take it back, wished she could go back to Ethan's and tell him they could work it out and get Lincoln back, she knew she needed to work on herself first.

Because she wasn't doing this right. She never did.

She had been a distraction all right, a distraction for herself. And she couldn't do that again.

She wouldn't.

CHAPTER EIGHTEEN

Lincoln tossed himself into his work, tired of looking at a blank canvas, weary of looking at the art that he'd almost destroyed.

He took another swig from the bottle of Jack and just painted.

He wasn't drunk, but he was past buzzed. And if he *kept* drinking, he'd slide right into inebriated. And he didn't want to be that artist. Didn't want to have to rely on alcohol. But for today, he would pretend.

Because it had been four fucking days since he'd seen them. Since he had walked out and pretended that he was fine.

But he was a mess. If Damien hadn't been in Lincoln's life, then Ethan would be okay. Holland wouldn't have been threatened. But she had been, maybe not to her face, but she *had* been, and Ethan had ended up in the fucking hospital.

Lincoln was going to blame himself. Damien was behind bars and facing God only knew what charges because of his obsession with Lincoln. And Lincoln was in the middle of it all with everyone. If he pulled himself out of the situation, then things would be better. But he had to work. He had to focus on his art.

Because before, he'd been able to blame the fact that he couldn't create on his love for Ethan and how he couldn't do anything about it. Now? Well, he had done something about it. And it hadn't been enough. He had tried—tried so fucking hard—and it hadn't been enough.

Because Damien had ruined it all.

And Lincoln had been there to light the whole thing on fire at the end of Damien's fall from grace.

He just needed to work. Needed to focus on his art because, apparently, having Ethan in his life the way he had always dreamed of hadn't been enough for him to break through his block. Having Holland, someone that completed him in a way he never thought possible hadn't been it either.

No, it was him. He was the one blocking his art. He was the one standing in his way. He was the one who had to fix it. He needed to remember why he did this, and it wasn't Damien. It wasn't selling his art. It wasn't doing anything for Holland's shop like he'd promised. Because he wasn't going to be able to do that now, was he?

He wouldn't be working on that piece for Francine like he wanted to for her birthday. He'd be doing none of that. But he needed to focus on why he wanted to paint, why he liked drawing, why he enjoyed being an artist. Because, in the end, it would be the only thing he had left.

If he couldn't have the people that he loved, he needed to at least have something.

Though maybe he didn't deserve it.

He added more paint to the canvas, filling in curves and lines. Adding more until a shape began to manifest, and he saw her eyes.

It was Holland, the side of her, lying on a bed. But not a realistic portrait. More abstract, where you could tell it was a woman, but only he could tell it was Holland. His client wouldn't know.

They wouldn't know that look was for him and Ethan. Wouldn't know that it meant everything in the world to Lincoln.

They wouldn't know that he had walked away from that look because he had been too chickenshit about everything else that had happened.

But there was no going back now. And he knew that.

There was a knock on the door, and he froze, swallowing hard.

He had changed the locks the day after Damien showed up, but he still felt like he needed to do it again, even though that wasn't realistic at all.

And then there was a click in the lock and the turning of a key, and he knew who was there. The only person who had access. And it wasn't Ethan. Not anymore. Because Lincoln had ruined that, just like he wrecked everything else.

No, he knew who it was. And he knew damn well it was the only person he had left.

Because he'd walked away from everyone else.

"I didn't want to use the key, but I didn't think you were going to let me in." Lincoln turned to face Madison as she walked in, closing the door behind her before locking it.

"I'm just checking on you."

"I'm fine." He knew the words were gruff, knew he was being an asshole, but he didn't care. He needed to work.

"And I hate interrupting you when you're working but I'm so worried about you, Lincoln. You're like my brother, and I don't like seeing you in pain. How can I help?"

"You can go away."

"And you can stop being an asshole and talk to somebody."

"I'm finally painting, Madison." He tossed his paintbrush in the cleaner, knowing he needed to soak it first before dealing with the next step. He was at a place where he could pause, and that was good, so he turned to his cousin and glared. "What? What the hell do you want from me?"

She just stared at him, her chin raised. Then she took a few steps forward.

"I want you to talk to me. Or someone. Damien came into your home and hurt you. Just like he hurt Ethan. But you're not talking about it. Nobody is. Nobody's talking about the fact that you had a black eye and bruises on your face and a cut-up lip. No one's talking about the fact that he hurt you in more ways than one, or that we can't get to you. You won't even let your parents come. I know they said they were going to come out here for you, but you yelled at them and said you didn't need them."

"I don't."

"You're lying. You're lying to yourself and to everyone else. Talk to Ethan. He's up and about now."

"You've seen him?"

"His brother Aaron called me. Apparently, Ethan makes sure everyone in his circle has everyone's numbers for emergencies."

"You know Aaron. You've met him a few times."

"Yes, but we weren't friends before this. Though we're becoming so now. Because our family is hurting, and we can't fix it. Help us fix it. Talk to Ethan. This wasn't your fault, wasn't his either. This was Damien. You two and Holland were so good together, and I don't know why you're not *still* together. It doesn't make any sense to me."

"It doesn't have to make sense to you. You're not part of it."

"I know that. But you are my family. Therefore, I get to be the one who tells you to get up off your ass and talk to the man you love. Talk to the woman you love. You walked out on Holland, too. You thrust that woman into a relationship that was so unlike anything she'd ever been in before, and then you just left her. You let those cops and those nurses look at her with disdain and judge her, and you didn't help her. Weren't there for her."

"Do you think I don't know that? That's why I'm gone. The two of them can be together, and they can figure shit out. Then maybe, one day, they'll forgive me enough to be friends with me again. I never want to see that look on Ethan's face again, the one where he's scared and pissed off. And I never want to see that look on Holland's face, when someone's judging her for who she's with or who she is."

"First off, you knew that going into this. And the rest of that's on everybody else. Fuck them and their opinions."

"It's easy to say when you're not part of it."

"Yes, I guess it is. But you have never been alone in this. We have all supported you. Yes, any unconventional relationship's going to be hard, but you just need to communicate. And you're not doing that. And secondly? Why the hell do you think Holland and Ethan are still together?"

"What do you mean?"

"Holland left right after you did, and Ethan couldn't run after her because he was still on the damn couch. That's what Aaron said anyway."

Lincoln swallowed hard.

"She's gone?"

"Yep, she blamed herself or some shit, thought she was getting in the middle of you two and ruining things. You need to fix this, Lincoln. Because Holland's an amazing person, and she's alone now. And you are pushing everyone away so you can be alone, too."

"I just need to focus."

"Focus on your art, sure, I get that. It's your craft, your passion, your job. But don't lose everything else because of it. Don't lose yourself. Don't lose your happiness. What you had with those two only comes around once in a lifetime. And sometimes never. Don't lose it."

"I don't know if I ever really had it."

"Then you're far more idiotic than I ever gave you credit for."

"Nice," he barked.

"I love you, Lincoln. You're my favorite family member, and you know it. But right now, I don't really like you much."

"I don't like myself either."

"Then fix it. You can fix this."

"I can't."

"Why not?"

"Because every time I close my eyes, I picture Ethan dying. I picture Damien coming after Holland like he promised. All to get them out of the way. For me. And what am I? Not fucking worth it, that's what."

"Lincoln."

"No. I don't want to talk about this anymore. I just want it to be over. They'll figure things out. I know they will. Holland will always want to run. Now, she only has to run from one of us."

"Lincoln, you know that's not the case."

"Just go. I can't do this. I don't have anything left. I have nothing for them. I am the reason they were hurt. They can figure it out together. Because I don't deserve what I had."

As Madison just stared at him, Lincoln wasn't sure there was anything else to say. His cousin swallowed hard, grabbed her bag, and then walked away.

And he honestly didn't know if she would be back. Apparently, he was good at pushing everybody out of his life.

And he didn't know how to fix that. Didn't know if he should.

He went back to his work. Hours passed, and he switched to water, figuring that getting drunk wouldn't fix anything. Maybe, just maybe he had his art worked out, though.

He was still working on that commission piece, but it meant nothing.

Because he didn't even have the contact information for the client.

Damien had set it up, and now he'd have to figure it out on his own.

He had a scheduled art show coming up, and that was probably gone, too. All because he had let Damien handle it for him, and now he was fucked.

But, he probably deserved it. And more.

His phone buzzed on the table, and he almost ignored it, except for the fact that he didn't recognize the number. It wasn't anybody he knew.

He tapped his brush against his thigh as he stared at his artwork, then picked up the phone.

"Is this Lincoln McClard?"

Lincoln frowned. "Yes? Can I ask who I'm speaking with?"

"Oh, good, I'm so glad this is your number. This is Frank Statham from the Statham Projects."

Jesus Christ, the client.

Lincoln sat down on his rickety stool and licked his lips. "Oh, I remember you guys. Shit. Um, sorry for cursing. It's been a long day."

"I'd assume so." There was a pause. "I heard about what happened with Damien. I'm really sorry you and your partners were hurt in that. Well, that Ethan was hurt and Holland almost was."

Partners. Well, that was a nice way to put it. Though the guy didn't sound put off in the least by it. That was good.

"Me, too. Hell. It caught us all by surprise. I didn't have any of your information, and the cops still have all of Damien's computers and stuff, so I haven't been able to get ahold of you."

"Well, I didn't have your information either because the agent always protects the artist."

There was an awkward pause.

"Sorry."

"No, *I'm* sorry. I'm late on my project with you."

"I didn't have a set deadline. If I'm doing something commercial, then I'm very particular about due dates, but this was an art piece that I wanted from an artist I admire. With that said, if you can't get it to me for a decade, honestly, that's okay. But I still want it." Lincoln paused, swallowing hard as he looked at the piece that was finally coming together after so many months. "I'm working on it right now, actually, but I'm not agented currently."

"That's fine. I'm sure you'll find one. The world wants your art, Lincoln. People in my circles have been talking about how they want more from you and were afraid you would stop producing after this whole mess. You're not going to stop, are you?"

Lincoln was silent for so long, it was Frank's turn to curse.

"Please, don't stop."

"I'm not. I'm just trying to figure out what I want."

"Well, if you want to continue working on that art piece, we can talk about it. I can give you the same deal you had before, but this time without your agent. I'm going to call that contract null and void."

"I don't know, I need to think about it."

"Then you think about it. And when you're ready, we're here. You have my information now. Lincoln? Please don't quit. I quit doing what I loved before because of some crap in my life that you don't need to hear about. But I almost lost a couple of things that were very important to me. Don't let that happen to you."

Lincoln said a few things, but he wasn't a hundred percent sure what, then he hung up, remembering to save the man's contact info.

He couldn't quite understand what had just happened, but it seemed he might have a deal. He looked down at his phone, and then at the canvas, and didn't know what to do. He felt as if he were two steps behind again, trying to catch up. And maybe that was okay. Perhaps he needed that. But for the first time in a while, he had an idea, he had art, he had purpose. He just didn't know how to fix everything else he'd fucked up.

He set down his phone. Once again, someone knocked at the door. He looked over. But no one put their key in the lock. It wasn't Madison. Fear crawled up his spine, but then he remembered it wasn't Damien either. It couldn't be.

Another emotion slid over him. He was really afraid that it was someone he didn't want to see. Someone that he'd walked away from and hurt.

But he still headed towards the door. When he opened it after looking through the peephole, he swallowed hard and faced the one person he'd always loved. The one who'd been one third of everything for him.

And he froze.

***

Ethan stood there, his hands on his waist as he tried to act and look as if he weren't shaking inside. He'd had to wait until he was physically able to stand at Lincoln's door to yell at him for leaving. Because Lincoln didn't get to do this.

But now that Ethan was here, hell, the man looked so good. Tired, but good. There was paint in his hair, on his cheek, and on his clothes. He looked so fucking sexy but exhausted.

Well, good. He deserved to look as bad as Ethan felt.

"Ethan," Lincoln breathed. Just that one word, the sound of his name on Lincoln's lips, made him want to go to his knees and beg.

He wasn't going to beg. But there would be some damn groveling from Lincoln. He deserved at least that much.

"Lincoln. Can I come in?"

Lincoln looked like he wanted to say no, and Ethan ignored the hurt he felt at that. Because, damnit, he was going to make it inside.

He would go in and look at the place where Lincoln had been hurt. Where Damien had been apparently lying prone on the floor and tied up.

He wanted to see it.

"So…" Lincoln said, and then his voice trailed off as he closed the door behind them.

Ethan looked around, noticed the paint smell in the air even with the ventilation fans on, and turned to look at Lincoln.

He loved this man. He'd always loved him.

And Ethan missed him. But what was worse, he missed Holland. He missed her smile, the way she laughed with him.

He wasn't whole without her, and he sure as hell wasn't complete without Lincoln. He needed them both. Call him selfish, but what the fuck ever. People could love in many ways. Because finding that emotion, that frail piece of love that you could attach yourself to and want and desire and have for the rest of your life was something that didn't come around often.

He had been searching his entire fucking life for it and it had been right in front of him. And it wasn't until he had seen Holland that everything clicked, and he realized why he had waited so long for Lincoln. Because he had been waiting for her.

He and Lincoln hadn't been ready for each other without her. She completed them. But before they could go to her, Ethan needed to fix this. He needed to get Lincoln on the same page. And that meant he needed to figure out what the fuck was going on in his best friend's head.

"I see you're painting again."

"I am."

"Good. I'm glad Damien didn't take that from you."

Lincoln flinched, and Ethan raised his chin.

"Damien. Damien, Damien, Damien, Damien. Yes, the same name as the son from that Antichrist movie, and I don't even care."

"I thought it was *The Omen*."

"I thought *The Omen* was about the Antichrist."

"I don't think we watched the same movie."

"Who the fuck cares? He is out of our lives forever. Yes, he hurt me. I get that. And you can flinch and hate that and hate what he did. But you don't get to hate me for it."

Ethan was yelling at this point, moving so close to Lincoln that he could smell him, could feel the heat of him. Lincoln didn't back away, but he did flinch.

Ethan hated that.

"I don't hate you."

Lincoln whispered the words.

And yet Ethan felt like they were a shout.

"I don't hate you either. I never could. But, honestly, I did hate you a little bit. When you walked away? When you gave up on us without giving us a chance."

"I gave us a chance. And I ruined it. Damien attacked you because of me."

"He attacked me because he lost something. He cracked. He's insane. Whatever word and label you want to put on him, he likely deserves it, that's what he is. But...he has nothing to do with us."

"He has *everything* to do with us."

"No. He doesn't."

"He threatened Holland. If I hadn't stopped him, he would've hurt her. Or worse."

The blood in Ethan's veins ran cold.

"He did?"

"He did. I left her. I left you both so you could figure things out together. Where I wouldn't be a part of it.

Because she was threatened, and you were hurt. Because of me."

Ethan threw up his hands and growled.

"No, it wasn't you. It was all Damien. You need to get that through your thick skull."

"But if I hadn't brought Damien into the relationship by his association with me, this wouldn't have happened."

"If Damien hadn't become obsessive, then it wouldn't have happened. There's a lot of fucking things that could hurt us at any moment in time, Lincoln. It's not all on you. You walked away. *That's* what hurt us. More so than Damien."

"And I can't fix that."

"Bullshit. You know what? I work too much. We know that. I hurt you guys every time I missed a date, and I was trying to fix it. And when I go back to work—because I'm going to—I'm going to fix that, too. I'm not going to work as many hours. My boss already knows that. Everyone there knows. We're all trying to work at it so we can be with our loved ones. Because I fucking love you, Lincoln." Lincoln's eyes widened. "Don't look so surprised. I've loved you since before I kissed you. But it took Holland coming into our lives in such a grand way for me to realize that I needed to tell you. That I needed to be with you. But I need her, too. And I know it doesn't make sense to outsiders, but it's the way it is with the three of us."

"I love you, too," Lincoln whispered.

"And you're a fucking asshole. You don't get to push me away. You don't get to do that to Holland either. She walked out on me because she thought that she was a distraction. For us. That she was in the way. And I'll never forgive myself or you for letting her think that. But we can get past it. We need to fix this group, and to do that, we need to be together. No, you don't get to leave me. Because you're my best friend. Forever. We carved our names into that tree when we were little, saying we would be best friends forever. We don't get to go back on that."

Ethan knew he was ranting and rambling, but he couldn't help it.

Lincoln's lips twitched, and Ethan flipped him off.

"You're bringing up the tree?"

"You're damn right, I'm bringing up the tree. I'll bring it up whenever I need to. Because I fucking love you. And I want to spend the rest of my life with you, and not just as your best friend but as your lover and your husband or whatever else comes at us. We can deal with all the technical things after we get Holland back in our lives, because we really need her."

Lincoln took a step forward. He came so close that

Ethan wanted to grab him and kiss him and never let go. But he didn't. He held back.

"I'm an idiot."

"Yes. Yes, you are."

"I was so scared. You looked all bruised and bloody, and there was nothing I could do."

"Excuse me, but I saw you with a busted lip, too."

"You were far more hurt than I was."

"Well, he hit me from behind, I didn't have a chance to fight back."

Lincoln shuddered. "All I meant was that you were hurt more than I was, and therefore, I wanted to kill Damien. I had more rage."

"I have a hell of a lot of rage when it comes to him, too. But that's fine. We don't ever have to talk about him again. I want nothing to do with that man. But what I do want, is for you to say that you're not going to do this again. You're not going to get scared and run away. Because you're the steady one. I'm supposed to be the one who freaks out."

"That's not the case. You're the solid one in the family."

"Because I have you to lean on. I can be steady for everyone else because I've always had you. Now, I'm going to need you again. Because we need to get to Holland."

"I can't believe she left." Lincoln paused.

"No, I actually believe she did. She always seemed to have one foot out the door, and I blame myself for that."

"Hey, don't steal all the guilt, I have some, too. We spent so much time trying to figure out what we were to each other and having fun that I don't think I put enough energy into figuring out what I felt for her. She didn't know what I felt for her because I couldn't formulate words to tell her."

"I love her," Lincoln whispered.

"I love her, too. Now, before we go get our woman, because it's going to take both of us, I need to know, are you going to run away when things get hard again?"

Lincoln shook his head. "I had it in my head that you two would be better off without me. That I was worthless. That I was just going to fuck things up."

"And that's stupid. Next time you have that idea, come to me and I'll kiss it out of you. Or go to Holland. Because we're going to get her back."

"And you came to me first because you think I'm less complicated because I'm a man?" Lincoln asked, and Ethan pushed at his shoulder gently.

"Fuck, no. I've just known you longer." He swallowed hard and tried to smile as if he hadn't a care in the world. But, fuck, he'd been so afraid that he was going to lose Lincoln. Lose Holland. Both of them. "And I think that I could tie you up and drag you to her if I had to."

Lincoln just shook his head, and Ethan took a step forward and kissed him gently on the mouth. Lincoln stilled for a moment and Ethan was afraid that he was going to back away, but then he moaned and leaned into the kiss.

He tasted of booze and coffee, but Ethan didn't care. He'd missed this. Had missed this man.

The days that he hadn't had Lincoln in his life were the worst of his entire existence. He never wanted to do that again.

But now, they needed to do the hard part.

"We need to figure out how to make sure Holland knows exactly what she is to us."

"I hope to hell we can figure it out on the way."

"Me, too. Because I never want her to think that she is the lesser part of the three of us."

"She can't be. She's what makes us work. She's the one who makes me less serious and you more so."

"True, and she's the one who pushes us to be better. We better make sure she figures out what she means to us."

"I love you, Ethan."

"You need to say those words often. Because, at

some point, I'm going to expect groveling. I almost made you get on your knees."

Lincoln just shook his head, a grin growing on his face. "Let's make sure we grovel to Holland first, and then I'll get on my knees for you. Anytime you want."

Ethan kissed him again and then turned to look at his art. "You're so fucking talented."

"Remind me of that, too."

"Always. I'll always be here for you. I always have been, and I always will be. Now, let's go get our woman."

"And hope she stays put."

"Deal."

CHAPTER NINETEEN

The next time Holland had to look in a mirror and tell herself she was fine, she was going to tattoo the damn phrase on her forehead.

Just big block letters of *I'm fine*. Because she was. Fine. She wasn't wallowing. She wasn't sobbing. No, all she was doing was focusing on cleaning the house. Because today was her day off, even though she would have rather been in the store. However, both Steven and Fiona had kicked her out.

They had decided that maybe she'd been a little stressed out lately, a little high-strung. But it was her store. Right? Wasn't she allowed to be that way?

Okay, maybe she didn't need to rearrange the entire store overnight while nobody was there, and she should have been sleeping. Perhaps she didn't have to do inventory over and over again to make sure that what she was doing was right. And maybe she didn't need to make sure that every piece of art was placed exactly where it needed to be so the light shone perfectly on it, and someone would want to buy it. Okay, the latter was probably something she should be doing. And while she thought she had done things correctly before, she had rearranged it all anyway.

She focused so much on work that she didn't have to think about what the hell was going on in her personal life. And she was fine.

See? Fine. Big block letters and all.

The fact that she had actually sold more art than normal told her that she had made the right decision. The fact that it had already been in the back of her mind for the past year or so to do what she had done was okay, too. Yes, she had actually planned to have Steven or Fiona there to help her list things. And, if she were honest with herself, when she had first thought about it, she had planned to have Dustin help her, as well. Not that he would have wanted to. He'd never really liked her shop. He had been very focused on work and didn't have time for her "*little dreams.*"

"Dear God," she mumbled to herself. There was a

reason she wasn't married to Dustin. And it wasn't just because her sister was now going to marry the man. No, they just hadn't fit. She had been complacent in her demise, and she knew that.

But she was over him. And she was finding herself.

As she looked down at her old t-shirt and jean shorts with their pockets hanging below the bottom hem and frays everywhere, she figured...okay, this was her life now. Scrubbing her house from top to bottom, the smell of lemons and bleach and Pine-Sol filling the air. She had on those bright yellow rubber gloves that went up to near her elbows, and her hair was piled on top of her head. She hadn't even put in her contacts that morning, so she was wearing her big glasses, and not even her newest prescription since she couldn't find her good pair. She had put them somewhere when she reorganized the night before and couldn't find them.

Because that made total sense. Since she had no idea where she'd put them, she now had on her huge glasses that were a little too big for her face and made her look like a bug.

But that was fine. See? She was fine.

She put her cleaning rag down and sighed. She really looked like a mess. The only jewelry she had on were her two toe rings, and that was because she never took them off.

She really should get out of the house, find new friends, and be the Holland she needed to be.

But then she looked over at the shirt she had folded after carefully laundering it, and tears sprang to her eyes.

Lincoln had left it at her place, probably because he knew he would need it the next day. Then, he'd never picked it up.

Ethan had a pair of shorts here, too. There were even two extra toothbrushes at her place, still in their packages. Ones that she had pulled out for them so they didn't have to bring over any extra things. So they would always have stuff at her house. She didn't even want to think about what she had left at their places. Had she left anything?

There it was again, the complacency in her own demise.

This was all her fault.

She shouldn't have run, but it was safer than being walked out on. She'd already had it happen twice, once physically, and once emotionally. She didn't want to go through it again.

She wiped her eyes with whatever part of her skin wasn't covered in cleaning solution and went back to scrubbing the baseboards. Her knees ached, and she knew she probably should have put knee pads on or something, but that would have put her look over the top.

When the doorbell rang, she blew her hair from her eyes and looked through her fogged-up glasses, trying to think who might be visiting her.

No one. That's who.

Because...pity party, table for one.

She put the rag back into the bucket and stood up, trying not to slip on the puddle she had made. Then she took the dry rag, wiped up her puddle, and *then* made her way to the front of the house right as someone rang the doorbell again. Sighing, she opened it without looking and froze.

There they were. The men of her dreams, and of her waking nightmares. Of her past. Because they had to be firmly in her past.

She couldn't have them.

She really couldn't.

But, there they were. Lincoln looked tired. Ethan looked a little worse for wear. But they were here. Honestly, she really wanted to close the door and never see them again.

What was she supposed to do? Say?

"Oh."

Good, that was good. Great way to start it. Gah, why didn't she just say something like, *"Hello, how are you guys doing? You're back together again? Oh, good. I'm so glad for you. Goodbye."*

But...no, she couldn't say any of that.

"Did we catch you at a bad time?" Ethan asked, rocking back on his heels.

She shook her head, then remembered exactly what she was wearing and figured...why not? "Well, I was just cleaning the house, and I know I look ridiculous. Anyway, what can I do for you guys?" She knew she sounded like she was losing her mind, but that was fine. Because...she was fine.

"Can we come in?" Lincoln asked. She just stood there, her rubber-gloved hand gripping the edge of the door.

"Why?"

"We need to talk, babe," Ethan said.

She looked over at him, frowning.

"No, we don't. It looks like the two of you guys are together again, and that's great. I should go." She tried to close the door, but Lincoln put his hand in the way, stopping her. He was so big, so strong that she knew she wouldn't be able to close the door on him. But she also knew that if she asked again, he *would* leave. He would do as she asked because he wasn't the type of man to force things.

Neither was Ethan.

If she requested it, they would go, and she would never see them again. Why that hurt even more than when she had left in the first place, she didn't know. But she wasn't crying. She was done doing that. But her knees still shook.

"Please," Lincoln whispered. "If only for me to apologize for being a dick. Please, let us come in and talk to you."

The word *dick* got to her, and not for the usual reason. Because Lincoln really did look apologetic. She took a few steps back and gestured them in with her rubber-gloved hand.

The guys walked past her, their shoulders a little hunched. She didn't know what they were about to say. Maybe they were here to say goodbye and thank you for all the sex.

Dear God, she really wanted this to be over. That way, she could just cry again. Even if she told herself she was done doing that.

She hated that she just wanted to weep. That's not who she was. She was stronger than this. But she sure as hell didn't feel like it right then.

"I need to apologize," Lincoln said, his hands in his pockets.

"Okay."

See? She was fine. But she'd hurt Ethan with her

words before, she knew that. Somehow, she had to make things right, but she wasn't sure what to say.

Lincoln took a breath. "I shouldn't have left like that. I blamed myself for what Damien did, and I left because, in my mind, you were going to get hurt."

"How? It wasn't your fault. That was all Damien."

"You're right. It was. And I'm still trying to get that through my head. It's probably going to take a little bit of time, and a lot of both of you—hopefully—for me to figure that out."

Both of them. No, that couldn't be right. Because it was over between the three of them. It had to be.

"I need to apologize for what happened. With Damien. With you. With everything. I shouldn't have walked out like I did, but I was so afraid, felt so guilty about what happened with Damien, that I just reacted. I'm never going to forgive myself for that."

"What Damien did is not your fault."

"It feels like it. I introduced him to you guys. You know he threatened you, right?"

She froze and shook her head. She hadn't heard about everything that had happened when Damien confronted Lincoln. It seemed like a concerted effort that they'd shielded her.

"He threatened you and was going to do something worse to you than what happened with Ethan. He was determined to kill you. I could see it in his eyes. And I couldn't let that happen."

Fear clawed at her, but she pushed it away. Damien was behind bars. She was safe.

"It's still not your fault."

"I introduced him to you at that art event. It's damn well my fault that he was in our lives."

"Fuck that noise," Ethan said, and she looked over at him, giving him a nod.

"Exactly. Fuck that noise."

Lincoln just shook his head.

"I'm going to work through that, I swear. Ethan's going to make sure that happens."

"Damn straight."

She looked over and smiled at him. When he smiled back with heat in his eyes, she turned away. She was afraid to want more. Because she couldn't.

Not when she knew that they were meant for each other, not her. She was only there to love them from afar.

She couldn't have anything more.

"And I'll never forgive myself for the way that I hurt you guys. For leaving the way I did."

"Lincoln," Ethan growled.

"No, let me say this. I left because I thought I was doing the right thing. I was wrong. So fucking wrong.

And I'm going to try to make up for that." He let out a breath.

"Because I love the man at your side."

Her eyes widened, and she nodded, even though she was breaking inside. Of course, he loved Ethan. She had known it from the start. It was always going to be the two of them. And that was fine. Just like she'd said before. She was fine. She wasn't breaking inside.

"He's been my best friend for as long as I can remember. And I think I've loved him for just as long."

Ethan moved closer to her and slowly slid off her rubber glove so he could grip her hand. And because she was so numb, she let him.

"Look, the thing is, I know who I am. I know I have the power to love more than one person within me. And hell, baby, I love you, too. It's not just Ethan. It's you, Holland. You're a part of this. Maybe the most important part. I hope you know that."

She shook her head, wanting the words to be true but too afraid to hope.

"You are what makes us whole. You're the glue. You let us open up and figure out what's beneath the surface. I never would have had the courage to tell Ethan anything. I never would have opened up. And that's because of you. You make me a better person,

Holland. And I'm going to do everything in my power to make sure you understand that."

"But it's you two. It's always been you two."

Her voice was steady, even though she felt like crying.

Ethan slid off her other glove and then cupped her face in his hands, forcing her to turn to him.

"It might have started out that way, but in reality, we never would have had that without you."

"Don't think of me, then. At least, not in the future. I can be the person who brought you together, but I'll always be on that sideline." Now, she was crying, and she hated it.

Ethan slid his thumbs across her cheeks, wiping away her tears.

"And that makes me a fucking asshole for making you feel that way. Because it's not just me and Lincoln. It never was. You make us smile. You make us explore parts of ourselves we never thought of. You make us stop and look around and realize how we're living and what we need to be. You are our future. And I'm going to spend the rest of my life making sure you know that."

"And I'll be right by his side, making sure you know that, too." She looked over at Lincoln as he slid his hand down her back.

"You're our future, Holland. And if you let us, we'll

spend the rest of our lives making sure you understand that. We want to ensure that you know that you're cherished, cared for, and seen."

She swallowed hard. "But I ran," she whispered. "I ran."

"We know. But run to us now," Ethan said. "Because I fucking love you, Holland."

"And I love you, too. I hope to hell that you can find something within you for both of us. Because while Ethan and I could work by ourselves, we wouldn't be who we need to be without you. I want to spend the rest of my days waking up in both of your arms, realizing that I can be a better person because of you. And because of him. But it won't work without you. It'll never work without you."

Her hands shook as she clasped them in front of herself, and then she pulled away. Both men looked a little dejected, but she needed to think.

"I wasn't expecting this. I was just going to clean."

"The first thing we need to hear though is how you feel about us," Lincoln said, his voice smooth. "You don't have to say anything. Maybe just give us a nod that you're open to it. We all moved a little fast, though not fast enough in some cases."

"But know this," Lincoln continued, "I'm going to fight for you. I'm never going to run again. And I hope to hell that you trust us enough to believe that." Holland's hands shook again, and she turned away, trying to compose herself. She took in deep breaths, filling her lungs. She almost coughed at the lemon scent in the air. Her house smelled so clean, and her place of business was spotless and organized, as well. Everything was wonderful in her life. Except for this.

This part, the part she'd been running from, was a mess.

"Holland?" Ethan asked, a little bit of fear in his voice.

She had done that. She had put that there. And she kept doing things like this. Kept hurting them. She didn't know what to do. She turned.

"I have so much baggage," she said with a laugh. Lincoln's brows rose.

"Ah, hello?"

"We're sort of all baggage. It's what we do. But, fuck it. You're ours," Ethan said.

"It's the three of us, not just the two. This is how it works. We're going to fight, we're going to get annoyed with each other, and we're going to talk it out. Do you remember what we first said when we started this?" Ethan asked, and she nodded. "We said we'd communicate. And we're not doing that. We're going to have to do better. Because as much as I love kissing you, as much as the sex is the best thing that's ever happened in my life, that's not really the important part."

She frowned.

"Are you saying the sex isn't great?" Lincoln asked, and Ethan flipped him off.

"Shut up. I'm not great at words."

"You're doing just fine," she whispered.

Ethan let out a breath. "Oh, well, what I meant to say was that being with you two, knowing that I get to see you guys nearly every day and work at what we have, *that*'s the best thing. I want to work this out. I want to figure it out. I want to love you until the end of my days. Just one day at a time. No running. Not anymore."

"You met me while I was running," she reminded them.

"And you found us," Lincoln said. "Or maybe we found you. Whatever. We found each other, that's what matters. Tell us you want this. Tell us you want a future. You don't have to love us yet. But I'm going to spend the rest of my days making sure you do."

As the tears fell, she took a step forward, then another, and put her hands on both of their chests, feeling their heartbeats beneath her palms.

"I'm afraid," she whispered, her hands curling into fists.

"And we'll be here to assuage those," Lincoln said, taking her wrist in his hand and gently squeezing.

Ethan reached out and caressed her face, and she leaned into his touch.

"Trust us. Please."

"Please let us show you that we deserve this. And then maybe, one day, you can love us, too."

She shook her head, and the expression on both of their faces fell.

"You don't have to wait. Even though I told myself I needed to run, that I needed to have a way out because you guys are so perfect for each other, I fell for you both. I love you, both of you, and I know I told myself I shouldn't. But I do. Though I don't know what to do next. I just know I want to do it with you. Both of you."

The men's eyes widened, and they grinned before leaning in. Lincoln took her lips first, and then Ethan kissed her. This was home. This was the next phase of who she was meant to be.

She didn't know what would happen next. She didn't know if she was going to be able to fix everything in her life. But she knew she wouldn't be doing it alone.

Because, all along, they had been right here. She'd been the one taking two steps back.

She didn't want to do it anymore. As she leaned into Lincoln's hold, and Ethan held her from behind, she breathed in their scents and knew this was home. She could do this. She really *was* fine. More than.

She had fallen in love with a Montgomery and his best friend, and she never wanted to let go. And as they held her, she knew she didn't have to.

Finally.

EPILOGUE

Lincoln slid his hands down the front of his shirt, making sure it was at least somewhat straight, while Holland did the same to her dress. Ethan, holding a stack of gifts and a specially made canvas bag filled with three bottles of wine, just rolled his eyes at the two of them.

"You guys have met these people before, right? I mean, it's my family, but we're standing in front of the house. Lincoln practically lived here. And, Holland, you know them."

Holland looked over at Lincoln, who just snorted and shook his head.

"We're nervous," Lincoln said, and Holland nodded before sliding her hand into his.

She looked up at the house and then leaned into

Lincoln a bit. "I mean, this is sort of a meet-the-parents thing."

"You know my parents. And the rest of the family."

"Yes, but this is our first birthday event as a throuple."

"I really hate that word," Holland said, and Lincoln nodded.

"I do, too. I don't know why I even said it. And I don't like the word *threesome* because that just makes me think of sex, and then I get a hard-on while in front of people, and it gets weird."

Lincoln looked down at his crotch and winced.

"Well, think of baseball."

"Thinking of baseball just makes me think of those men in those pants of theirs with their very fine asses," Lincoln said, looking over at Holland, who snorted.

"Okay, think of the person that you hate the most playing baseball. Or...rotten fish. Or candy getting stuck to your teeth where you can't pick it out, and then you need to get a cavity filled, and they have to do a root—"

"Okay, okay, okay." Lincoln shuddered. "I hate teeth. You *know* I hate teeth."

"And? Did I help?" Holland asked, grinning.

"Yes, and I hate you a little bit right now. But thank you. And I love you." He leaned down and kissed her on the lips. She just grinned at him.

"You're so sweet."

"Are you two done yet? Because these things are really heavy."

Lincoln winced and took the larger of the items from Ethan, while Holland took the bag of wine as Ethan held up the other three gifts in his hands.

"I don't know why we got so much stuff for my mom," Ethan mumbled. And then he froze and looked over his shoulder. "Don't tell her I said that."

"You're fine. Nobody's looking," Holland said. "And we got so much for your mom because she's amazing. And when she last came into the store, she looked at some of these pieces, and they made her smile. But she didn't get them for herself because, as you said, she never gets anything for herself."

"Well, my mom is pretty amazing."

"Yes, she is," Holland said, grinning.

Lincoln just looked down at the two of them and held back a sigh. The Montgomerys had been his family for long enough that it didn't seem weird to think of them that way. Holland was just getting used to it. He had never met her parents or her sister and didn't think he ever would. Wasn't sure he wanted to. And while she didn't hate them anymore, she never talked about them and didn't want them in her life. And he was just fine with that. Cutting toxic people out of your life was good. Maybe if he had done that with Damien long before everything changed, the man wouldn't be locked in a cell, facing years in prison for attempted murder.

Lincoln's parents were actually coming to town in the next couple of weeks, something that had shocked him. He didn't mind going to visit them, but his dad was actually thinking about retiring, and that meant he wanted to come and visit his son and the two loves of Lincoln's life. There had been no judgment, just absolute glee in his mother's voice at the thought of him settling down. Not only with Ethan, a boy that they both loved, but also with Holland—in his mother's words, the woman who put a smile on his face and a twinkle in his eyes.

Apparently his parents were on board.

However, today was not about his family. Or Holland's. It was about the Montgomerys.

And it was Francine's birthday.

"Why are you guys standing out there?" Bristol asked, coming out to help, taking a package from Ethan's hands. "Plus, with all this stuff, you're going to make us look bad," she said, laughing.

"We can't help it, we like trying to be the best and outnumber everybody," Holland said.

"Well, it's super easy when you already have one

more person than every couple in there. I don't know how you ended up with two men while I have none."

Holland started walking up with Bristol, both of them talking about who Bristol needed to start dating and the fact that her love life was completely boring.

"Is Holland going to start setting Bristol up with people?" Lincoln asked as he and Ethan made their way into the house.

"I don't know, man. I always thought she'd fall for her best friend like I did."

Lincoln leaned down and pressed a kiss to Ethan's lips before looking up to watch Marcus scowling at Bristol.

She scowled right back and stomped on his foot as she passed. Lincoln's brows rose.

Okay, that was interesting.

"Happy Birthday, Mom," Ethan said, leaning down to kiss his mother on the cheek.

"Happy Birthday, Francine."

"You need to start calling me *Mom*. So does Holland. I like being called Mom."

"But I bet you want to be called Grandma more," Aaron said, lifting his mother up from behind and twirling her around the room.

"Aaron Montgomery, you put me down right now," she said, laughing.

Aaron smacked a kiss to his mother's lips and then shot off before his dad hit him with his newspaper.

"I'm fine, I'm fine," Francine said, fixing her dress. "That boy, though."

"He loves you, just like we do. And you've always been Mrs. Montgomery to me. It took the past what? Two years for me to start calling you Francine without cringing?"

"You'll get used to Mom." She paused. "And if you're ready, Grandma. I'd love to be called Grandma." Her eyes twinkled, and everyone laughed. "I can't help it. Of course, I call myself Grandmother to Jasper, the cutest dog ever." She leaned down and kissed the top of the white Siberian Husky's head. "Who's my favorite grandpuppy? Who's my favorite grandpuppy?" she sing-songed, and Lincoln snorted.

"Maybe we should get a cat," he told Ethan.

"There's that foster sale coming up. The one where all the foster parents bring their cats in and try to get them adopted out. We could look."

"What are we doing?" Holland asked, coming up to them and taking the last package from Ethan's hands.

Aaron ran by, stealing the present from her and running, and they all just rolled their eyes.

Aaron was insane, but they loved him.

"We were thinking about getting a cat," Ethan said.

"Well, which house would he or she stay at?" Holland asked, her brows raised. "That's a lot of cat hair, and even though I really, *really* want one, it wouldn't be fair for him or her to keep moving from house to house."

Everybody got really quiet, and Lincoln cleared his throat.

"Okay, we'll talk about that when we get home." A pause. "Let me figure out what that home is first."

Francine started clapping her hands, as Holland blushed, and Ethan coughed into his fist. To disperse the awkwardness of the moment because he was pretty sure they were about to all move in together finally, he turned to Francine and handed over the very large, rectangular package. "This is for you."

Her eyes widened, and she looked down at it. "What on Earth?"

"I know it's not present time, but you should open it," Ethan said, and Holland nodded.

"Please, Mrs. Montgomery."

"I am Francine, Franny, or Mom. You decide." She said the words, but she was looking down at the package, shaking her head.

"If this is what I think it is, young man, I'm going to hurt you."

"Don't hurt me, just open it."

Timothy came and took the package from her, and they opened it together. Lincoln sucked in a breath as Francine started weeping over it.

It was their home. The place filled with love, heart, and all of the Montgomerys. He had painted it over time, with it all coming out in a whoosh at the end, with the shadows of the trees where they had all played, and individual long shadows for each of the Montgomery clan.

There were toys on the grass, actual replicas of what they had played with as children.

It was everything that Ethan, and later Lincoln, would come to call home.

The Montgomery home.

"It's wonderful," she whispered. "You did this for me?" she asked, looking over her shoulder.

"Of course. I wanted you to have a little bit of home."

"And a Lincoln McClard original," Aaron said.

"Pricey," Bristol said. "Way to show us up."

Francine waved them off and turned so she could reach up and pat his cheek.

"I love you, my son."

"And I love you too, Mom." She started crying, and he held her close as Ethan wrapped his arm around Holland. When Timothy took his wife, Lincoln went over to Holland's side and gripped her hand while she leaned into Ethan.

He looked over at the people that were his family and smiled. He'd have to bring Madison over soon. He knew she needed this, too. She was working today, so she hadn't been able to make it, but he'd force it the next time.

Because of the Montgomerys, Lincoln had found his home, and he'd found the love of his life.

The loves of his life.

Ethan had always been his rock, his compass, but Holland...she was their lighthouse, the one who illumi-nated where they needed to go. And he knew that, no matter what happened, he'd be between them, loving every single moment of it.

THE END

Next in the Montgomery Ink: Boulder series?

It's Bristol's turn in EMBRACED IN INK.

WANT TO READ A SPECIAL BONUS EPILOGUE FEATURING ETHAN, LINCOLN, & HOLLAND? CLICK HERE!

A NOTE FROM
CARRIE ANN RYAN

Thank you so much for reading **SATED IN INK.** I do hope if you liked this story, that you would please leave a review! Reviews help authors *and* readers.

It's been a couple years since I wrote a menage romance, and I knew I needed to go back to it in the Montgomery world. Writing so many relationships within a single relationship is complicated and SO worth it. I loved this book and this triad. Ethan, Lincoln, and Holland had their issues and I adored figuring them out and fixing it.

As for who is next? Bristol is finally getting what she deserves in Embraced in Ink. Maybe. Possibly. Okay, hopefully. Just ask her best friend.

The Montgomery Ink: Boulder Series:

Book 1: Wrapped in Ink

Book 2: Sated in Ink

Book 3: Embraced in Ink

Book 3: Moments in Ink

Book 4: Seduced in Ink

Book 4.5: Captured in Ink

Book 4.7: Inked Fantasy

Book 4.8: A Very Montgomery Christmas

WANT TO READ A SPECIAL BONUS EPILOGUE FEATURING ETHAN, LINCOLN, & HOLLAND? CLICK HERE!

f you want to make sure you know what's coming next from me, you can sign up for my newsletter at www.CarrieAnnRyan.com; follow me on twitter at @CarrieAnnRyan, or like my Facebook page. I also have a Facebook Fan Club where we have trivia, chats, and other goodies. You guys are the reason I get to do what I do and I thank you.

Make sure you're signed up for my MAILING LIST so you can know when the next releases are available as well as find giveaways and FREE READS.

Happy Reading!

ALSO FROM
CARRIE ANN RYAN

The Montgomery Ink Legacy Series:

Book 1: Bittersweet Promises (Leif & Brooke)

Book 2: At First Meet (Nick & Lake)

Book 2.5: Happily Ever Never (May & Leo)

Book 3: Longtime Crush (Sebastian & Raven)

Book 4: Best Friend Temptation (Noah, Ford, and Greer)

Book 4.5: Happily Ever Maybe (Jennifer & Gus)

Book 5: Last First Kiss (Daisy & Hugh)

Book 6: His Second Chance (Kane & Phoebe)

Book 7: One Night with You (Kingston & Claire)

Book 8: Accidentally Forever (Crew & Aria)

Book 9: Last Chance Seduction (Lexington & Mercy)

Book 10: Kiss Me Forever (Brooklyn & Reece)

Book 11: His Guilty Pleasure (Dash & Aly)

Book 12: Maybe it's You (Riley & Gage)

The Cage Family

Book 1: The Forever Rule (Aston & Blakely)

Book 2: An Unexpected Everything (Isabella & Weston)

Book 3: If You Were Mine (Dorian & Harper)

Book 4: One Quick Obsession (Hudson & Scarlett)

Book 5: Pretend it's Forever (Sophia & Carson)

Book 6: Wish it Were You (Flynn & Luna)

Ashford Creek

Book 1: Legacy (Callum & Felicity)

Book 2: Crossroads (Bodhi & Kiera)

Book 3: Westward (Atlas & Elizabeth)

Book 4: Patience (Teagan & Rush)

Clover Lake

Book 1: Always a Fake Bridesmaid (Livvy & Ewan)

Book 2: Accidental Runaway Groom (Jamie & Sharp)

Book 3: His Practically Fake Proposal (Galen & Addy)

The Wilder Brothers Series:

Book 1: One Way Back to Me (Eli & Alexis)

Book 2: Always the One for Me (Evan & Kendall)

Book 3: The Path to You (Everett & Bethany)

Book 4: Coming Home for Us (Elijah & Maddie)

Book 5: Stay Here With Me (East & Lark)

Book 6: Finding the Road to Us (Elliot, Trace, and Sidney)

Book 7: Moments for You (Ridge & Aurora)

Book 7.5: A Wilder Wedding (Amos & Naomi)

Book 8: Forever For Us (Wyatt & Ava)

Book 9: Pieces of Me (Gabriel & Briar)

Book 10: Endlessly Yours (Brooks & Rory)

The Falling for the Cassidy Brothers Series:

(Formerly the First Time Series)

Book 1: Good Time Boyfriend (Heath & Devney)

Book 2: Last Minute Fiancé (Luca & Addison)

Book 3: Second Chance Husband (August & Paisley)

Montgomery Ink Denver:

Book 0.5: Ink Inspired (Shep & Shea)

Book 0.6: Ink Reunited (Sassy, Rare, and Ian)

Book 1: Delicate Ink (Austin & Sierra)

Book 1.5: Forever Ink (Callie & Morgan)

Book 2: Tempting Boundaries (Decker and Miranda)

Book 3: Harder than Words (Meghan & Luc)

Book 3.5: <u>Finally Found You</u> (Mason & Presley)

Book 4: <u>Written in Ink</u> (Griffin & Autumn)

Book 4.5: <u>Hidden Ink</u> (Hailey & Sloane)

Book 5: <u>Ink Enduring</u> (Maya, Jake, and Border)

Book 6: <u>Ink Exposed</u> (Alex & Tabby)

Book 6.5: <u>Adoring Ink</u> (Holly & Brody)

Book 6.6: <u>Love, Honor, & Ink</u> (Arianna & Harper)

Book 7: <u>Inked Expressions</u> (Storm & Everly)

Book 7.3: <u>Dropout</u> (Grayson & Kate)

Book 7.5: <u>Executive Ink</u> (Jax & Ashlynn)

Book 8: <u>Inked Memories</u> (Wes & Jillian)

Book 8.5: <u>Inked Nights</u> (Derek & Olivia)

Book 8.7: <u>Second Chance Ink</u> (Brandon & Lauren)

Book 8.5: Montgomery Midnight Kisses (Alex & Tabby Bonus(

Bonus: Inked Kingdom (Stone & Sarina)

Montgomery Ink: Colorado Springs

Book 1: Fallen Ink (Adrienne & Mace)

Book 2: Restless Ink (Thea & Dimitri)

Book 2.5: Ashes to Ink (Abby & Ryan)

Book 3: Jagged Ink (Roxie & Carter)

Book 3.5: Ink by Numbers (Landon & Kaylee)

The Montgomery Ink: Boulder Series:

Book 1: Wrapped in Ink (Liam & Arden)

Book 2: Sated in Ink (Ethan, Lincoln, and Holland)

Book 3: Embraced in Ink (Bristol & Marcus)

Book 3: Moments in Ink (Zia & Meredith)

Book 4: Seduced in Ink (Aaron & Madison)

Book 4.5: Captured in Ink (Julia, Ronin, & Kincaid)

Book 4.7: Inked Fantasy (Secret ??)

Book 4.8: A Very Montgomery Christmas (The Entire Boulder Family)

The Montgomery Ink: Fort Collins Series:

Book 1: Inked Persuasion (Jacob & Annabelle)

Book 2: Inked Obsession (Beckett & Eliza)

Book 3: Inked Devotion (Benjamin & Brenna)

Book 3.5: Nothing But Ink (Clay & Riggs)

Book 4: Inked Craving (Lee & Paige)

Book 5: Inked Temptation (Archer & Killian)

The Promise Me Series:

Book 1: Forever Only Once (Cross & Hazel)

Book 2: From That Moment (Prior & Paris)

Book 3: Far From Destined (Macon & Dakota)

Book 4: From Our First (Nate & Myra)

The Whiskey and Lies Series:

Book 1: Whiskey Secrets (Dare & Kenzie)

Book 2: Whiskey Reveals (Fox & Melody)

Book 3: <u>Whiskey Undone</u> (Loch & Ainsley)

The Gallagher Brothers Series:

Book 1: <u>Love Restored</u> (Graham & Blake)

Book 2: <u>Passion Restored</u> (Owen & Liz)

Book 3: <u>Hope Restored</u> (Murphy & Tessa)

The Carr Family Series:

(Formerly the Less Than Series)

Book 1: Breathless With Her (Devin & Erin)

Book 2: Reckless With You (Tucker & Amelia)

Book 3: Shameless With Him (Caleb & Zoey)

The Fractured Connections Series:

Book 1: Breaking Without You (Cameron & Violet)

Book 2: Shouldn't Have You (Brendon & Harmony)

Book 3: Falling With You (Aiden & Sienna)

Book 4: Taken With You (Beckham & Meadow)

The Campus Roommates Series:

(Formerly the On My Own Series)

Book 0.5: My First Glance

Book 1: My One Night (Dillon & Elise)

Book 2: My Rebound (Pacey & Mackenzie)

Book 3: My Next Play (Miles & Nessa)

Book 4: My Bad Decisions (Tanner & Natalie)

The Ravenwood Coven Series:

Book 1: Dawn Unearthed

Book 2: Dusk Unveiled

Book 3: Evernight Unleashed

The Aspen Pack Series:

Book 1: Etched in Honor

Book 2: Hunted in Darkness

Book 3: Mated in Chaos

Book 4: Harbored in Silence

Book 5: Marked in Flames

The Talon Pack:

Book 1: <u>Tattered Loyalties</u>

Book 2: <u>An Alpha's Choice</u>

Book 3: <u>Mated in Mist</u>

Book 4: <u>Wolf Betrayed</u>

Book 5: <u>Fractured Silence</u>

Book 6: <u>Destiny Disgraced</u>

Book 7: <u>Eternal Mourning</u>

Book 8: <u>Strength Enduring</u>

Book 9: <u>Forever Broken</u>

Book 10: Mated in Darkness

Book 11: Fated in Winter

Redwood Pack Series:

Book 0.5: <u>An Alpha's Path</u>

Book 1: <u>A Taste for a Mate</u>

Book 2: <u>Trinity Bound</u>

Book 2.5: <u>A Night Away</u>

Book 3: <u>Enforcer's Redemption</u>

Book 3.5: <u>Blurred Expectations</u>

Book 3.7: <u>Forgiveness</u>

Book 4: <u>Shattered Emotions</u>

Book 5: <u>Hidden Destiny</u>

Book 5.5: <u>A Beta's Haven</u>

Book 6: <u>Fighting Fate</u>

Book 6.5: <u>Loving the Omega</u>

Book 6.7: <u>The Hunted Heart</u>

Book 7: <u>Wicked Wolf</u>

The Elements of Five Series:

Book 1: From Breath and Ruin

Book 2: From Flame and Ash

Book 3: From Spirit and Binding

Book 4: From Shadow and Silence

Dante's Circle Series:

Book 1: <u>Dust of My Wings</u>

Book 2: <u>Her Warriors' Three Wishes</u>

Book 3: <u>An Unlucky Moon</u>

Book 3.5: <u>His Choice</u>

Book 4: <u>Tangled Innocence</u>

Book 5: <u>Fierce Enchantment</u>

Book 6: <u>An Immortal's Song</u>

Book 7: <u>Prowled Darkness</u>

Book 8: Dante's Circle Reborn

Holiday, Montana Series:

Book 1: <u>Charmed Spirits</u>

Book 2: <u>Santa's Executive</u>

Book 3: <u>Finding Abigail</u>

Book 4: <u>Her Lucky Love</u>

Book 5: Dreams of Ivory

The Branded Pack Series:

(Written with Alexandra Ivy)

Book 1: <u>Stolen and Forgiven</u>

Book 2: <u>Abandoned and Unseen</u>

Book 3: <u>Buried and Shadowed</u>

ABOUT THE AUTHOR

Carrie Ann Ryan is the New York Times and USA Today bestselling author of contemporary, paranormal, and young adult romance. Her works include the Montgomery Ink, Redwood Pack, Fractured Connections, and Elements of Five series, which have sold over 3.0 million books worldwide. She started writing while in graduate school for her advanced degree in chemistry and hasn't stopped since. Carrie Ann has written over seventy-five novels and novellas with more in the works. When she's not losing herself in her emotional and action-packed worlds, she's reading as much as she can while wrangling her clowder of cats who have more followers than she does.

www.CarrieAnnRyan.com

www.ingramcontent.com/pod-product-compliance
Lightning Source LLC
Chambersburg PA
CBHW072003110726
47910CB00005B/1636